MW01121900

Always

D. A. LAWSON

Always

a novel

TATE PUBLISHING & *Enterprises*

Always
Copyright © 2011 by D.A. Lawson. All rights reserved.

No part of this publication may be reproduced, stored in a retrieval system or transmitted in any way by any means, electronic, mechanical, photocopy, recording or otherwise without the prior permission of the author except as provided by USA copyright law.

This novel is a work of fiction. Names, descriptions, entities, and incidents included in the story are products of the author's imagination. Any resemblance to actual persons, events, and entities is entirely coincidental.

Scripture quotations are taken from the Holy Bible, New Living Translation, copyright ©1996. Used by permission of Tyndale House Publishers, Inc., Wheaton, Illinois 60189. All rights reserved.

The opinions expressed by the author are not necessarily those of Tate Publishing, LLC.

Published by Tate Publishing & Enterprises, LLC
127 E. Trade Center Terrace | Mustang, Oklahoma 73064 USA
1.888.361.9473 | www.tatepublishing.com

Tate Publishing is committed to excellence in the publishing industry. The company reflects the philosophy established by the founders, based on Psalm 68:11,
"The Lord gave the word and great was the company of those who published it."

Book design copyright © 2011 by Tate Publishing, LLC. All rights reserved.
Cover design by Kellie Southerland
Interior design by Nathan Harmony

Published in the United States of America

ISBN: 978-1-61739-900-8
1. Fiction: Romance: General
2. Fiction: Christian: Romance
11.02.08

Dedication

This book is for Brad; I'll always love you. And for Jennifer, thanks for everything.

Prologue

Kentucky
April 1989

Julie McCourt stared at the phone as the ringing stabbed through the early morning quietness of her grandmother's house. She knew who was on the other end. She could see him in her mind. He was 250 miles away, pacing like a caged tiger, his cold blue eyes flashing angrily as he waited for her to answer. The same thing had been going on for weeks now. He waited until he knew she was alone. He had always made sure he knew her schedule.

After the first few times, she stopped answering. Today she had to answer. She didn't know why. Maybe this would be the day he would finally listen to reason and leave her alone.

She slowly brought the handset to her ear. "What do you want, Jeremy?" she asked evenly, forcing herself to stay calm when she really wanted to scream.

"I just want you—to talk to you. I love you," he said with forced softness.

"You don't know what love is. It's over, Jeremy. Leave me alone. Please, just leave me alone."

"I can't leave you alone. You're mine. Do you understand? Mine. Always mine," he answered, his tone becoming harsh.

Julie had heard all this before, over and over and over again. Since she had told Jeremy she needed space and time, he had been trying to change her mind. She started dating Jeremy Beavens in 1986, when she was only sixteen. She had invested—no, wasted was more like it—nearly three years of her life in a relationship with him.

When he had given her the ring on Valentine's Day and asked her to marry him, she had said yes. It was what she was supposed to say. It was what he wanted. He always got what he wanted when it came to Julie, but not this time. The ring had made it hit home. She knew there was no way she could spend the rest of her life bound to Jeremy Beavens by marriage.

At nineteen, Julie was too young to get married. She wanted to focus on college, be accepted into pharmacy school, go on and get a doctorate degree, and have a career in pharmaceutical research. Had he given her time and stopped pressuring her to marry, she might have believed that he cared for her. Possession had been all he cared about. She had finally figured it out.

To make matters worse, she had discovered he'd been dealing and using drugs. She didn't know what kind or for how long, but he admitted it when she had confronted him. Julie felt betrayed. If he had been caught and she had been with him, she would have had to kiss any career in pharmacy good-bye. That's when she gave him back the ring and told him it was over. She was finished being manipulated and controlled by him. Jeremy apparently had different plans. She had broken their engagement the end of February, and he still wouldn't leave her alone.

"No, Jeremy," Julie answered, briefly closing her eyes and taking a deep breath, "you do not own me."

"There's somebody else, isn't there?" He started ranting, the volume of his voice growing louder. "Are you sleeping with him? You're sleeping with him, aren't you? You slut! Nobody else can have you. I won't let him have you…"

Jeremy was still screaming and cursing at her when she quietly hung up the phone. Julie knew this wouldn't be the end of it. *God, would it ever be over?*

Chapter 1

Julie cried as she gathered her books and stuffed them in her backpack. She asked herself how it had come to this. She didn't know how in the world she had let her life get in such a wreck. She must be stupid.

She knew she wasn't stupid, though, not intellectually speaking anyway. She had graduated as valedictorian from high school, had been accepted to every college she had applied, and had a 3.87 GPA so far in a rigorous pre-pharmacy program. So, no, she wasn't stupid. She was too trusting, though—way too trusting.

It was hard not to go back through the last three years and ask a lot of what-ifs. What if she hadn't started working at the restaurant where Jeremy was a cook? What if she had kept going out with Steve, the guy she dated a while right before Jeremy? What if she had just told Jeremy no when he'd asked her out? What if she hadn't stopped writing to Robert, her friend from church camp? What if she could still talk to Ned, a friend she'd known all through school? What if she had listened to the alarms in her head? What if? What if? What if? The past couldn't be changed, and she knew that. Success in the future required moving on from her past and planning. Planning she could do.

Julie always had a plan. She thought things through, weighed the options, made a decision, and stuck to the plan. Except Jeremy Beavens had definitely not been part of the plan.

Julie had started working at Johnson's Restaurant the summer after she turned sixteen. Her mom had said, "Julie, you're sixteen now. You've got your driver's license. Don't you think it's time you got a job?"

So Julie got herself a job as a hostess and waitress. It was the summer before her junior year in high school. The summer started out to be a good one. Working gave her money. She saved some every week to put toward college and still had some to spend. She had time to spend with her friends from school, and she was making new friends at the restaurant.

In the beginning Julie didn't know many of the people working there. She went to a different school than the other kids who worked the same shifts she did. Julie made friends quickly at work, though. She always tried to be friendly, and she was genuinely interested in other people. People had often told her that she was easy to talk to.

Even guys told her she was easy to talk to. At that point she hadn't had a serious boyfriend, which was the way she liked it, but she had dated quite a bit.

Up until Julie met Jeremy, dating had been fun and carefree. Before Jeremy, she had remained friends with the guys she had gone out with. In fact, she and Ned had dated off and on even before they could officially date, meeting at ball games and school dances, sitting together at lunch, writing letters to each other during summer breaks, attending church functions together. She and Ned had dated each other, as well as other people, but still remained close friends.

Jeremy had changed that, that and many other things. He had changed her, twisting her and manipulating her until she wasn't sure who she was anymore. It was a gradual thing. Little by little he had taken over parts of her life.

It was odd, but in the beginning, when they had just started going out, Jeremy told her that he would not be the one she ended up with. He told Julie the guy she fell in love with would be the luckiest guy in the world. She was gullible enough to find that charming.

He was so different than any other guy she had ever been interested in. He was older for one thing, three years older than her. He had already graduated high school and had taken some college courses at IUPU in Fort Wayne.

Jeremy's appearance was vastly different from the other guys she had been attracted to. The most notable characteristic was his startlingly blue eyes. They were so sharp, so intense, that they nearly took her breath away the first time she saw him. He was tall, with hair that was almost black. He wore it spiked on top and long in back. It nearly reached his shoulders. He even had an earring. They had literally been the proverbial bad boy and the girl next door. She'd been that crazy, never thinking that anything even remotely serious would come from dating him.

But serious things did come from dating him. Seeing it in retrospect, Julie could pick out the events that led to the loss of her control.

The first happened when they had been dating for about a month. They were watching a movie in her parents' living room. The rest of her family had gone to bed. Jeremy started kissing her. They had kissed before, several times in fact. He was much more forward that way than any of her other boyfriends had ever been. She found herself constantly pushing his hands away from areas she didn't think he should have them. That night, he pushed her further than anyone ever had. As they lay together on the floor, he very subtly touched her in a very intimate area, in a very intimate way. She gasped and stiffened. This was totally foreign to her. She knew about kissing. She had some idea of what happened when people had sex. This in-between stuff was totally unknown. He kissed her more deeply. Then he kissed her along her jaw up to her ear.

"Just let me touch you. I won't hurt you. I promise," he whispered.

An alarm was going off. Julie knew she should stop him, but somehow she couldn't. He sounded so desperate, so tender. She relaxed a little as he continued kissing her and touching her. She could feel her own wetness as he continued the unfamiliar caress. She wasn't completely sure she liked it, but it didn't exactly feel bad either. He touched and kissed her for several minutes until, finally, he slowly pulled his hand away and just held her.

"There's a special bond between us now, Julie. You'll always remember this and remember me for doing it to you."

The alarm was sounding again. If only she had listened! What he had done to her had nothing to do with caring about her or even anything to do with lust or desire. Unfortunately, it would be much later until she discovered that he had done it as a way to have control over her, just like everything else he did.

She didn't respond to what he had said, just looked back at him and gave him a small, weak, and somewhat bewildered smile. After a few minutes of his intense gaze, Julie found her voice. "I guess you better go. It's getting late."

"You're right. It is late," he said, taking his eyes off hers and glancing at the clock on the wall. He looked back at her and said, "I'll call you tomorrow."

He stood up and helped Julie to her feet. He kept his grip on her hand as she walked him to the door. Turning toward her, he said, "I'll be thinking about you. I always think about you."

He kissed her gently and walked out the door toward his car. Julie shut the door behind him and turned the lock. She waited until she heard his engine start and then turned off the porch light. She walked back down the hall toward the bathroom and started getting ready for bed.

Upstairs in her room, she continued to turn over the events of the evening in her mind. She couldn't shake a feeling of guilt for what had happened. She had never gone that far before. On the other hand, it wasn't exactly sex. She was still a virgin, after all. She rolled her thoughts over and over in her mind, finally convincing herself it hadn't really meant anything.

The next few days sailed by easily. Julie was busy packing to go to Wisconsin for church camp. She would be gone for a week. She had gone to the same camp the previous year and had loved it. It had been a mountaintop spiritual experience, and she was looking forward to a spiritual renewal. One bad thing about having a job was not being able to go to church. Church had always been a big part of her life, but working at the restaurant had made it impossible for her to attend with any regularity. Being away from the norm and having time to focus on God was going to be good. She was also hoping to rid herself of the guilt poking at her from the back of her mind.

She had said nothing about what had happened and neither had Jeremy. He didn't try anything else like that either. The night before she left for camp, he took her out for ice cream. When he took her home, he didn't come inside. He told her he hoped she had a good time at camp and kissed her good night.

Camp was indeed awesome. Julie made new friends. She even met a guy from Missouri named Robert Worth. She hadn't meant to meet a guy, but it happened. They fell into a fast friendship. Robert was hurting. A drunk driver had killed his older brother a few months before. He was angry, angry at the drunk driver for taking his innocent brother's life, angry at his brother for dying, angry at his parents for not being able to help him because of their own grief, and even angry with God because he didn't stop it from happening.

Julie cared for hurting people. She hated for others to suffer. She was no counselor, no psychologist, but she was a good listener. Robert talked, and she listened. She listened and let him know she cared about him. She helped Robert talk about his brother, to remember his brother without the pain and to laugh about things they had done together.

She even told him about Jeremy—not everything but some of it. He listened without passing judgment. She told Robert she was afraid Jeremy was more serious than she was, and she didn't really know what to do about it. She didn't want to hurt Jeremy, but she didn't feel right about continuing a relationship with him either.

After talking to one of the camp counselors about her situation with Jeremy, she finally decided she would break it off with him when she returned home. Julie didn't share specific details with the counselor; she just explained how he made her feel uncomfortable and that she was always stopping him from doing something to her he shouldn't. The counselor pointed out that if he truly cared about her he would respect her enough not to push her into something she didn't really want to do. Julie agreed, and, with that decision made, she felt the guilt lifted.

Toward the end of camp, Julie and Robert made plans to write to each other. They discussed the possibility of attending Purdue University together. Julie was already planning to apply there for pharmacy school, and Robert was interested in engineering.

One night they went out on the golf course with some other campers to lie on blankets and watch the Perseids meteor shower. It was a great place to see it. There was very little light pollution in that part of Wisconsin, and the golf course was a large open space with no trees to block the view. The shooting stars zoomed through the sky so fast, one right after the other, that it was almost like watching fireworks go off.

As Julie lay next to Robert on a blanket, watching the meteors whiz overhead, and listening to the quiet murmuring of the friends around them, she felt his warm hand slide over hers and gently squeeze it. She squeezed back and turned to look at him. He was watching her. She could tell even though she was unable to make out his expression in the dark. After a while he leaned toward her and kissed her. Not a passionate kiss, but a slow, gentle kiss, filled with friendship, trust, and appreciation. It was a sweet kiss. It was a good kiss. Julie closed her eyes and kissed him back. It felt much different than when Jeremy kissed her.

When he ended the kiss and pulled away, he smiled. She couldn't see his smile, but she could feel it. She smiled too.

"That was nice," he said quietly.

"It was very nice," she answered and let out a little sigh of contentment. She snuggled closer to him, and he put his arms around her. They both turned their faces toward the sky and watched quietly as the rest of the stars shot across the blue blackness of the Wisconsin sky.

After the meteor shower was over, people began to stand, stretch, and pick up their blankets in preparation for the trek back to the dormitory rooms. Robert and Julie held hands all the way along the path toward the buildings. He walked her to her building and down the hall to her room. He told her roommates good night and then kissed her softly after they had all gone into the room.

"Good night," he said. "Sweet dreams."

Julie grinned up at him and reached to brush back his almost-blond hair that the breeze had blown across his forehead. His hazel eyes seemed to glow in the soft light of the hallway.

"Good night to you," she said through her grin.

"I'm glad I met you, Julie McCourt," he said softly, his eyes studying her face.

"I'm glad I met you too. I'll see you at breakfast in the morning."

Julie reluctantly stepped through the door and shut it behind her. She smiled as she listened to the fading sound of his whistling as he made his way down the hall.

On the last morning of camp, there was a throng of people in front of the main building. Some were laughing; some were crying. Everyone was making noise. There were shouts as youth group leaders worked to gather their kids together and load them in their respective vans for the ride home. Most groups had several hours of traveling before they would make it home that night, Julie and her group included.

Julie hugged the many friends she had met. Her eyes were shiny with tears. When she turned and found herself facing Rob, a single tear slid down her cheek. Robert brushed it away with his thumb.

"Don't cry, Julie. I don't think I can stand to see you cry."

Julie sniffed and swallowed hard. "Oh, I cry all the time," she said, trying to smile.

"I'll miss you, Julie. You've helped me so much. I feel like I've known you for years instead of just a few days."

"I know what you mean. You're a very special friend. Be sure to write to me. I'll write to you. I promise."

They hugged each other, squeezing tight, neither one wanting to let go. Julie lifted her head and kissed his cheek.

Rob brought his lips to her ear. "I wish I could really kiss you," he whispered.

Julie blushed.

Robert wrote. Julie wrote. They talked on the phone. They both received letters a few days after getting home. Julie hadn't seen Jeremy since she'd returned. She had talked to him on the phone, but she had not wanted to end it like that. She'd rather do it in person. It seemed better that way. At the time she didn't know what a mistake she was making.

School had started, so she wasn't working nearly as much, two evenings after school and every other Saturday and Sunday. Thankfully, her path hadn't crossed Jeremy's much. Not long enough for any discussion anyway. Her luck ran out one Friday night. She'd gone to the local park with a group from the restaurant. A bunch of the guys got up a game of basketball. Julie and her friend Amy sat on nearby swings watching and talking.

Julie saw Jeremy's car pull into the parking lot. She immediately felt her body tense. He walked past the basketball court, calling out to some of the guys playing. Several of them joked back and forth with him for a few minutes. Then he saw Julie and began walking toward her, never taking his eyes off her face. When he reached the swings, he leaned against one of the support poles.

Amy was the first to speak. "Hey, Jeremy. How's it goin'?"

"I'm good, Amy. How 'bout you? How's Trent?"

Julie noticed he didn't look at Amy as he spoke. His piercing stare remained focused on her.

"He's still finishing up at the restaurant. Fridays are always busy. Lots more dishes to wash," Amy answered, looking from her friend to Jeremy.

"Say, Amy," he said, his eyes still fixed on her face, "do you mind if I talk to Julie for a while? Alone."

Amy glanced at her, questioning with her eyes. Julie gave her a nod. Amy looked at Jeremy and back to Julie and then slowly walked over to sit on a bench by the basketball court.

Jeremy looked over his shoulder as if he was checking to make sure they were out of earshot. Julie took a deep breath. "Jeremy, I need—"

She stopped as he turned back toward her. His blue eyes were full of tears. His face twisted with emotion. He was holding something in his hand. He had pulled it out of the pocket inside his jacket. It was an envelope with her name and address on it. It was from Robert, but this was the first time Julie had seen it. The envelope had been opened. From the creases and the ragged look of the paper, she could tell the letter had been read and reread and folded time and time again. Anger immediately sprung up inside her. Her face was red with rage.

"How did you—"

He cut her question off, tears pouring down his face. "How could you have done this to me? Don't you know how I feel about you? Don't you know how I care? I love you, Julie. I love you, and you cheated on me."

"I did not cheat on you. I never made you any promises—"

He wasn't listening. "Remember the night in your parents' living room? You gave part of yourself to me that night. How could you be with someone else? How could you let him hold you and kiss you when I was here waiting for you? I'll always be here waiting for you, Julie. Always."

She was beginning to get confused. He sounded so hurt. "I don't remember giving you anything, Jeremy. It's more like you took it." She finally forced out the words.

He dropped to his knees on the ground in front of her. He grabbed both of her hands in his, the envelope holding Robert's letter still clutched in his fingers. He held on to her as if he was a drowning man and she was the only one who could save him. He was sobbing now, his shoulders shuddering uncontrollably.

"Don't say things like that! You make what we did sound bad, dirty somehow. Please don't ever say that!" He moaned.

Julie had never seen any man act like this, not even in a movie. She started to feel sorry for him.

"Julie, you have to understand. You are the only one I want. You will always be the only one I want. What we did, you can't undo it. You can't take it back. Promise me I'll be your only one. Promise me forever, Julie."

He was squeezing her hands now, tightly, very tightly.

Julie opened her mouth to speak, but nothing came out. She was so confused. At camp everything had seemed so different. She had known what she needed to do about this, but now he had her so twisted up that she didn't know anymore. He made it sound like she'd done something terribly wrong and the only way to make it right was to stay with him, to promise. So she promised. It was the biggest mistake she ever made.

Julie grabbed a tissue, wiped her tears, blew her nose, and forced her thoughts back to the present. She looked at the clock on the microwave. She still had time to stop by the elementary school and see her grandmother for a few minutes before heading to class. She grabbed her loaded backpack and her keys and headed out into the Kentucky sunshine.

Chapter 2

Kevin Sanders awoke suddenly to loud banging and cursing. With a great deal of effort, he opened his eyes just wide enough to see his roommate Paul Gray staggering through the room. Paul slammed his foot into the corner of his dresser, cursed in pain, and finally collapsed face first onto his bed, muttering something about pom-poms. Apparently Paul had had a very good time last night.

Kevin lifted his head and looked at the clock on his desk. He had to stare at it for a while before it would come into focus. It was seven o'clock in the morning. He did not want to get up yet. He had already planned to skip his first class this morning. Kevin let his head fall back onto his pillow and closed his eyes. Then he heard it. Paul was snoring loudly. Unable to go back to sleep, Kevin got up and shuffled to the showers down the hall. As the hot water flowed over his dark hair, he became aware of a dull ache in his head. Coffee, he needed coffee.

After showering and dressing, he headed back to his room. Paul hadn't moved. His feet were toward the head of the bed, and his head was hanging slightly off the end of it.

Kevin moved quietly to his desk, put his notebooks in his backpack, grabbed his wallet, and put on his jacket. When he turned to leave, he noticed Paul was not only snoring but was also drooling. Kevin moved back to the other end of the room, out the door, and into the hallway, closing the door silently behind him. He chuckled and shook his head, thinking about how much worse Paul's head was going to feel than his.

Kevin's own head had reason to hurt after last night. Last night had been a Thursday, the traditional party night for pharmacy students. Tests were usually on Thursdays, and afterward most pharmacy students needed to cut loose a little.

The University of Kentucky College of Pharmacy had a demanding program. Just being accepted was difficult. In Kevin's class there had been one hundred slots available and over three hundred applicants. Of course, getting in was only the beginning. Once in, students faced eighteen-hour semesters of almost all 800-level courses.

So he deserved a little recreation, but maybe he had had a bit too much. He'd had a few too many beers on top of too many Jell-O shots, on top of some kind of concoction some of the fourth-year students were dispensing from an IV bag. Admittedly, he may have allowed himself a little too much fun this entire semester.

This was his first year in pharmacy school, so he was referred to as a third-year student. Technically, the pre-pharmacy work should take two years to complete, but few students were able to handle all the courses required in two years. Kevin had; he was quite capable when he put his mind to something. In the fall semester his grades were good, but he had let them slide this spring, especially since he'd turned twenty-one. He was certainly not in any danger of not graduating, but he wasn't going to graduate top of his class either. Life was too short not to have some fun.

Kevin pushed through the doors of his dorm building and stepped out into the cool April morning. The grass and sidewalks around the Kirwin-Blanding complex were wet from last night's rain, but the sky was clear this morning. The sunrise looked promising. Kevin sleepily surveyed the familiar surroundings. There were few other people out this early. He smiled wryly to himself and wondered if pharmacy students were the only ones with eight o'clock classes. Of course, after last night, he didn't figure too many of his classmates would actually show up at eight. If it hadn't been for Paul and his pom-poms, he wouldn't be making it either.

Kevin glanced at his watch as he walked across campus. He still had time for coffee. He cut through Chandler Medical Center, went into the hospital cafeteria, and ordered a large black coffee. The coffee here wasn't bad. It was strong, and that's what he needed this morning. He closed his eyes and inhaled the soothing aroma. He took a gulp and headed out the door.

Outside, medical students, residents, and physicians were heading toward the hospital. Kevin noticed students entering the nursing building across the street. There was much more activity on this side of campus. Healthcare majors must be the only ones with eight o'clock classes.

He made his way across Rose Street, weaving his way through the early morning Lexington traffic.

Reaching the door, he held it open for a couple of women in his class. They murmured their greetings, and he smiled as he nodded in reply. They had been at the party last night too. One of them teasingly asked him how he was feeling this morning.

"I'll be good as soon as I get the rest of this coffee down," he replied warmly.

Foregoing the elevators, Kevin headed to the stairs and took them up to the third floor. He took his usual seat in the back row and started going through the papers that had been in his mailbox as he waited for class to begin.

Kevin noticed Carl, one of his married classmates, come in and take a seat in the row in front of his. Kevin was surprised to see him since he'd been at the party last night—without his wife—having way too much of the wrong kind of fun for a married guy. Carl often bragged about picking up women after slipping his wedding band in his pocket. Kevin thought Carl was disgusting. He didn't understand getting married if you were going to carry on like that.

After the lecture had already begun, Kevin's friend Dave, still panting from his run up the stairs, slipped into the seat next to him. The professor turned from the huge boards at the front of the room, glared at Dave, cleared his throat, glared at Dave some more, and turned back to the board to complete his lecture outline.

Dave was older than Kevin and, like Carl in the next row up, was married. Unlike Carl, Dave was faithful to his wife. Lately Dave, who was normally wound a little too tightly, was acting even more stressed than usual. Dave's wife, who was also a UK student, was expecting their first child. With finals approaching and the baby due in late May, the man was just about frazzled.

"How's the wife?" Kevin whispered.

"Oh, she's as big as a barn and moody as hell," he muttered in reply. "But," he said with a big grin, "we're gonna have a boy! We found out yesterday during her ultrasound. We're naming him Kyle."

In Dave's excitement, he forgot to whisper and was practically yelling by the time he got to "Kyle." All eyes were focused on the back of the room. Dave smiled meekly and gave a little wave. If looks could kill, the professor would have rendered poor baby Kyle fatherless.

Once everyone else had returned their focus to the professor, Dave turned back to Kevin and told him quietly about shopping for hours buying blue sleepers, blue blankets, blue bibs, blue everything. Kevin hadn't realized there were so many blue things to buy for a baby. When Dave, still grinning from ear to ear, finished telling about blue this and that, he turned his attention to the professor and tried to catch up on the notes he'd missed.

Kevin was happy for his friend but realized he felt a stab of something that might be envy. He wondered what it would be like to find someone to share life with. He seriously doubted he would ever know.

Chapter 3

Julie parked her tiny car at the rear of Howevalley Elementary School and got out. She headed up the concrete steps, opened the heavy back door, and stepped into the storage area behind the kitchen. She walked between the shelves filled with all sorts of large cans, bottles, and jars used to fix the breakfasts and lunches served at the school.

Julie's grandmother, Ann Young, had worked at the school her entire adult life. She had started as a cook back when her own mother had been the lunchroom manager and then took her place when she retired. All of this had taken place before Julie had even been born. Grams loved to cook, and she was good at it. Julie had not inherited any of those genes because she couldn't boil water.

As Julie stepped into the bright, stainless steel kitchen, she called out a cheerful, "Good morning, ladies."

She received happy greetings from the women scattered in different areas of the large room as they performed various tasks involved in either cleaning up the morning meal or preparing for the noon one.

Julie went around the corner to find her grandmother in her small office going over menus and writing up her weekly food order. Her grandmother looked up as she heard her approach. Julie watched her grandmother's smile fade before it had completely formed. Julie could tell her grandmother knew she had been crying. What she said told Julie she also knew why she'd been crying.

"He called again. Why did you answer the phone?"

"Oh, I don't know. I enjoy the verbal abuse I guess," Julie answered, trying to lighten the serious situation.

"You know, I really don't think this is funny. I don't see how you can joke about it. I'm afraid Jeremy is going to come down here and do something violent. The man is clearly not stable."

"I don't suppose you would consider changing your phone number?" Julie asked hesitantly.

Grams had probably had the same phone number for decades.

"Changing the number wouldn't stop him from coming down here."

Julie shrugged and gave her grandmother a wry look in response. Seeing the concern in her grandmother's soft blue eyes reminded Julie of the main reason she had left Wells County, Indiana, given up going to Purdue or Butler, and moved to Kentucky. Before Julie had moved in with her grandmother, Grams had lived alone for four years. Julie's grandfather had died after a hard, nine-month battle with cancer. Julie's grandmother had tirelessly cared for him throughout his entire illness, taking him to his appointments, feeding him, bathing him, and holding his hand as he wretched helplessly after chemo treatments. Even during his many hospitalizations, she stayed right by his side.

Grams had taken a leave of absence from work so that she could care for her husband night and day. She had lost both weight and sleep. Her hair turned almost completely gray, where there had been no gray before, and for the first time in her life, she actually looked her age.

Julie knew her grandparents had loved each other. They had shared a strong and rare devotion to each other, even though they had married when they were both very young.

Losing her husband nearly crushed Grams's spirit. Because of that, Julie moved in with her after high school and was attending the community college in Elizabethtown to do her pre-pharmacy course work.

Julie had been foolish enough to think that she and Jeremy might be able to share a love like her grandparents had shared. Aside from his overpossessiveness and jealousy, he had been good to her, or so she thought, until she found out about the drug problem. But even before the drug issue, she was uncomfortable with his lack of trust. It really wasn't until she moved away from him that she realized how he had been totally monopolizing her life.

The jealousy worsened after Robert's letter was stolen. Despite Julie's fervent assurances that she would stay true to her promise and date only him, Jeremy made it impossible for her to have friends who were male. He stood over her while she wrote to Robert, telling him that she could never write him again, being sure Julie made it clear that Jeremy was the reason.

A few days later, Julie remembered sitting on the sofa in her parents' living room, working on homework. Jeremy was sitting near her, watching television. When the phone rang, Julie's mom answered.

"Julie, it's for you. I think it's that Robert boy from church camp."

Real smooth there, Mom! Thanks.

Before Julie knew it, Jeremy was leaning heavily against her. He pressed his mouth hard against her ear and clamped down on her upper arm with his fingers so tightly that Julie knew it would leave a bruise. "You tell him you never want to speak to him again," he rasped angrily so only she could hear. "You tell him, or I will. Do you understand? I don't want you talking to any other guy, especially not him."

Julie nodded, and he released her to go to the phone in the other room. "Hello?" she said quietly into the receiver.

"Julie, it's Robert. I got your letter today. I don't understand. Tell me you don't mean this."

"Robert, please. I can't do this," Julie said, choking back a sob.

"Julie this is not you. Jeremy put you up to this. I know he did. Let me help you. It doesn't have to be this way."

"You're in Missouri. What could you do?"

"I don't know. Maybe I could—"

Julie took a deep breath and cut him off. "Robert, I'll be fine. Just let it go. We cannot be friends anymore. Please don't ever call or write me again. Please. I'm so sorry, but this is the way it has to be. Good-bye, Robert. I hope you won't hate me."

She quietly hung up the phone and took a moment to compose herself before returning to Jeremy in the living room.

Thankfully, Jeremy left without argument or further conflict. When he was gone, Julie went straight to her room. Once inside with the door secured behind her, she let the tears come.

That night Julie realized she would have to avoid any of her friends who were not female. She feared that if she didn't, one of them might speak to her when Jeremy was out with her somewhere. She didn't know what he might do, but she knew she didn't want to find out.

She stopped speaking to any males except when it was absolutely necessary. The only guys she talked to were Jeremy's friends. She went out of her way to avoid anyone she didn't think Jeremy would approve of. Julie knew it bothered Ned that she was avoiding him, but she didn't know what else to do.

One night she and Jeremy went to a football game. When he brought her home, there was a note written in soap on the glass portion of the door.

> *Julie,*
>   *I really did love you. I wish I could've told you. If I wasn't such a jerk, we could still be friends.*
>   *Love always,*
>   *Slim*

Slim was Ned's nickname. Julie's heart was breaking. Ned thought he had done something wrong. When she saw

Jeremy's expression, her eyes went wide with fright. He was about to completely lose control.

He stomped up on the porch, staring at the words. He was physically shaking with rage. He spun around, thrusting his face to hers until their noses almost touched.

"Who wrote this?" he roared.

Julie backed away, shaking her head. "I don't know," she lied, thanking God Jeremy did not know Ned's nickname.

After that Jeremy changed his work schedule so that he could take her to school every morning and pick her up every afternoon. He would be waiting for her by her locker every day after her last class. He told her he wanted to save her money. She'd be able to save more money for college if he drove her everywhere. After school he either took her home or to work. After work he was always waiting for her when she got off.

At the time she convinced herself that his jealousy showed how much he cared for her and that he was really trying to help her save money for college. Looking back, she could see it was all part of his desire to control her. She wished she had seen it when it was happening.

Grams's voice brought Julie out of her reflections. "Julie! Julie, are you listening?"

Julie gave her head a little shake and focused on what her grandmother was saying.

"Something has to be done before this goes any further. After I get done here at school, I am going to make some phone calls. Maybe we can get a restraining order or something."

"Oh, Grams, a restraining order? Wouldn't that be embarrassing?"

"Better to be embarrassed than hurt. Or worse!"

Julie couldn't disagree with her there. She glanced at her watch. "Well, I better run, or I won't make it to my first class on time."

"Okay, honey, but be careful. Have you eaten? No, I know you haven't eaten. Grab a cinnamon roll left over from this morning and eat it on the way."

Chapter 4

At 8:50 a.m. there was a large influx of third-year students entering the lecture hall. Pharmacy students were the type that might skip a class here and there, but never would they miss an entire day.

Included among the incoming masses was a friend of both Kevin and Dave. Dave noticed Mitch Collins first, nudged Kevin in the arm, and nodded toward their friend as he strolled into the room. Kevin saw Mitch grinning slyly as a pretty, petite blonde whispered something in his ear. The blonde was a fellow classmate named Cindy. Since the beginning of third year, she had mercilessly been throwing herself at Kevin, who had brushed off her advances. He just wasn't interested. Apparently she was finally moving on.

Mitch threw himself in the seat next to Kevin, and Cindy moved on down the aisle. As she took a seat with some of her girlfriends, she turned to give the three men a coy smile and a little wave. Dave and Kevin looked at each other knowingly and then looked together at Mitch. He was smiling smugly and examining his nails.

Mitch sat up suddenly and said, "Hey, Kev, were you here at eight?"

When Kevin nodded, Mitch continued, "After last night, I can't believe you were able to drag your butt out of bed that early!"

"I must admit my early arrival was due entirely to my scholarly roommate."

"Yeah, right!" Mitch scoffed. "What'd he do? Come in drunk this morning and wake you up in time for class?"

"Pretty much," Kevin admitted and told the story about Paul's drunken beating and banging and muttering about pom-poms.

Both Mitch and Dave laughed out loud. "I will definitely have to hear the story behind the pom-poms when next I see your dear roommate," Mitch said. "Let me see your notes from this morning."

Kevin handed him the notes he had taken. Mitch frowned. "Man, I forgot you write in hieroglyphics! I can't make anything out of this." Mitch handed the sheets back to Kevin.

"Copy Dave's then. He doesn't know any ancient Egyptian. Hey, Dave, tell Mitch your news," Kevin said, turning from one friend to the other.

"We're having a boy and naming him Kyle," Dave blurted as he handed over his neatly written notes.

"Hey, that's great, Dave. Congratulations!"

The three were quiet as Mitch copied what he had missed in the first lecture.

After Mitch finished and handed back Dave's notes, he turned to Kevin. "You got any plans this weekend?

Cindy's cousin is coming to Lexington for the weekend, and I thought we could double date."

"So are you and Cindy a thing now?" Kevin asked.

"We hooked up last night at the party. I went home with her afterward. Jealous?"

"Not at all," Kevin answered honestly. "She's not my type."

"If drop-dead-gorgeous-I-want-to-fool-around-and-no-strings-attached isn't your type, then what is?" Mitch asked, openly astonished.

"I don't know what my type is, but if you're not careful, you're gonna catch something!"

"Hey, you know me," Mitch replied. "I take precautions. I saw too much nasty stuff during my summer rotation at the Fayette County Health Department. So, *anyway*, how 'bout this weekend?"

"Can't. I've got tennis matches in Louisville Friday afternoon and most of Saturday and Sunday. It's a tournament."

"All weekend? How 'bout the evenings? You're not going to stay in Louisville, are you?"

"No, but I'm sure I'll be poor company after playing tennis all day."

"Whatever," Mitch grumbled. "You are totally blowing my weekend. I know Cindy won't go out if I can't find a date for her cousin."

"I'm sorry," Kevin said, which was true. He did feel a little guilty, but not guilty enough to go out on another one of Mitch's blind dates. "Why don't you give Paul a call? I remember him saying something about being around this weekend. He might be interested."

"Okay. I'll call him. I still don't get you and chicks, man. I've set you up so many times, and you have never shown interest in any of them. I set up quality dates too. Babes, even. What's the deal with you?" Mitch answered his own question. "You're holdin' out for *the one*, aren't you? Man, when you fall, you are gonna fall so hard! I just hope I'm around to see it."

Kevin could not think of one snappy comeback that might wipe the cocky, know-it-all expression off his friend's face. He sat there speechless as the next instructor came in and began passing out handouts for her class.

The rest of the day went by—more instructors, more lectures, more notes, break for lunch, compounding lab. As Kevin walked back to his dorm, he couldn't help but think about what Mitch had said.

He'd never really thought about it before. He had dated several girls in high school, but no one seriously. In fact, he couldn't remember going out on more than one date with any one girl. The same had been true in college so far.

The fact that he was still a virgin didn't bother him. He'd never really thought about it one way or the other. It wasn't as if he hadn't had chances to lose it if he'd wanted to. It seemed that there had always been girls like Cindy who made it quite clear just how far they would let him go. He'd met girls at parties and spring break trips to Florida too—girls from Canada and Australia even.

But none of those girls had interested him at all. That brought him to Mitch's question. What was his type? Thinking about it, he still didn't know. He guessed he wanted her to be attractive. But Mitch was right about that. The women he had set him up with had been good looking. So it wasn't just attractiveness he was looking for. He wanted someone who was genuine, someone real, someone who was more than what she was on the outside.

Kevin didn't want to think anymore about women or *the* woman, as the case may be. He had lived this long without one, and he didn't see any reason to change that in the near future, maybe ever, for that matter. He hit the stairs, taking two at a time, up to his floor, hoping Paul was sober. He was going to drag him to the tennis courts.

Chapter 5

Julie was hot, sweating hot. She couldn't breathe. She was suffocating. Someone was pressing down on her, crushing her. She was trying to move, but she couldn't break free. She wanted to scream, but someone's mouth covered hers. There were legs and arms tangled with her arms and legs. He was over her, all around her, inside her. She jerked her head from side to side, finally breaking the hold he had on her.

"Let me go! Please let me go." The words came out as a hoarse whisper, even though she was trying to scream.

"Oh, I can never let you go, Julie. You belong to me. You will always belong to me."

She knew that voice. His mouth was right next to her ear. It couldn't be, but it was. It was Jeremy.

"No!" she screamed, her eyes flying open.

She was in her bed. She was alone. She was covered in sweat, her heart was pounding in her chest, and she could barely catch her breath. It was a dream, a nightmare. It wasn't real.

She was unable to move, still frozen in fear at the seeming reality of the dream. She tried hard to take deep breaths, to calm herself and slow down her heart rate. She still wasn't fully awake but became aware of a noise coming from another place in the house. The phone. The phone was ringing. She came to her senses. She stumbled into the living room next to her bedroom in her grandmother's basement. She staggered to the phone and picked up the handset.

"Hello," she croaked. Her throat was hoarse from sleep and her nightmare.

"Hello, Julie. Have you been dreaming about me?"

Jeremy. Oh my God! How could he know? Julie dropped the phone and ran upstairs. She wanted to run and never stop. She ran as far as the kitchen door. She looked down. She was wearing only her pajamas—an old, holey, oversized T-shirt that came down just far enough to cover her underwear. She started laughing. She may have been on the verge of hysteria, but she couldn't help it. When she thought of herself running through the fields and yards around her grandmother's house half dressed, she lost it. Boy, wouldn't the neighbors get a load out of that!

Finally shaking herself completely free of her nightmare and the laughing fit that followed, Julie looked at the clock on the kitchen wall. It was early yet, but she might as well hit the shower and start getting ready for class.

She headed back to her room to turn off her alarm and grab some clothes. As she walked through the living room, she remembered the phone and replaced it in the cradle. She prayed it would not ring again.

For the last two weeks, he had called only twice instead of every morning. Two weeks ago Julie and her grandmother had gone to the Hardin County Sheriff's office to see about a restraining order. The secretary there knew Grams and suggested a letter threatening a restraining order. She said in similar cases the letter worked without all the legal red tape. Julie's faith that the letter would work were fading.

He called right after he got the letter. Julie had known he would, and, as she had also known, he'd been royally ticked off. She took that call, hoping beyond hope it would be the last time she would have to talk to him.

He had made no more calls until today. Anytime the phone rang in the morning on weekdays, Julie knew it was him. No one else ever called in the morning. He had started calling and harassing her daily after she broke off their engagement. She was sure he chose mornings because he knew she would be home alone. She made a point of ignoring the phone ringing at that time of day. Today he caught her off guard.

If she could just make it through finals week, he wouldn't know her schedule. Once she started her summer classes and started working more hours at her part-time job, there would be no way for him to track her. Then, once she got through next year, she would be in Lexington. He would never find her there.

As she showered, unbidden memories—spurred by her nightmare—came flooding into her mind. She had given Jeremy her virginity, and, at times, it was as if she could still feel his touch on her skin. She scrubbed harder in an effort to get clean and to wash his effect off of her.

She hadn't wanted to become sexually involved with Jeremy. It was another way he had manipulated her. It wasn't until close to the end of their relationship that she had finally given in to his constant badgering. They loved each other, he reasoned. They were going to get married anyway. They had been together for almost three years. He told her she was so unfair to him to hold herself from him when he loved and wanted her so much. So she had finally given in and had been regretting her decision ever since.

It hadn't even been enjoyable. Julie was pretty sure sex was supposed to be enjoyable, but in her experience it had not been. In fact, it had been downright painful, the first time especially. The times following the first experience were not much better. She thought it could be different if the experience was shared with someone who truly cared for her. Instead of feeling loved and treasured, Jeremy made her feel like something he only wished to control. There was no gentleness or compassion, only conquest.

She secretly suspected he wanted her to get pregnant. What twisted reason he would have for that, she did not know. She hated the thought of Jeremy being anybody's father, much less her child's. Thank God she didn't have to worry about that. She had been on birth control pills for a while before she even started dating Jeremy, and not for the prevention of pregnancy. Her physician started her on them because of her terribly irregular and difficult menstrual cycles. It just turned out that, for a while, the pills had served a dual purpose.

She wouldn't have to worry about preventing pregnancy now. She had absolutely no intention of becoming involved with another man. For one thing, she didn't think she could let herself be that close to anyone ever again. For another thing, she felt she would be cheating any other man because she was no longer a virgin.

Julie knew she was being old fashioned to feel that way, but she couldn't help it. Being free of any male restrictions would give her freedom to do what she wanted, and that wasn't old fashioned. She wanted to find herself again. All she wanted was to focus on school and then her career. She didn't need a man to do that. One would only get in the way.

Chapter 6

It was nine o'clock when Kevin got back to Lexington Sunday evening. His tennis tournament had gone well. He was pleased with his performance.

Tennis was something he enjoyed. He didn't obsess about it like some of the people he played against. Some guys he knew spent hours on lessons and training. Kevin didn't do that. For him, tennis was recreational, something to do for fun and exercise.

A few years ago, he and some high school buddies bought rackets and taught themselves how to play. He'd been playing ever since, spending his free time playing with friends and entering U.S. Tennis Association matches from time to time. It kept him in shape and helped relieve stress.

After the announcements of the winners this evening, Kevin showered and changed in the locker room at the tennis center. Going out to his car, his gear slung over his shoulder, he noticed he was the only one walking out alone. The other tennis players all seemed to have someone there with them. Kevin suddenly felt a pang of loneliness.

He'd never noticed it before. He'd often come to matches alone. Sometimes he and a friend would sign up for matches together, sometimes not. It had never been a big deal. Tonight he found himself wondering what it would be like to bring someone special with him to watch him play. Silently, Kevin cursed Mitch. This was his fault. All that talk Friday about holding out for a perfect woman had put all these crazy thoughts in his head.

Kevin tried to shake the undesired thoughts out of his mind as he stowed his gear in the trunk of his Mustang. He got in and started his car. He pulled out of the parking lot and drove until he found a fast food restaurant. After grabbing something through the drive-thru, he made his way to I-64. As he ate and drove toward Lexington, he still couldn't get rid of the lonely feeling.

When he entered the dorm room, Paul was at his desk with an opened book. "Well, will wonders never cease?" Kevin said. "Have I ever seen you reading a book?"

"Ha, ha, very funny. I happen to be an okay student. I just don't let my studies interfere with my social life. A guy has to have priorities," Paul replied, turning away from his book toward his friend. "How'd the matches go today?"

"I placed second in the men's singles for my division," Kevin answered as he took his sweaty tennis clothes out of his bag and added them to his pile of dirty laundry in the closet. The pile had grown rather large. He was either going to have to do laundry or go home soon. He hated doing laundry.

"Well, you missed out on a great redhead while you swatted away at green, fuzzy tennis balls. But your loss was my gain. I had a very good weekend thanks to you."

"I'm so happy for you. She probably enjoyed your company more than she would've mine anyway." He still didn't regret not going out on the blind date.

"Oh, hey, before I forget, your mom called earlier. She said for you to call her back tonight. It didn't matter how late it was. She was going to wait up for your call."

Kevin glanced at his watch. It was almost nine thirty. His mom was a nurse at Hardin Memorial Hospital in E-town, and Kevin knew she got up early to go to work. "Thanks. I better go ahead and call before it gets too late."

Kevin made his way to the desk at the end of his small dorm-sized bed and sat down. The phone only rang twice before his mother answered.

"Hey, Mom. Paul said you called earlier. I just got in."

"How was your tennis tournament, son?"

He quickly relayed the details of the tournament, answering her questions about his serve, specific games, points he'd won, and his opponents.

"Your dad will be so proud, Kevin. I'm proud of you too."

"Thanks, Mom. How is Dad?"

"Oh, he's good. He's always good."

Kevin could hear the sound of contentment in his mom's voice. He knew his parents loved each other. Even though they had been married for nearly thirty years, it was obvious they still enjoyed spending time together.

"Kevin, I called because I wanted to talk to you about something. I know you and Paul have plans to get an apartment in Lexington this summer, and what I'm suggesting won't change that. The hospital wants to hire a pharmacy student for the summer to work mostly in the IV room and some in unit dose. Sam Jones, the pharmacy tech supervisor, asked me if you would be interested. You would need to work thirty to forty hours a week and every other weekend. This would be a good chance for you to get some clinical experience. The pay sounds like it would be pretty good. You can stay here. Your old room is the same as always."

Kevin knew what his mother was doing. Last summer he'd stayed in Lexington most of the time while he was enrolled in UK's summer program for students interested in careers in the healthcare field. Since this year had started, he'd only been home one weekend out of ten and only part of the holiday breaks. The time for him to permanently move out was rapidly approaching. His mom was trying to keep him close a little while longer.

She was right about his work experience. He did need some exposure to hospital pharmacy. With school and tennis, he hadn't had time yet to hunt for a job in Lexington. Money was something he was in need of too. He had worked for an independent pharmacy all through high school and the two years he'd gone to the Elizabethtown Community College, saving as much money as possible, but he hadn't worked since he started pharmacy school. His parents were helping him with tuition, but still his bank account had dwindled substantially.

"Kevin, honey, are you thinking about it? Sam said he would like to meet with you. Could you make it to the hospital by three o'clock Friday afternoon? I've got his phone number. Why don't you give him a call to set up the appointment for Friday?"

"Okay, Mom." What did he have to lose? Kevin took down the number and propped the slip of paper next to the lamp on his desk. He would call Mr. Jones tomorrow after class.

"Listen, Mom. I have some laundry—"

"Bring it," she said. "You can stay the night Friday. I'll cook and see if your sister can come for dinner."

"Sounds good. Tell Dad hello for me. I'll see you Friday."

After Kevin hung up the phone, he spent some time talking to Paul. Kevin, struggling to stifle yawns, listened as Paul recounted his weekend with Cindy's red-haired cousin. When Paul was finished with his tale, Kevin went to bed.

Chapter 7

When Julie pulled her compact car into a parking spot behind the hospital, she was happy. She couldn't remember the last time she felt happy. It felt good actually.

Things were going her way for the first time in a long time. Finals were next week, and she was ready for the exams. She was also ready to have another long, hard semester under her belt. Each one brought her closer and closer to her goal of pharmacy school. She'd also gotten the two summer classes she wanted. One was a morning class she could attend on her day off, and the other was an evening class she would go to after work. Best of all, she hadn't talked to Jeremy in several days. The phone had been silent every morning. Each day without a phone call caused her to relax more and more. She hadn't even realized how oppressed his calls had made her feel until they had stopped.

Feeling lighthearted, she actually caught herself humming as she walked through the parking lot toward the back door of the hospital. She glanced at her watch. It was almost four thirty. Her days were longer on Friday because of chemistry lab. The technicians she usually worked with in unit dose would already be gone for the day, but Sam would still be here.

She had been working in the pharmacy since last semester. She had worked every other weekend and picked up extra hours during spring and Christmas breaks. Her cell biology professor, who was also the advisor for all pre-pharmacy students, had announced the job opening. She had called and set up an interview along with at least two other pre-pharmacy students attending the community college. She had been hired for the job over the other applicants because of her previous work experience.

During high school she had taken a health occupations class. In the course, students studied anatomy and physiology and medical terminology. Part of the course allowed students to gain actual work experience in their desired field of healthcare at Caylor-Nickel Clinic, a hospital in the county where Julie went to high school. Everything from respiratory therapy to nursing to radiology was offered. Julie had been the only student to choose pharmacy and was able to work in both the clinic's inpatient and outpatient pharmacies. She had learned a great deal during her rotations. That knowledge had helped her get the job at Hardin Memorial.

She opened the back door of the hospital and turned down the hallway to the right. The pharmacy was on the bottom floor of the hospital behind the cafeteria and across the hall from the morgue. Dungeon-like, the pharmacy only had one small window that opened to the hallway, allowing the pick up of stat orders without allowing non-pharmacy personnel entry into the pharmacy itself. Security was priority in a pharmacy, and the heavy metal doors allowing access to the pharmacy and IV room required a key code to open.

Julie entered her code, pushed hard to open the door, and stepped into the main room. Stan, a grandfatherly man and one of the pharmacists who frequently worked the second shift, was sitting on a high stool entering orders into the computer while the second shift tech filled the orders to be checked.

Stan turned and greeted Julie with a smile. "Hey, Julie. Are you here to give me the night off?"

"Not yet, Stan. Give me a few years; then I'll be ready. Is Sam still here?"

"I think he's in his office."

Before Julie could make her way back to Sam's office, someone called out to her from the IV room. "Julie, come in here a minute before you go back." It was Lisa Simmons, one of the IV technicians who was a few years older than Julie.

Julie stepped into the IV room and was hit immediately by the strong vapors of isopropyl alcohol. Lisa was methodically wiping down the work surface of the IV hood as she prepared to mix the IVs for the evening run she would deliver later to the patient floors.

"Hi, Julie," Lisa called loudly so that Julie could hear her over the sound of the hood's filtering unit. "Are you here to get your check?"

"Yes," Julie called from behind her, "and the first schedule for summer. Finals are next week."

Lisa finished wiping the hood's surfaces and tossed the alcohol damp gauze in the trash. She took more sterile gauze from a package on the counter and began the same process on the work counter between her and Julie. She was smiling as she worked. Lisa was excited. Julie had worked with Lisa for several months now, and excitement seemed to be a common emotion for Lisa. She was an upbeat person and very likable. She was also a deliriously happy newlywed.

Lisa pulled off her gloves, tossed them in the trash, and glanced toward the doorway as she came around the counter toward Julie. She grabbed Julie's sleeve and pulled her toward the other side of the room, away from the doorway connecting the IV room and the rest of the pharmacy.

Lisa's eyes sparkled as she huddled close to Julie. Julie suspected this had something to do with a guy. Lisa had been trying to get Julie to notice guys that worked at the hospital since Julie had started working there. Julie hadn't shared much about Jeremy, but it was enough for Lisa to form an opinion of him. Lisa made it clear that she thought Jeremy was a loser and was glad that Julie had broken up with him. The only problem was that Lisa thought Julie needed another guy. She pushed the issue every chance she got, despite Julie's adamant position that she didn't want any guy. Lisa was constantly telling her that she was young, she needed to get out more, and she needed to have more fun. A new guy, in Lisa's opinion, would solve all of Julie's problems.

Lisa looked around, turning her head from side to side, as if she expected someone to be spying on them. Julie braced herself, all the while trying hard not to laugh out loud at her friend's behavior.

"Sam's in his office, but he's not alone. He's talking with a pharmacy student he just hired. The guy's hot and looks athletic. His name is Kevin. He's finishing his first year of pharmacy school. His mom is Joann Sanders. She works on the second floor in the orthopedic unit. Do you know her?" Lisa stopped for breath then continued. "When I saw him, I immediately thought of you. This is what you need, a summer romance—nothing serious, just fun. You two would surely have a lot in common with both of you interested in pharmacy."

Julie shook her head, trying to take in all that Lisa had said. "Lisa, you know I have no interest in guys, especially right now. Less than three months ago, I was engaged to a maniac. The last thing I need is another boyfriend—even a summer one—messing with my mind. And no, I don't know his mother."

"Well, you need to get your check from Sam anyway. It's not gonna hurt to scope him out while you're back there. It never hurts to look."

"Whatever you say, Lisa." Julie said over her shoulder as she walked through the door toward Sam's office at the back of the pharmacy.

As she rounded the far work counter in the unit dose area, she could hear people talking. She recognized Sam's voice. The other was unfamiliar but very nice. She quietly took a few more steps, trying not to be seen. Sam and the "hot pharmacy student" were sitting beside Sam's desk. The younger man's back was to her, and Sam was facing her. She stood and silently observed what she could of his back since neither one had noticed her yet.

The pharmacy student had short, neatly combed dark hair. He was dressed in a white dress shirt and khaki pants. She couldn't help but notice he had rather broad shoulders under the white shirt. She heard Sam clear his throat.

Julie immediately averted her eyes and looked at Sam, who apparently had stood while she was checking out her new co-worker. His mustache was twitching, and he looked like he was trying very hard to hold something back. Julie figured it was laughter. She couldn't help blushing, feeling like a kid caught with her hand in the cookie jar. She noticed the younger man shift in his chair to look at her, but she kept her eyes on Sam.

"I'm sorry. I didn't mean to interrupt. I finished with lab a little while ago and came by to get my paycheck and schedule."

"That's all right. This is actually perfect timing. I'd like you to meet Kevin Sanders. He's in pharmacy school at UK and will be working with us this summer."

Kevin, still looking at Julie, stood and turned to fully face her. He wasn't extremely tall, but he was taller than she was.

"Kevin, this is Julie McCourt. She's a pre-pharmacy student at ECC and has been working here for several months now."

"It's nice to meet you," Kevin said, holding out his hand in greeting and smiling pleasantly. "Are you a freshman or sophomore?"

Julie smiled in return, placed her hand in his, held it firmly, and gave it a short, polite shake before releasing her hold. He had warm, strong hands. "I'm finishing up my freshman year."

Their eyes met and held during the exchange. He had pleasant brown eyes.

She turned back toward Sam. He was sifting through a stack of papers and envelopes on his desk. He found what he was looking for in a matter of seconds and held a sheet of paper with the tech schedule on it and an envelope containing her paycheck. He stepped toward her with his arm outstretched, handing her the two items.

"I've scheduled you off on Tuesdays for your class. Is that the right day?"

Julie nodded.

"Later on I'll need a tech to work some evening shifts to cover vacations. Would you be able to do that?" Sam asked.

"Sure. I've got an evening class on Thursdays, but any other night would be fine."

Sam stepped back to his desk and made a note. "Thanks, Julie. Have a nice weekend. I'll see you bright and early the Monday after next. Good luck with finals."

"Thanks," she said as she turned to walk away. She returned the smile Kevin gave her as she left.

When Julie returned to the front of the pharmacy, Lisa was leaning on the counter watching Stan typing an order into the computer. She looked at Julie expectantly.

"Well?" Lisa said.

"Well, what?" Julie said.

Lisa rolled her eyes and pulled Julie into the IV room. Lisa stared at her for a moment. "I want to know what you think of Kevin."

"Well, he is a pharmacy student," Julie said simply, trying not to smile.

"And?"

"You were right. He is hot."

"I knew it!" Lisa said before doing a little victory dance.

"But," Julie interjected, "I am still not interested."

Lisa stopped dancing. "Girl, you are such a party pooper."

"Please, Lisa, do not try to set me up with him. It would be so embarrassing."

"Oh, honey. Don't worry," Lisa said, giving her a quick one-armed hug. "I won't do anything to embarrass you. I promise."

"Well, I better head home. Grams will be worried if I'm too late. I'll see you later."

Julie walked toward the door and waved bye to Stan and the tech still working at the front counter. Julie went to her car and started toward her grandmother's home located outside of Cecilia.

Chapter 8

Kevin's meeting with Sam was over about fifteen minutes after Julie left. Kevin shook Sam's hand, thanked him, and made his way to his car. He had parked near the employee lot and found himself looking around for Julie. There was no sign of her, and Kevin was disappointed that she'd already left.

From what Sam had told him about her and the other employees, Julie was the youngest person in the pharmacy. He figured she must be about two years younger than he was.

She was pretty too. Not glamorously gorgeous, but beautiful in a wholesome way. Her eyes had really caught his attention. He didn't know why. They were brown, which was common enough. He had brown eyes after all, but there was something different about hers. For one thing, they were so dark they were almost black. They also had a definite sparkle to them, almost as if one could see whatever she was feeling or thinking.

He shook his head as he approached his car. He removed his tie and unbuttoned the top two buttons on his shirt. He could not for the life of him ever remember noticing so much about somebody's eyes. He was still trying to figure it all out as he drove his car toward Hodgenville and his parents' home.

Hodgenville was a tiny town in LaRue County, southeast of Louisville, and a twenty-minute drive east from Elizabethtown. Its big claim to fame was being the birthplace of Abraham Lincoln. On the square in the middle of town there was a statue of Lincoln, and just outside of town there was a national park. It was a nice park with the original log cabin where Lincoln was born, housed in a huge building. There were lots of trees and grassy areas. As a student at Hodgenville Elementary, Kevin had been on many a field trip to Lincoln Farm.

Besides the park, Hodgenville had a grocery store, a couple of gas stations, a bank, a few family-owned restaurants, a motel near the park that was made to look like a log cabin in the front, an elementary school, and a high school. There were no stores for shopping unless it was for food, no movie theater, and no places to even rent movies. Basically, there was nothing to do in Hodgenville.

Even though Kevin had lived there his whole life, he was so glad when he was accepted into pharmacy school and was able to move to Lexington. There was always something to do there.

He would have attended UK in 1986, right after high school, to do his pre-pharmacy work if it hadn't been for the money. He lived at home his first two years and took the classes he needed at Elizabethtown Community College. That allowed him to keep working at his job in E-town; plus, he didn't have to pay rent. It made his mom happy too.

She'd be happy about his taking the job at the hospital as well. Kevin couldn't help taking a job that practically fell in his lap. He would still have every other weekend off and could spend those in Lexington. He was going to have a week off after finals were over too. That would give him time to get his stuff moved into the apartment he and Paul were going to rent. Paul was going to work and stay in Lexington for the summer, so the apartment wouldn't be empty.

Kevin took his bag and his basket full of dirty laundry out of the backseat and headed into the house. He opened the side door and stepped into the kitchen. From the smells he could tell his mom had been cooking all day. His stomach growled. Kevin silently crept up behind her and said, "Boo!"

Joann Sanders screamed and jumped about a foot into the air. "Kevin! You scared me to death. I almost burned myself. You nut!"

Kevin couldn't help it. He loved to do stuff like that to his mom. It was so easy. He was laughing as he said, "When's dinner? I'm starved."

"At six, as long as your sister is here on time."

That, Kevin knew, meant they would be eating closer to six thirty or even seven. His sister was always late. Kevin left his bag and laundry by the refrigerator and grabbed an apple out of the bowl on the counter. He started eating it as he walked into the living room to find his dad. His dad was in his favorite recliner watching TV.

"Hey, Dad," Kevin said as he took a seat on the sofa.

"Hey, Kev. I thought you might be here when I heard your mother scream."

"Oh, John!" Joann said as she hustled past the living room carrying Kevin's bag. "I'm going to put this in your room, Kevin."

"Thanks, Mom."

When his mom returned, she started asking about the hospital job.

"I decided to take it," Kevin answered.

His mom's face glowed with pleasure. "I'm glad. It will be good to have you around some this summer."

"Do you know many of the pharmacy employees?"

"Well, I know all the pharmacists and Sam, of course. Most of the technicians I know at least on a first-name basis. There are a couple of younger technicians that I don't really know. I think they may be students at ECC and work mostly weekends. I've seen them from time to time, but I've never talked to them much. Why do you want to know?"

"Oh, just curious about the people I'll be working with this summer." He wondered if the other student was male or female. He wondered if Julie was dating anyone.

Kevin finished his apple and wasn't surprised when his mom whisked the core out of his hand on her way back to the kitchen. The men sat in the living room discussing everything from sports to politics while Joann finished up in the kitchen and put in a load of Kevin's clothes to wash.

Before long, Kevin heard a ruckus coming from the kitchen. Kevin knew that meant his sister and her family had arrived.

"Well, it's time to eat," his dad said, smiling as he stood.

Kevin followed his dad into the kitchen. Almost immediately a forty-pound, blue-eyed, blond-haired human missile ran into Kevin.

"Kevin!" his nephew, Derrick, screamed.

Derrick was an energetic six-year-old, who was only quiet when he slept. He could talk almost nonstop. Kevin often wondered why he didn't pass out from lack of oxygen.

Kevin hadn't been able to spend much time with Derrick since he had moved to Lexington. Spending time with his nephew would be another benefit of being home this summer.

After Derrick moved on to greet his grandfather, Kevin was free to say hello to his brother-in-law and give his sister a quick hug. His sister didn't look much like him. While Kevin had dark hair and eyes, his sister Kelly had blonde hair and eyes that were sometimes blue, sometimes green. She was quite a bit shorter than Kevin too. Right now she was almost as wide. Kelly and her husband were expecting their second child, a girl due sometime in July.

As the commotion of greetings and settling around the table ended, Kevin faced his sister across the table. "How's my niece?" he asked.

"Oh, she's fine. It's your sister you should be concerned about," Kelly answered.

Kevin noticed Doug, his brother-in-law, reaching out to pat his wife's hand. He was a good guy who pampered his sister to no end.

"I am so ready to get this over with. I don't remember the last time I saw my feet, and my back is killing me."

Doug moved his hand between Kelly and the back of her chair and began to gently massage her lower back.

Kelly looked at her husband and said, "Thank you, dear. You are too good to me."

Doug rubbed her back a few moments longer and then continued eating.

Kevin sat there during dinner and quietly observed those around him. He made comments from time to time, listened to Derrick chatter on and on, and watched his family. He noticed the glances his parents shared, as if they knew some little secret that was only for them. He watched his sister and brother-in-law murmur to each other, saying things that were for their ears only.

It occurred to him, sitting there with people who loved him, that he was lonely. There was something missing in his life. He was ready to find whatever it was he needed to fill this void. He just wasn't sure how yet.

Chapter 9

Julie made it through finals week and felt pretty good about her grades. She knew getting into pharmacy school would be tough, and a large part of it hinged on the old GPA. She'd gotten a B in Calculus I last semester, but she had received As in all her other classes. She was eager to get her grades for this semester, but it would take a few days. She had a couple weeks until her summer classes started. Both of them should be easy As, and neither should require much work outside of class.

Besides her classes and work, Julie planned to do some babysitting for her aunt and uncle and spend time with her friends. One thing Julie was not going to do during the summer was date. She hadn't had any offers since she broke it off with Jeremy, and that was fine with her. After being with someone so controlling, it was nice to be on her own.

It was such a relief not to have heard anything from him. A relief, but then again it was unnerving. He had pursued her for so long, even to the point of being threatening. It was hard to believe that, just like that, he would leave her alone. It made her wonder what he was up to.

When she was out or even at home alone, she found herself wary of her surroundings. She was constantly looking around her, fearful that she might see his face. She had nightmares about him from time to time too. She couldn't shake the feeling that something terrible was going to have to happen before he would leave her alone for good.

Kevin sailed through finals week without too much damage to his GPA. He had hopes that he might have even raised his grades a bit. After the torture ended for the semester, he let loose and enjoyed the pharmacy party. It was one last get-together for the pharmacy students before everyone went his or her separate ways for the summer. Because UK had the only pharmacy school in Kentucky, students came from all over the state and a few came from out of state. Most students went home for the summer, so it was nice to have time to party before everyone split.

Paul and Kevin settled into their apartment the week after finals. It was a two-bedroom townhouse. The bedrooms and a bath were on the second floor, while the first floor had a living room, a kitchen, a dining area, and a half bath. It wasn't anything fancy, but it would do for two single college guys. There was even a small deck out back that would be perfect for storing beer kegs during a party.

They had their first party later that week with an ample supply of alcohol and snacks, plus more people than Kevin could count. The party was a success. The night was warm, and both the front door of the apartment and the sliding glass door leading out to the deck were open to let air circulate. Paul and Kevin met several of their neighbors. The open doors with music pouring out sent an open invitation to those who heard it.

Kevin was out back getting another beer when he heard Paul calling for him. "Kev-vin!"

Kevin stepped through the opened back door into the crowded living room. He saw Paul through the throng coming down the hallway with two attractive girls in tow. "Right here, Paul," Kevin called out over the music and voices.

"Kevin, I'd like you to meet two of our neighbors. Their apartment is in building B. This is Mindy Cooper and Nina Lane." Paul put a hand on each girl's shoulder as he said her name.

Mindy was the shorter of the two and had short, bouncy curls. Nina had long blonde hair and the bluest eyes Kevin had ever seen. Both girls were thin with form-fitting tank tops, short shorts, and flip-flops.

"Hello, Mindy, Nina." Kevin looked each young woman in the eye with his greeting. "Are you students at UK?"

It was Nina who spoke. She had a soft, lilting Southern accent. "We are. Mindy is in special education, and I'm an architect student."

Mindy went off with Paul while Nina stayed to talk to Kevin. Kevin took her to sit on the stairs so that they would have a quieter place to talk.

"Architect, huh? You must be very creative. What kind of things are you going to design when you graduate?" Kevin asked after they were seated next to each other on the steps.

Nina shrugged a bare, tan shoulder. "I haven't decided yet. I enjoy designing about any kind of structure. Paul said you are a student too. What's your major?"

"I'm in pharmacy school. I have two years left until I graduate."

"Pharmacy. Wow. You must be pretty smart."

"Sometimes." Kevin laughed.

Nina and Kevin shared about their hometowns and what had brought them to the University of Kentucky. They talked about classes they'd taken and what their upcoming semesters would be like.

Nina was very pretty, and when she looked at him with those big, blue eyes, Kevin knew she wanted him to kiss her. He looked at her lips. They were full and pink. They would be good lips for kissing. He looked back at her eyes. Yeah, she wanted him to kiss her. As he leaned toward her, a very strange thing happened. It was something Kevin had never experienced before. Another face popped into his mind. It was a wholesome, beautiful face with dark, down-to-the-depths-of-your-soul brown eyes.

He couldn't do it. He couldn't kiss Nina with Julie's face in his mind. He pretended to be leaning over to check the contents of her cup. Thankfully, it was nearly empty. "Nina, you need something else to drink. Let me go get you another beer."

"Wait, Kevin. You don't—"

He slipped the plastic cup from her fingers and went down the stairs and through the hall as if the place was on fire. *Oh, wouldn't Mitch have a field day with this!*

Once he was out on the patio, Kevin took a deep breath and let it out slowly. He took his time filling two cups with Bud Light and then slowly zigzagged his way back through the people in the living room. He noticed Paul in the corner, lip locked with a curly-haired brunette—Mindy. They were gonna be busy for a while.

When Kevin returned to Nina, she was quietly sitting there waiting for him. He handed over her full cup and sat down a couple of steps below her instead of next to her as before.

"Thanks," she said, taking the cup, disappointment apparent in her eyes even though she kept a pleasant smile on her face.

They talked for quite a while longer. Nina was smart and funny. They had a lot in common. She even played tennis. So why was it he could not get Julie McCourt out of his head the whole time he talked to her? He'd only met Julie once. Once! They'd only spoken for a few minutes, about nothing.

"Do you know what time it is?" he heard Nina ask during a lull in the conversation. "I need to be at work tomorrow at noon. I better get some sleep."

Kevin stood and leaned over the banister to get a look at the microwave clock in the kitchen. "It's twelve thirty," he replied.

"Well, I should find Mindy and let her know I'm heading home."

"She and Paul were in a very deep discussion when I went for our beers," Kevin told her teasingly.

"A *discussion*, huh? Did this discussion involve anatomy by any chance?" Nina asked, her eyes twinkling with mischief.

"Anatomy? Well, yes, actually, I do believe it did."

They found Mindy and Paul in the same corner where Kevin had spied them earlier. They were still very busy with their discussion. Nina and Kevin stood in front of them, unnoticed, for a few moments before Kevin cleared his throat. The second time he cleared his throat, they came up for air.

Nina and Kevin looked at each other and then at the couple huddled together in the chair. Kevin tried hard not to laugh out loud; Paul looked annoyed and glared hard at him while Mindy flushed bright red with embarrassment.

Nina spoke first. "Mindy, I'm sorry to…um…interrupt." She paused and bit her lip. "I'm heading home. I wanted to tell you so you wouldn't worry when you couldn't find me."

"Oh, okay," her friend answered, her cheeks almost back to their normal color. "I won't be too much longer, but I'll be quiet when I come in so I don't wake you."

"I'll walk you home," Kevin said to Nina.

Kevin guided Nina through the remaining partiers, out the front door, and into the night. It was only May, but already the air was still warm after midnight. The two of them walked across the dimly lit parking lot to Nina's building. Nina fished her keys from her pocket.

After she unlocked the door, she turned to Kevin. "I get off work tomorrow at six. How would you like to play a couple games of tennis?"

"Sounds good. Does Mindy play? I could bring Paul along, and we could play doubles."

"Mindy plays. That's a great idea actually. Where do you usually play?"

"I've always played on campus, the courts by the aquatic center. I lived in Blanding, so those courts were close."

"That's where we play too."

"I'll talk to Paul and Mindy when I go back over. How 'bout I give you a call in the morning before you leave for work?"

"That'd be good. I probably won't see Mindy tonight or in the morning. I usually leave here at 11:40. That gives me time to get through the Nicholasville Road traffic. I work at Fayette Mall in the sporting goods store, the one near the food court."

"I know the store. I've shopped there before."

"Come on in, Kevin. I'll write down my number for you."

Kevin followed her into the apartment. It appeared to be laid out exactly like his and Paul's. Unlike theirs, this one looked lived in. They had pictures on the wall in the hall and in the living room. The end tables on each end of the couch were scattered with books and photographs in matching frames. Kevin picked one up and looked at it as Nina sat down in a chair next to the phone to write down her number. The picture featured a group of blond-haired, blue-eyed people who had to be related standing in front of a large barn. He recognized one as the person in the room with him.

"Oh, that's me with my family on our horse farm in Tennessee," he heard Nina say. "My parents breed and train Tennessee Walking Horses. Those four guys are my brothers. I have two older and two younger. I'm the only girl, stuck smack dab in the middle of all those boys."

"Nice family," Kevin said as he replaced the photo on the table. "I better get back."

Nina stood and handed him a piece of paper with her name and phone number neatly printed on it. She led him out to the entryway. When she reached the door, she turned to look at him.

"Kevin, I had a really nice time with you tonight. I'm looking forward to tomorrow."

She was looking at him again with those blue, blue eyes. He took a step closer, bringing himself inches from her upturned face. He leaned his head down and gave her a soft kiss on her left cheek.

"Good night, Nina. I'll call you in the morning."

Kevin opened the door and let himself out, closing it softly behind him. He walked back across the parking lot toward his own building. He strolled into his apartment through the still open front door. He found Paul in the dining room with a group of lingering guests, playing a drinking game. Mindy was on his lap, which was actually a necessity because they didn't have enough chairs for everybody. In fact, there were other people who had pulled coolers up near the table to act as makeshift seats.

Kevin told Paul and Mindy about the tennis idea. They both seemed to like it. The three agreed to meet at Paul and Kevin's apartment about seven the next night. Kevin told Mindy he would call Nina in the morning and let her know what they had decided. He left the group around the table and made his way through the now empty living room and out onto the patio.

He emptied the keg of the remaining beer and drank it. He brought the keg into the living room and set it by the back door. Under the kitchen sink, he located the garbage bags. He pulled out one and headed back to the deck. He picked up the empty cups and bottles that had been scattered. Back inside, he laid the partially filled bag next to the keg then shut and locked the sliding glass door. He looked around the room and decided the rest of the clean up could wait until tomorrow.

As he passed through the kitchen, he fixed himself a glass of ice water. He leaned against the frame of the opening between the kitchen and the dining area and quietly watched his friends.

Paul seemed to be really taken with Mindy. Kevin didn't figure Paul would come back home tonight after he took her to her apartment. He glanced at another of his friends and his wife. He was a graduate student in some kind of engineering field and a genius too. He and his wife had been married about a year now, and it was obvious they were very happy. It made Kevin feel, once more, that hole in his life wanting to be filled.

He heard Paul laughing and realized he was laughing at him. "What did you say, Paul? I didn't hear you."

"No kidding, lover boy? I was asking if you were thinking about Nina," Paul said, grinning from ear to ear, "but your dreamy expression answered my question."

Kevin gave him a half smile. The group around the table burst into laughter.

As the party finally broke up, Kevin and Paul walked their last guests to the door and told them good-bye. Mindy excused herself, explaining that she needed to use the restroom before she walked back. Kevin and Paul were talking as they waited for her in the kitchen.

"Are you going to stay with Mindy tonight?" Kevin asked as he refilled his glass with water. "I wondered if I needed to go ahead and lock the door after you leave with her."

"No, don't lock it. I'll be back shortly."

In answer to the obvious shock on Kevin's face, Paul went on. "This one's different, Kev. I don't want to mess this up. I don't want this to be a one-night stand. I don't think Mindy is that kind of girl anyway. She's different. Do you know what I mean?"

Kevin could tell his friend was serious. In all the time he'd known Paul, he had never heard him talk like this about anything, much less a girl. "I think I do."

They heard Mindy enter the room. "All ready, Paul. Thanks, ya'll, for the great party. I had a good time." The last sentence she said with a faint blush on her cheeks as she looked at Paul. She turned to Kevin. "It was really nice meeting you, Kevin. I guess I'll see you tomorrow evening at seven."

"Nice meeting you too. I'll see you tomorrow. Good night, Paul."

Kevin could hear them whispering and heard Mindy's soft laughter as she and Paul went out the door. Kevin shut the door, leaving it unlocked for Paul, and headed upstairs.

He brushed his teeth in the bathroom then went to his room and stripped off his shorts and T-shirt. He slid between the sheets and leaned over to set the alarm clock beside his bed for eleven in the morning. He wanted to be sure he was awake in time to call Nina about the plans for tomorrow night.

Chapter 10

The next morning Kevin woke even before his alarm went off. He looked at his clock—nine forty-five. He had over an hour until the time he had planned to call Nina.

He got out of bed, throwing the blankets over his pillow in an attempt at making it up. He switched off his alarm, grabbed clothes, and headed to the shower. As the hot water splashed over him, he thought about what needed to be done today.

After showering, shaving, and dressing, he went downstairs. Paul's door was still shut, and Kevin was careful not to wake him. He made his way to the kitchen and fixed a cup of instant coffee. As he drank it, he straightened up the kitchen, throwing away trash left from last night and placing dirty dishes in the dishwasher. He was wiping off the counters with a new dishcloth when Paul walked in.

He was still wearing the worn T-shirt and pajama pants he had slept in. His feet were bare. He shuffled wordlessly to the cabinet next to the microwave, pulled out a mug, filled it with water, heated it in the microwave for two minutes, stirred in instant coffee granules, and began to drink with his eyes closed. Halfway through his coffee, Paul opened his eyes and, for the first time that morning, acknowledged Kevin who was leaning against the counter watching him.

"What're you looking at?" Paul asked crossly.

"Buddy, you better have some more coffee. Maybe it'll improve your mood. What's the matter? Hung over?"

Paul finished the rest of his coffee before he answered. "No, I'm not hung over, but I think last night was a life-changing experience for me," he said seriously.

"You mean Mindy?"

"Yeah, Mindy. I can't stop thinking about her. Do you think it's possible to fall in love this fast?"

Kevin thought before he answered. "I don't know. I've never been in love before so I'm certainly not an expert source of advice on the subject. But I would think it's like you said last night; you don't want to mess it up. Maybe you should take it one day at a time and see what happens. Things have a way of working out."

"I think you're right. One day at a time. That's what I'll do." He put his empty mug in the dishwasher and said, "I'm gonna head up and shower. Then we can clean up this mess."

When he left, Kevin looked at his watch. It was ten minutes after eleven. He went to the phone and dialed Nina's number. She picked up on the first ring.

"Hello," Nina said quietly.

"Were you sitting on the phone or what?" Kevin asked, laughing.

"Well, you said you would call. I didn't want the phone to wake Mindy, so I was right beside it, waiting. Don't let it go to your head, big guy."

After Kevin finished explaining the arrangements for that evening to Nina, he and Paul started working on the mess from the party. Once the apartment was passably clean, they loaded the keg into Kevin's car, returned it, and bought tennis balls. It was four o'clock when they got back to the apartment complex.

Mindy was standing in front of her building as they pulled up to theirs. She waved to them as they got out of the car. Paul walked over to her. Kevin noticed that they both had goofy smiles on their faces as he unlocked the apartment and went inside.

He went upstairs to his room and put the new balls in his tennis bag. He laid out the clothes he would need for the next two weeks. He packed everything up and loaded his car.

Kevin spent the rest of the afternoon alone watching television. He didn't mind being alone. He enjoyed it actually. It was nice to have quiet, especially after the crowded party last night. Kevin enjoyed parties but preferred small groups to large ones. He caught himself wondering if Julie liked big groups or small ones. When he heard the sound of the front door opening and voices in the hall, he forced the thoughts of Julie from his mind.

He stood as Paul, Mindy, and Nina came through the hallway. The girls were decked out in tennis dresses. They each wore coordinating sweatbands on one wrist and were carrying their rackets. Nina had her long hair pulled back in a ponytail. She looked good in tennis garb. After their greetings, Kevin ran up the stairs to grab his bag.

"Could you drive?" Kevin asked Paul when he returned. "I've already loaded my car for tomorrow."

"Where are you goin' tomorrow?" Nina asked before Paul could answer.

"This summer I'm working in the pharmacy at the hospital in Elizabethtown. It's close to my parents' home, so I'm staying there through the week and every other weekend. My first day is Monday, so I'm heading out sometime tomorrow."

"Oh," Nina said quietly, looking at the floor, "that will be good experience for you."

"It will. I've only worked retail so far."

Paul laid a hand on Nina's back. "He'll be here every other weekend," he told her. Turning to Kevin, he said, "I can drive."

They left the apartment and loaded into Paul's Corolla. Kevin and Nina sat in the back while Mindy sat up front next to Paul. As they made their way to the campus tennis courts, Mindy and Paul chatted quietly between themselves. Kevin turned to Nina. She was looking out the window. "Rough day at work?" he asked.

She turned to look at him. "Oh, we were busy. We always are on Saturdays. I'm just disappointed that you're not going to be in Lexington this summer." She gave him a small smile and kept talking. "I was hoping we could get to know each other better this summer."

Kevin took a deep breath and blew it out.

"Nina, I really like you, but I don't want you sitting around all summer waiting on me."

They looked at each other for a while, just looked at each other. Kevin watched as Nina's eyes lit up.

"You're already seeing someone," she said.

"Well, not exactly…"

She reached over a patted his hand, her smile reaching her eyes this time. "That's okay. She's a very lucky girl, Kevin, a very lucky girl."

They played several games of tennis. Sometimes Paul and Kevin were against the girls. Sometimes Mindy and Paul took on Nina and Kevin. Kevin didn't lose a single game. The other three gave him a hard time.

"What can I say?" was Kevin's cocky answer. "I'm just that good."

Nina swatted him on the butt with her racket. Sweaty and breathless from playing and laughing, the foursome headed back to Paul's car. It was almost nine o'clock. They were hungry but too sweaty to go into a restaurant. Paul suggested they head back to the apartments and order a pizza.

"I rented a movie today. We can bring it over to your place and watch it while we eat," Mindy said.

They all agreed to both suggestions. After Paul parked his car, the girls headed to their place to change and grab the movie, and the guys went in their apartment. Paul went straight to the phone and ordered a large pepperoni pizza, and Kevin went up to change into clean clothes. Paul met Kevin in the hall upstairs.

"So what's going on with you and Nina?" Paul asked. "It looked like you two were having some kind of deep discussion in my backseat. She acted upset that you weren't gonna be around this summer."

"Well, nothing's really going on," Kevin answered. "Nina's under the impression I'm seeing someone else."

"But you're not. Are you?"

"Not exactly," Kevin told him. Then he explained about meeting Julie.

"So let me get this straight. You're giving up something with a great girl who is right here because of someone you met one time and know absolutely nothing about."

"It sounds crazy, I know."

"I hope you're not making a big mistake. I also hope you aren't ruining my chances with Mindy. They grew up together, you know. They've known each other their entire lives."

"I don't think anything I do or don't do is going to affect you and Mindy," Kevin said honestly.

The doorbell rang. "I'll get it," Kevin said. "You go change so you won't be all smelly when Mindy gets over here."

Paul lifted an arm, sniffed his armpit, and grimaced. He turned and dashed into his room. Before Kevin could even get the front door opened, he heard the shower start. He couldn't help laughing to himself. The pizza delivery guy was waiting when Kevin opened the door. The girls were right behind him. After paying the guy and taking the pizza, he greeted Nina and Mindy. He headed to the kitchen with the pizza and directed the girls to the living room.

"Paul decided he stunk and needed a shower," Kevin called from the other room. "What can I get you two to drink?"

Both girls laughed. "Diet something," they said together.

Kevin took four Diet Cokes into the living room and returned to the kitchen. Paul came downstairs then, his hair still damp from his shower. He helped Kevin load paper plates with pizza and the two of them carried them, along with napkins, into the living room.

Paul and Mindy snuggled on throw pillows on the floor while Kevin sat with Nina on the sofa. Kevin sat close enough that he and Nina could talk quietly, but they weren't touching. They laughed at the same scenes in the movie. Kevin felt comfortable with Nina, and she seemed to enjoy his company. He told himself—more than once during the night—that he had made the right decision in not pursuing a romantic relationship with her.

When the movie was over, Paul and Kevin walked the girls back to their apartment. Paul and Mindy walked in front, arms linked around the other's waist, talking and laughing quietly all the way across the parking lot. Nina and Kevin walked slowly behind them trying to give them as much privacy as possible. They didn't touch and spoke very little as they followed the couple in front.

Finally, Nina said, "I've enjoyed these last two days, Kevin. I wish you luck in Elizabethtown."

"Thanks. I've enjoyed it too."

When the foursome reached the door of the girls' apartment, Paul went inside with Mindy. Kevin told Nina good night outside and watched her go through the door.

Inside his own apartment, Kevin cleaned up from supper and unloaded the dishwasher. As he turned the light off in the kitchen, he heard Paul come in and lock the door.

"Perfect timing! I just finished cleaning up," Kevin teased when they met in the hallway.

"You know, I stayed over there with Mindy just so you'd have time to get all that done." His face grew serious before he said, "Man, I hope you know what you're doing. I really hope you know what you're doing."

"Me too," Kevin answered just as seriously as they walked up the stairs to their bedrooms. "Me too."

Chapter 11

For the most part, Kevin's first day at HMH was long and boring. He was glad to see Julie again and meet more of his co-workers when he got there at eight o'clock. He stood at the back of the unit dose area waiting for Sam, who was going to escort him to the occupational health nurse for his drug screen and physical. He quietly waited and listened to the technicians working.

He realized something about Julie as he waited for Sam. She had a dazzling, contagious smile. Her whole face lit up. Even though she was working, she smiled a lot.

It was obvious the technicians were comfortable and familiar with each other. They worked steadily, moving and reaching around each other, talking and laughing without losing their focus. Kevin specifically listened to Julie and Jim—the other ECC student—interact. Even though Jim didn't talk as much as the others and was extremely soft spoken, Julie was able to get him to talk and laugh more than he would for the other, older technicians. Kevin got the impression that Jim and Julie took classes together at ECC and that Jim was a pre-pharmacy student too.

As he pondered, Sam walked into the unit dose area, greeting his techs as he came through. When he saw Kevin he said, "Good morning. I'm running a little late. Sorry about that, but I forgot I needed to be here early to get you over for your physical. I usually don't come in until nine o'clock." He walked into his office and picked paper work up off his desk. "These are the forms we need for your physical. Come on and I'll walk you over to the employee health nurse."

Kevin followed Sam back through the pharmacy. He wasn't positive, but he thought he saw Julie watching him out of the corner of her eye.

Kevin made it through the physical and drug screen before heading upstairs to the conference room for orientation meetings with other new employees. He listened to boring speeches and watched boring videos. He missed having lunch with the rest of the pharmacy employees and ate lunch alone in the cafeteria. After lunch he listened to more boring speeches and watched more boring videos.

During the hospital tour, he got another glimpse of Julie. She and Jim were on the fifth floor exchanging the unit dose carts. They were leaving the boxes filled with each patient's supply of meds for the next twenty-four hours and removing the used boxes. The used boxes, Kevin figured, would be the ones he would help fill tomorrow. Then the whole process would be repeated.

From the back of the tour group, Kevin watched Julie work. The gray metal boxes were fairly large with several individual patient drawers in each one. They looked heavy, and Kevin wondered how Julie could lift them. He noticed she didn't struggle as she pulled a filled box from the pharmacy off the large rolling cart and exchanged it with the used one she took off the nursing cart. She must be stronger than she looked. As she worked, trading out the nursing cart closest to the orientation tour group, she noticed Kevin watching her. She gave him one of those heart-melting smiles. He smiled back.

She leaned toward him and quietly asked, "How's orientation?"

"Boring," he whispered confidentially.

She laughed quietly. "It'll be better tomorrow. You'll get to do this," she said sweeping her arms toward the rolling cart. Sounding more serious, she said, "This really is a great place to work. I love my job here." She glanced over to where Jim was finished and waiting for her. "I better get back to it. See you later, Kevin."

Jim and Julie both waved to him from the other side of the nurses' station. He waved and watched them steer the cart to the staff elevators, Julie pulling from the front and Jim pushing from the rear.

Kevin envied Jim. Then he realized he would never get to work alongside Julie. He wouldn't get to talk and joke with her like he heard the technicians doing this morning. His only day in unit dose would be Tuesday. That was Julie's day off, and she didn't work in the IV room. Kevin really, really envied Jim.

When Julie and Jim returned to the pharmacy, they straightened the unit dose area and restocked the drug bins that needed it so that everything would be ready to go for tomorrow. Once the carts were exchanged, the unit dose technicians were pretty much done for the day. The only thing left to do was clean their work area, take their afternoon break, and help out front if they needed it.

When the other techs got back, Jim went with them to the cafeteria for their break. Julie spent her break in the IV room talking to Lisa as she worked.

Lisa wasted no time before asking about Kevin. "Did you see Kevin today? Today was his first day, wasn't it?"

"I saw very little of him, which is fine. Somebody that looks like him probably has dozens of girls after him anyway. I'm sure he wouldn't be interested in me."

"Well, guess who gets to start training him in here Wednesday? Me," Lisa said without waiting for an answer. "I could find out about him. Drop some hints to spark some interest in you. Not that it would take much, as cute as you are."

"Lisa," Julie said, trying not to lose her patience, "I've already told you. I cannot do this right now. After psycho Jeremy I may never have another boyfriend. I don't think it's worth the risk you have to take."

"Is he still calling you every day?"

"Not every day. Only occasionally now, which makes it worse almost. I don't know when not to answer the phone. It gives me the creeps. I have a terrible feeling he's up to something. Once I get into pharmacy school and move to Lexington, I'll get an unlisted phone number. He won't be able to find me then. Only when I know I am completely free of him can I even begin to think about dating someone else. Do you understand?"

"I do understand you feeling that way, but not letting yourself be happy is letting him keep control over you."

"I am happy. I've got school, work, and friends. I don't need a guy."

"What if Kevin Sanders is *the one* for you?"

Julie laughed. "That's a bit dramatic, don't you think?"

Kevin's second day was better than his first, but his third day beat both of the others. Wednesday he started in the IV room. Lisa Simmons started training him. Lisa was an angel in disguise.

She asked him what he thought about the different pharmacy employees. She was very subtle, asking about techs and pharmacists, males and females. When she got to Julie, she must have picked up on his interest.

After that, the entire time she was instructing and training him, she dropped little bits of information about Julie. By lunch he'd learned that Julie had grown up in northern Indiana, had moved down here when she graduated high school to live with her widowed grandmother, and that she had once been engaged to a guy from Indiana but had broken it off a few months ago. Lisa also told him that Julie wasn't dating anyone. That was the good news. The bad news was she didn't want to date anyone.

Kevin looked around the IV room as Lisa demonstrated again how to clean the hood. They had restocked the refrigerator with the most common doses of IV meds, had the morning run filled and delivered, and had the mess cleaned up. Kevin had learned a lot already. What he made would be pumped directly into a patient's vein upstairs. The responsibility was somewhat overwhelming, and Kevin definitely took it seriously. There was no room for error. If he made a mistake, he could kill someone.

Somehow Lisa had been able to teach him thoroughly about the IV room while enlightening him about Julie. She did all this without compromising safety or efficiency. She performed all these feats with a pleasant attitude and a smile on her face. On top of it all, she made sure they were on schedule so that they could take their lunch break with the unit dose technicians.

Kevin walked with Lisa to the cafeteria and made his way through the line. Tray in hand, he followed Lisa to the table where the other pharmacy personnel were already seated. He took a seat directly across from Julie. She gave him a smile that made him feel that she was really happy to see him. He wondered if she smiled at everybody that way.

"Hey, Kevin. How do you like it here so far?"

"I like it. I've learned a lot already."

"I've never worked in the IV room. I'd like to. Tell me what it's like."

Kevin did. He and Julie talked the entire lunch break. They swapped stories about pre-pharmacy classes, and they learned that she had a lot of the same instructors and professors that he had had at ECC. Occasionally, he and Julie spoke to others at the table, but most of the time it was as if they were the only two people there.

He wanted to ask her out, but he knew he would not succeed if he pushed too hard. So he would wait. He had the whole summer to wait for an opening. Like he told Paul, things have a way of working out.

Chapter 12

For three weeks, Kevin and Julie ate lunch together every day they both worked. May was over; they were moving into the second week in June.

It wasn't like they were alone at lunch or anything, but Kevin still enjoyed the time and looked forward to lunches with her. Sometimes the two of them sat at a small table away from everyone else, but usually they sat with the rest of the pharmacy employees.

They talked about anything and everything. It didn't even matter to Kevin that she wasn't focused solely on him; he was glad just to be near her. The more he learned about her, the more he wanted to know. He didn't think the time was right yet to ask her out. He watched for signs that she was interested in him. She always had a smile for him and spoke to him specifically, but she didn't seem to pay any more attention to him than she did anyone else. He kept hoping that he'd come to lunch to find that she had saved a seat for him.

Several days he had been the first to reach the table and had saved a seat so that Julie could sit across from him.

Lisa—bless her heart—had been a big help. The times he came to lunch after everyone else had gone through the line, he found Lisa sitting near Julie. As soon as he arrived at the table, Lisa stood, giving one excuse or another for leaving, and offered Kevin her chair. She always gave Kevin a secret wink when that happened.

Not all his fellow employees were as gracious. In fact, whenever Curt, who was one of the pharmacists they worked with, ate lunch with the techs, he somehow managed to occupy the seat across from Julie.

That was the position Kevin coveted most.

Julie was having a frustrating day. It was a Friday, Kevin's day off. She was used to talking with him over lunch. Today she missed his company. She had hoped he'd come in to get his check like he usually did on Friday mornings, but he hadn't. He had told her that he spent his weekends off in Lexington. He must've left without his paycheck this time. He probably had a girlfriend to visit. She tried to figure out why that idea made her feel even crankier. She told herself again that she wasn't interested in him that way. She reminded herself she wasn't interested in anyone that way and did not want to be.

At lunch she sat alone in a corner, facing the wall. Lisa was also off today, which was just as well. Julie spent her lunch studying ancient civilizations. Her "cake" history class was kicking her butt.

She had chosen this particular class because the instructor was supposed to be easy. Well, the easy instructor had some sort of family emergency and was replaced at the last minute with Dr. Tomey. He was not at all easy. The man lived, breathed, ate, and slept history. He thought everyone else should too. He didn't care that this was a summer course; he crammed as much information in as would be required for a regular semester class. Apparently no one had told him that summer, filler courses were not supposed to require hours and hours of outside class time. Julie wouldn't be surprised if the man ignored his own syllabus. Instead on stopping in the midseventeenth century, he'd probably continue until he covered everything from the ancient Sumerians all the way up to the 1986 *Challenger* explosion.

She would never use this information in any kind of pharmacy career, but the course was required to earn the degree. The only thing remotely interesting so far had been the ancient Egyptians and their surgical techniques. She hated putting this much work into something she would never need to know again. She was bemoaning the fact that even Cal I hadn't caused her this much grief when a shadow fell across her book.

She glanced up to see one of the security guards looking over her shoulder. The man talked to her all the time and somehow knew her name. She didn't know how; she couldn't remember his. She smiled, trying to be polite, even though she didn't feel at all friendly at the moment. He smiled back, and to her regret, sat in the empty chair on the other side of the table. He stretched out his arm and lifted her book so that he could see the cover.

"Gross! What are you reading that for?"

"This is for one of the classes I'm taking this summer. I'm trying to study for a test next week," she added, hoping he would take the hint and let her concentrate.

It didn't work. Julie watched as he leaned back in his chair, hooked his thumbs through the belt loops of his uniform, and said, "I never liked school very much. It's not my thing."

"Hmm." She returned her focus to her history book.

"So, Julie, what are you doing this weekend?"

"Working," she said absently. "And studying."

"I thought maybe... if you wanted... you know... we could see a movie... or... I don't know."

"Oh," she mumbled, "I wouldn't have time for a movie."

A few minutes later, Julie sensed him move to a standing position. He cast another shadow on her book, making it difficult for her to read. She looked up, trying not to let her irritation show.

"Well, maybe some other time," he said as he turned to walk away. "I'll see ya around."

"Okay. See ya later."

Just as she was turning back to the text, she heard the sound of quiet laughter. She shifted her eyes toward the noise and saw Kevin standing a couple feet away by the Coke machine. Their eyes met, and she smiled in spite of herself. She watched as he bent to lift the can of Coke he'd bought from the machine.

He was wearing shorts, a T-shirt, and a baseball cap. His face looked like he skipped shaving that morning. He looked great. The man had to possess the best looking pair of legs God had ever put on the male species. They were tan and muscular. She told herself she only noticed the way he looked because he wasn't dressed in his usual shirt and tie.

As he came toward her, she closed her book and pushed it to the side. "What's so funny?" she asked as he sat down.

"You and Barney."

"Who's Barney?"

"The security guard whose heart you just broke."

"Is his name really Barney? I can never think of it when he talks to me."

Kevin laughed again. "No, his name's not Barney. He reminds me of Barney Fife. That's my nickname for him."

"Oh," Julie said, feeling silly. "How'd I break his heart?"

"You turned him down."

She had no idea what Kevin was talking about. "Turned him down for what?"

"He was asking you out on a date, Julie."

"No, he wasn't," she said as she shook her head and gestured with a wave of her hand.

"What do you think a guy's doing when he asks you what you're doing this weekend and mentions seeing a movie?"

She hadn't really paid attention to what he was saying. She thought back. He had mentioned a movie. She felt her face grow warm. "Oh, my gosh, Kevin. I was trying to study. I wasn't really listening to him. Was I totally rude? Should I find him and apologize?"

"My guess is that you'll end up with Barney at the theater tomorrow night if you do apologize. And, no, you weren't at all rude. You let him down gently. Besides, he's Barney; he has plenty of ego to sustain him. Of course, if you'd like to go out with him, I'm sure a smile from you would be all it would take for him to make another attempt."

She waved her hand again. "It's just as well. I don't date."

"Why not?"

"It's a long story, but basically, my focus right now is getting into pharmacy school."

He frowned at her. "There's more to life than school."

"Yeah, I know," she replied somewhat defensively. She reached for her book. Kevin reached for it at the same time. When her hand touched his, it felt almost like a current of electricity had gone over her skin. She jerked back. His eyes caught hers. He had an odd expression on his face.

After a second or two, he cleared his throat and dropped his eyes to her book. "You taking a world history class this summer?"

"Unfortunately," she grumbled.

"Ah," Kevin said, "the Phoenicians with their alphabet, the Lydians with their coins, the Assyrians, the two Babylonian Empires, Greece, Rome … It goes on and on."

"What? Are you some kind of history buff or something?"

"No, but I took this class my freshman year." He started flipping through the pages of the textbook.

"You still remember that stuff?" Julie could not believe he remembered anything from a stupid, worthless class he took two years ago.

"I guess so, some of it anyway. I don't know; stuff just stays in my brain. I'm full of all kinds of useless information."

"Wow," Julie said. She was totally impressed. "I don't suppose you had Dr. Tomey?"

"Tomey! Good Lord, no. No one in their right mind takes one of his classes unless they're a history major."

Julie felt her shoulders sag. She could not believe this. "Maybe I should drop it and try again in the fall."

"You're taking this under Tomey? Why? Didn't anyone tell you what he was like?"

"I signed up for Deloris Lodge, but she went on hiatus at the last minute, and I got stuck with Tomey. Now I'm gonna have to work my behind off in to get an A." She moaned.

"The world won't come to an end if you get a B, you know."

"I don't want some history class to keep me out of pharmacy school."

"What's your worst grade so far?"

"I got a B in calculus," she admitted.

"A B in calculus," he repeated with a grin. "Julie, you're not going to have any trouble getting into pharmacy school. If a B is the worst you've done, your GPA will sustain another one. Trust me. Plus, with the experience you have working here, as long as your PCAT scores aren't rock bottom, you'll be fine."

"PCAT," she mumbled. She'd forgotten about that.

"The good ole Pharmacy College Admissions Test," Kevin said. "Isn't it crazy the stuff we do to torture ourselves? We pay a pretty good chunk of change for that torture too."

Julie couldn't help smiling. Kevin smiled back at her.

"I've heard Tomey does all his lectures without notes and rattles off all those names and dates out of his memory," Kevin said.

"It's true. It's the strangest thing. He doesn't even have to pause to think about what he's saying."

"You know how he does it, don't you?" Kevin asked leaning toward her across the table.

His eyes were sparkling, and Julie leaned toward him without thinking about it. "How?"

"He lived through most of what he talks about. The man must be hundreds of years old."

Julie laughed.

"That's better," Kevin said as he sat back in his chair and studied her. "You shouldn't worry so much. Everything will work out. Stressing only makes matters worse."

"I know," she confessed. "I try not to, but I can't help it sometimes."

She watched as he opened his Coke. To her surprise, he slid it over to her side of the table. "You drink this one," he said as he jumped up and went back to the machine. He returned with another can.

"You didn't have to do that," she told him.

"I couldn't drink one in front of you when you didn't have anything."

"Thanks."

"You're welcome."

"I thought you'd be in Lexington," Julie said after taking a few sips.

"I'm heading that way in a little bit. I came to get my check. I had planned to grab a Coke and go, but I got distracted."

"I'm sorry," she said.

"It's not your fault. It was Barney's."

Julie laughed again.

"I'd be willing to help you study your history, if you want," Kevin said after a moment.

"I couldn't ask you to do that. You have better things to do with your summer than help me with a boring history class."

"You're not asking. I'm offering. Let me help you. I promise you'll get an A," he said.

Julie studied his face. She'd never had help studying before. She'd always been the tutor. She wasn't quite sure what to make of his offer, but he'd already shown he knew at least some of the material. "All right, but you'll have to let me do something nice for you sometime."

"That's a deal," he told her with a smile.

Chapter 13

Kevin drove straight to the Lexington Tennis Club after walking Julie back to the pharmacy. He was playing in the Lexington Invitational. It was a pretty large tournament with over one hundred entrants.

He sailed through his two matches on Friday, winning in straight sets in each of those. On Saturday, Paul, Mindy, and Nina came to watch him play. The morning match was another easy win. He had finished in time to watch the end of the match determining the opponent for his second one. The winner was a guy he'd played more than once. He was tough. Kevin had beaten the man before, but the man had also beaten Kevin a couple times. The afternoon match would be more of a challenge.

After lunch together, Kevin, Paul, and the girls watched some doubles matches and more of the men's singles matches. A few tiebreakers on the court Kevin was assigned pushed his afternoon match into the evening.

It was five thirty before Kevin was on the court. During warm-ups, he noticed his opponent was weak on his backhand side. Kevin took advantage of that. Even with the backhand advantage, Kevin had to work to win. But he did win. Not in straight sets, but winning was winning. That win put Kevin in position to play in the championship match the next day.

Paul and the girls seemed to be thrilled for him. Paul slapped him on the back, and Nina and Mindy both hugged him.

"This calls for a celebration," Nina said as he packed up his racket and towel and threw away his empty Gatorade bottles.

"I don't know. I'm pretty beat."

"Nonsense," Paul told him as they walked to the car. "You're tougher than that. Besides, you waltzed right through the first match. And that last one. Man! How many aces did you have?"

"Seven."

Paul whistled.

"I noticed his backhand was weak," Nina said. "That was a good move to keep hitting to it."

"Thanks," Kevin said as he smiled at her.

"So, are you up for a little party?" Mindy asked. "A very small party—just for four." She looked at him expectantly and smiled.

"Well, if it's just us, that would be okay."

"Good," Nina said, linking her arm with his as they walked along. "I worked very hard on something for you."

Kevin couldn't imagine what that could be.

At the apartments, Kevin dropped his friends at Mindy and Nina's door and then drove over and parked in front of his apartment. He took a quick shower, dressed, and headed over to join them. When he walked in the door, the girls showered him with confetti, and Paul was blowing one of those noise makers from New Year's Eve parties.

"What on earth are you all doin'?"

"Throwing you a party," Nina said.

"We knew you wouldn't have time tomorrow because you'd head back to Hodgenville after your match, and we wanted to celebrate your victory," Paul said.

"But I haven't won yet."

"You will," Nina told him confidently.

Kevin was shocked. The apartment was decorated, and Mindy had whipped up one of her great casseroles and a salad for dinner. For dessert, Nina had baked and decorated him a cake. It was shaped like a tennis ball, a three-dimensional tennis ball.

"I can't believe you made that," Kevin told Nina when she brought it to the table.

"Are you kidding me?" she teased. "I'm going to be an architect. This is nothing."

Dinner was nice. The four of them talked and joked throughout the meal. The cake not only looked good, it tasted great. It was yellow, his favorite.

After visiting a while longer, Kevin headed back to his and Paul's place. The girls refused to let him help clean up; he was ready to call it a night anyway.

Sometime later, he was in bed reading up on world history when he heard a knock at his bedroom door. It was Paul. Kevin put down the book.

"Are you sure you know what you're doing?" Paul asked from the doorway.

"What do you mean?"

"Not dating Nina," his roommate replied.

Kevin looked at him for a moment. "With Mindy, how did you know? What made her different? Why did you want to see her more than once, and why do you continue to spend time with her?"

Paul rubbed the back of his head and made a face. "I don't know. There's just a connection there. I've never felt it with anyone else before."

"Okay. Well, I like Nina. She's great, but I don't feel the connection. She's just a friend."

"So this pharmacy girl … What's her name?"

"Julie."

"Julie. Okay. Do you feel the connection with her?"

Kevin thought back to what it had felt like when their hands accidentally touched in the cafeteria yesterday. "Maybe. Probably. I'm not sure."

"Have you two gone out yet?"

"No, I haven't even asked her, but we've been talking at work. I really like her."

"Hmm." Paul looked at the book on Kevin's bed. "What are you reading?"

"Old World history. Julie's having some trouble with a summer class. She was expecting an easy time of it, but got stuck with the Attila the Hun of history professors. I'm gonna help her study."

Paul's eyebrows shot up. "You think the way to the woman's heart is through her mind?"

Kevin shrugged. "You never know."

Early the following afternoon, Kevin was warming up on the court when he saw Nina, Mindy, and Paul sit in the stands. He gave them a wave.

The guy he was playing today was really good. Kevin had never beaten him, hadn't even gotten close to beating him. He felt good about the match, though. He'd been playing well. He was ready.

Kevin got the first serve. Standing on the baseline on the ad side of the court, Kevin took several deep breaths. He blocked out everything around him but his opponent and the court. Kevin served the ball—an ace, not a bad way to start a match.

It got tougher. It was a hard match with a lot of tie breaks. The guy threw fits that would put John McEnroe to shame. He had distracted Kevin before with his antics but not today. Kevin was too focused. When Kevin finally won the final point to win the match, he became aware of the background noise for the first time since the match had started. He'd been so into his game that he had blocked out everything else.

After going to the net and shaking hands, he looked up to see his three friends hugging and high-fiving each other. Kevin smiled. They were great.

Monday evening Julie met Kevin at the ECC library. They settled at one of the tables in the back. Several other people were seated among the other tables, reading or talking quietly.

As she pulled her book and notes from her backpack, Kevin said, "Tell me why you want to be a pharmacist."

The question threw her off. She was ready to jump right into the work. It took her a moment to answer. "I don't want to just be a pharmacist," she finally said. "I mean, there's nothing wrong with being a pharmacist, and I plan to practice for a while. I'll need to in order to make enough money to continue my education. But I want to conduct research. I plan to get my doctorate. I want to develop new drugs, find cures for diseases."

"Wow. Ambitious, aren't you?"

"I don't know. I just want to make a difference." She watched him study her for a moment before she asked, "How 'bout you? Why are you in pharmacy?"

"My sister played tennis with a girl whose dad owns a pharmacy. The guy was looking for a delivery boy to deliver meds to the nursing homes he serviced. Kelly, my sister, arranged for me to meet with him. I ended up working there from the time I was sixteen until I moved to Lexington last year. At first I only drove and delivered. Later I worked in the pharmacy itself as a technician.

"I liked the work, and I liked that the owner of the store, and the pharmacists who worked for him seemed to have money and time to enjoy life. I was always good in science and math. I had to have a job doing something, so I chose to major in pharmacy when the time came."

They talked more about their work experiences. Julie told him about the health occupations class she took in high school and about working at the clinic in Bluffton, Indiana.

"So how did you end up here, hundreds of miles away from where you grew up, at a community college?"

"My grandmother. My mom grew up in Kentucky but moved to Indiana when she married my dad. His family's from Indiana. I was born in Indiana and lived there until I was eighteen. That's when I moved in with my grandmother.

"She'd lived alone since my grandfather died my freshman year of high school. She told me about UK's pharmacy school and about the community college. She didn't ask me to come, but I knew she was lonely. I had been accepted at Purdue and Butler. Butler's in Indianapolis if you've never heard of it. I really wanted to go to Butler, but I didn't think I'd be able to swing the cost. I came down and visited ECC and talked to the admissions counselor. I pay out-of-state tuition here, but it's still cheaper than Butler. I forfeited some of my scholarship money because I didn't go to a school in Indiana, but my grandmother's not alone anymore."

"Do you like it here?"

"I do. I always enjoyed visiting. Kentucky's a beautiful state."

Somehow, Kevin eased them into history. Before Julie knew it, she had the major ancient civilizations down, could describe their characteristics, and was able to recite their major historic contributions. Kevin had actually made studying fun.

As they walked together to the parking lot, Julie thanked him.

"You're welcome. It was my pleasure. Same time, same place tomorrow?"

Julie didn't think she needed another study session before her test Thursday, but she liked being with Kevin. "All right," she said. "Are you sure you don't mind?"

"I don't mind at all."

When Kevin got to the library Tuesday, there were even more people there than the day before. He found Julie already seated in the same area they'd used yesterday. He stood a short distance from the table watching her read. Her face was tense with concentration. He moved toward her and with his index and middle finger, he reached out to rub the area between her eyebrows, right above her nose. He'd apparently surprised her, but when she looked up and saw him, the tension eased from her face and she smiled. It was that warm, sweet smile that made him feel that she was happy to have him around.

"You're gonna have a wrinkle there before you're twenty-five if you don't learn to relax," he told her as he dropped his hand.

"Oh," she said waving off the comment. "No one will be around to care what I look like. How was work today?"

Kevin sat next to her and told about his day, including being pulled out of unit dose to work in the IV room. He told her about the unusual doses of Dilantin he'd prepared for a pediatric seizure patient and how he'd mixed his first Activase for a heart attack victim in the ER.

"Were you nervous? I mean, you have to mix that Activase and get it to the emergency room within minutes. Did the patient make it?"

"I wasn't nervous," he answered honestly. "There's no reason to get nervous. I just did what had to be done. It wasn't a big deal. I got orders for the guy later in the day. He'd been admitted, so he must've made it."

She placed her hand on his arm and squeezed. "That's a very big deal, Kevin. You helped save that man's life today."

He hadn't really thought about it like that. "Huh, I guess you're right."

They ended up talking more than they studied. It was obvious that Julie already knew the material. The fact they were doing this when she didn't need the help was encouraging.

For the second time in two days, they were the last two out of the library before the librarian closed for the night. As they went through the door, Kevin said, "How would you like to grab a hamburger tomorrow before we do this?"

She stopped moving and stood on the sidewalk looking at him. "I can't tomorrow," she said quietly. "I already have plans."

They started walking again. Something told him that she was disappointed in having to turn him down.

"My test is this Thursday. I think I'm ready. You don't need to waste any more time on me this week. I really do appreciate all your help, Kevin."

"I've enjoyed it," he said sincerely when they reached her car. "You know where to find me when you need to get ready for your next test."

"Thanks." She smiled before she got in her car. She told him good night before shutting the door and starting her engine.

Kevin waved as she backed out and then walked to his Mustang.

Chapter 14

If Julie had known Kevin's phone number the Thursday she got her history test back, she would have called him. She was that excited. She'd gotten a ninety-eight. Just like Kevin had told her, most of the students in her class were history majors, and she had scored higher than them on her test. Julie knew she had Kevin to thank for her success. Two of the essay questions had been issues that Kevin had discussed with her specifically, not to mention how he'd helped her learn the rest of the material.

She was on pins and needles all morning Friday while she watched and waited for him to drop by and pick up his paycheck. She was thoroughly disappointed when she came back downstairs after doing her narcotic counts and Lisa told her she had just missed him.

Monday morning was extremely hectic for both the IV and unit dose techs. Julie didn't have a chance to talk to Kevin except to say hi in passing. At lunch she found a table for two against the wall. Not long after she sat down, Curt walked over and started to join her.

"If you don't mind, I'm saving that for Kevin. I need to talk to him about the history class he's been helping me with." She smiled when she said it and was surprised when Curt grumbled something that didn't sound very nice as he turned away. It wasn't like it was the only available seat in the cafeteria. There were lots of empty tables.

Her lunch break was almost over when Julie spied Kevin coming through the line. He looked tired, but when he saw her stand and wave him over, he smiled.

"Are you having a rough day?" she asked him as he took his seat.

He shook his head. "Lisa being on vacation makes it tough on me. That woman carries way more than her own weight. To make it worse, the IV tech last night didn't mix up more than what she had to in order to cover the night run. Usually nights are slower, and the tech stocks the fridge with the common admixtures. The fridge was practically empty this morning, and I had to make twice as many IVs as usual."

"I'm sorry."

"That's all right. I don't mean to complain."

"It didn't sound like you were complaining. You were telling it like it is."

She waited for Kevin to take a few bites. She wished she knew how to work in the IV room. She'd help him if she could.

She looked at her watch. She only had a couple minutes left before she had to go back to work. "I got my test back last Thursday."

He stopped eating. "And?" he asked expectantly.

Julie felt her face break into a wide smile. "I got a ninety-eight," she said proudly. She reached across the table to squeeze his left hand. "Thank you so much, Kevin. I know I couldn't have done it without your help."

He squeezed her hand in return, smiled, and said, "I didn't do much, but I'd be happy to help you when the next test comes around."

Tuesday morning Kevin found the IV fridge more depleted than it had been Monday. Something was going on. No way could the night shift have had two nights in a row when they were so overrun they couldn't do their job. It was odd that this was happening the week he was the only one in the IV room.

At nine thirty, after working his butt off to catch up and missing his morning break for the second day in a row, Kevin went to find Sam to see if he knew what the deal was and to let him know there was a problem if he didn't.

Curt was in Sam's office. They were discussing the July tech schedule. The door was opened, and Kevin stood near the opening, waiting until they were finished. Sam gave him a nod and held up his index finger when he saw Kevin.

"Julie's working some nights this summer, isn't she?" Curt asked.

"Both she and Jim said they would pick up some nights to cover vacations," Sam replied.

"I'd like you to schedule Julie to work nights the third week of July. The ninth is her Sunday, isn't it?"

Kevin heard Sam say that it was.

"Put her on nights for the rest of that week. I'm covering Stan's vacation then. I'm Julie's preceptor, and I'd like to have some time working more directly with her."

Preceptor, my butt, Kevin thought. He heard the two men finishing up. Curt gave him a short nod as he left the office and Kevin went in.

"Okay, Kevin, what do you need?" Sam asked with his usual friendliness.

As Kevin explained the conditions of the IV room the last two mornings, Sam's expression grew serious. Kevin watched as he made a note on his desk blotter.

"I'm sorry you've had trouble," Sam said sincerely. "I'll talk to the night tech tonight when she comes in. You won't have the same problem tomorrow. I appreciate the work you've been doing. You're doing a fabulous job."

Kevin thanked him and headed back toward the front of the pharmacy. Curt surprised him by falling into step beside him.

"You're gonna have to get over that crap if you're gonna make it in the real world, Kevin," Curt said quietly so no one else could hear.

Kevin looked at him and felt his jaw tighten, but he didn't say anything. He went back into the IV room and focused on his work.

On Wednesday morning there was no improvement in the situation in the IV room. Kevin wondered why Sam hadn't taken care of the problem. Nothing was more irritating to Kevin than people who didn't do their job. Kevin didn't wait for Sam to get settled in his office this time; he caught him coming in the door.

"Sam, the stock levels were just as bad this morning," Kevin said, keeping the volume and tone of his voice very controlled.

The expression on Sam's face told Kevin that he was surprised. "I'm sorry. It shouldn't have been like that. I had to leave early yesterday. My mother fell at the nursing home. I had to go see about her. I asked Curt to speak to the night tech when she came in, but I guess he forgot."

Kevin was irritated before, but now he was angry. He doubted that Curt had forgotten anything. He wasn't going to lose his temper, though. Fits of anger were useless in his opinion. Even if he did feel like punching Curt, he wouldn't.

"Is your mother all right?" Kevin asked.

"Oh, she's fine. Thanks for asking. I think her blood sugar got too low. Her meds had been changed recently. I talked to her doctor and got everything straightened out."

Kevin followed Sam into the IV room and watched as the man looked through the refrigerator. Kevin could tell he was checking the labels to see when the bags had been mixed.

Turning from the refrigerator, he said, "I can tell you've worked your butt off this morning. You know what, Kevin? I'll call the tech responsible at home today. I'll make sure she knows what needs to be done during her shift. This will not happen again."

"Thanks, Sam. I appreciate it."

For the third day the time for Kevin's morning break came and went. He was barely able to stay ahead enough to get the morning run done. If he got many stat orders to mix, he'd never stay on schedule. At lunchtime he still had his head under the hood mixing away.

"How about some lunch?" he heard Julie call from behind him.

Kevin turned to look at her. "Can't. I'm still playing catch up from this morning."

"Is it the same problem as Monday?"

"Something like that," he said over his shoulder as he continued to work.

"Come on to lunch, Julie," Kevin heard Curt say. "Kevin's a big boy."

Kevin turned back and faced the hood to hide his smile when he heard what Julie said. She sounded as irritated as Kevin had felt that morning. "Don't be a jerk, Curt." Kevin felt her move right behind him. "I'm staying. There must be something I can do to help."

"Don't skip lunch on my account," Kevin told her.

"Nonsense. It's the least I can do for the world's best history tutor."

He checked over his shoulder as he worked. After asking him some questions, Julie printed his labels for the next run, pulled the IV bags from the refrigerator, and put the labels on the bags. "I'll get these checked by the front end pharmacist and deliver them to the floors. That way the whole run won't be late. I've left three labels on the counter. I didn't see them premade in the fridge. I think you may have to mix them."

Kevin finished up what he was doing under the hood. What he'd been working on filled the orders printed on the labels Julie had left for him. He took the bags upstairs and ran into Julie as she was making the last delivery. They walked back to the pharmacy together. She rolled the cart inside before they walked to the cafeteria to grab a quick lunch. They met the pharmacy staff that had already been to lunch as they were passing through the cafeteria doors.

Julie told Jim that she would be back to finish filling the carts as soon as she grabbed a sandwich.

"That's no problem," Jim told her. "I'll help you finish up. We'll get them upstairs on time. Don't worry."

Curt didn't say a word and had a sullen expression on his face.

As he sat down opposite Julie, Kevin thanked her for her help.

"I have another history test coming up. I'll let you return the favor."

Kevin laughed. He sure was glad she had ended up with Dr. Tomey.

Before Julie knew it, it was the Fourth of July. The summer was flying by. She had the holiday off from work and school. She hadn't had many breaks this summer, not with working a full-time schedule, taking classes, and babysitting for her cousins. She planned to enjoy Independence Day this year.

She had slept later than usual and was just getting out of the shower at ten o'clock. From the bathroom, she heard the phone ringing. Thinking it was her friend Shannon, who was going to meet her in E-town today, Julie ran to the phone with only a towel wrapped around her. Grams had already left to go to some kind of quilt show.

"Happy anniversary," she heard the voice on the other end of the line say.

Julie felt tears well up in her eyes. "Why are you doing this, Jeremy? Why won't you leave me alone?"

"You already know the answer to that question."

Julie felt the tears slide down her cheeks.

"Do you remember July 4, 1986?"

Julie closed her eyes, but the tears kept falling. She took a shuddering breath. "Yes, and if I could, I'd go back and change what happened. I wish I'd never met you."

Jeremy went on like she hadn't spoken. "I picked you up after work that evening. You were so excited to go out with me. So many guys at the restaurant wanted to date you, Julie. Did you know that? But you chose me. Why is that, Julie? Why me?"

She was openly sobbing now. "I ... I don't know."

Jeremy went on to remind her of every detail of their date—what she wore, the songs they listened to in his car as they waited for it to get dark, what time he took her home, the kissing. Julie continued to cry as Jeremy continued to talk.

Finally, he said, "I miss you, Julie. I'll see you soon. Know that I'm always thinking of you." With that the line went dead.

Julie stood in her grandmother's kitchen and cried for a long time. The words *I'll see you soon* echoed through her head. What if he was down here? What if he found her at the lake today? She thought about calling Shannon and canceling, but the thought of being alone scared her more. She'd rather take her chances in public.

Even though she knew the doors were already locked, she checked each and every one of them to be sure. After that she got dressed; she put an ice pack on her face for a few minutes, hoping to take down some of the swelling caused by the crying. She finished getting ready, grabbed her purse, and headed out the door.

As soon as Shannon saw her, she asked what was wrong. Julie told her about Jeremy's call and what he had said.

"He talked for a long while this time, huh?"

"Yeah, I guess he did," Julie answered.

Shannon smiled. "Well, at least he'll have one heck of a phone bill."

That made Julie laugh, and for a while she forgot about Jeremy. As Julie walked with Shannon through the park, he'd periodically pop back in her mind. She would get a glimpse of a tall man with dark hair in the crowd, and for a split second her heart would kick up a notch until she realized it wasn't him.

Julie and Shannon moved through the people and looked through the craft booths. Julie told Shannon about how difficult her history class was and how Kevin was helping her.

"Someone's helping *you* study?"

"What's that supposed to mean?" Julie asked as she laughed at the stunned look on her friend's face.

"You're usually the one with all the answers."

"I'm not the one who got an A in Cal I and went back for a second semester of torture with plans to keep repeating that process a couple more times."

"Touché. Well, what can I say? I'm good at math. You're good at everything else."

"I wish!" Julie said. "If I was good at everything else, I wouldn't need help with a history class."

Shannon grunted. Then she asked, "So what's this Kevin guy like? He's already in pharmacy school?"

"He just finished his first year. He went to ECC too. He talks about playing tennis all the time. You can tell too. He has great legs."

"Really?"

"Oh, shut up!" Julie said. "It's not like that."

Shannon stopped walking and looked at her. "So tell me what it is like."

Julie felt her face get warm.

"Ah hah! That's what I thought. Has he asked you out?"

"Not exactly."

"Explain please," Shannon said, mocking their chemistry professor. "How do you 'not exactly' ask someone out?"

"Well, after we studied one night, he asked if I'd like to grab something to eat before we started studying the next night."

"What'd you tell him?"

"I couldn't study or eat with him because it was a Wednesday. That's the night I teach the preschool class at church. I told him I couldn't."

"Hmm," Shannon said as they began to walk again. "I think I'd like to meet this Kevin with the great legs."

"You are absolutely hysterical, Shannon. Do you know that?"

Shannon bent her head back and laughed.

Tuesday afternoon Kevin met Jim at the bandstand at Freeman Lake Park. As the two of them walked around, Kevin looked for Julie. He didn't even know if she was planning on being at the lake for the Fourth of July events, but he still looked for her. It was Jim who spotted her. Kevin felt him nudge his arm as they snaked their way through the crowd.

"I see Julie over there with one of her friends."

"Where?" Kevin asked as he scanned the crowd.

"There," Jim said as he pointed, "with the blonde. She has some classes with us. They just bought something at that food stand."

Julie and the blonde were walking away from them. They were walking slowly, and it didn't take him and Jim long to catch up with them. Soon they were walking right behind the two women. Kevin had never seen Julie in shorts. She had nice legs. They were long and smooth.

Jim put an index finger to his lips. Kevin smiled and nodded. The two of them remained silent as they followed right behind Julie and her friend. Kevin had only meant to surprise her, but when he tapped her on the shoulder, she screamed and her funnel cake landed on the pavement. He reached out and grabbed her arm in an effort to balance her. She started to struggle. When he said, "Julie, it's me," she stopped, and Kevin felt her sag. She probably would've collapsed if he hadn't still been holding onto her arm. She covered her face with her hands. Kevin could hear her gulping for air. He wasn't sure if it was from embarrassment or if he had frightened her that badly.

"Julie, I'm so sorry. I didn't mean to freak you out like that. Are you okay?"

She only nodded, her hands still covering her face. Kevin felt terrible. He wanted to hug her but wasn't sure if it would help or make things worse. As he stood there watching Julie trying to bring herself under control, Kevin heard the friend with her say something. His eyes moved from Julie to the friend.

"It's not you," she said quietly. "She got a call this morning from her ex—"

Julie lifted her head at that. The look she gave her friend was very easy to read.

The blonde cleared her throat and mumbled, "Never mind."

After a few more minutes, Julie seemed more like herself. Kevin let go of her arm.

"Boy, I feel stupid," Julie finally said. Kevin heard her take a shaky breath. It sounded like she was trying not to cry.

"Don't feel stupid. It was my fault. I should've said something before I touched you."

"We wanted to surprise you two. We weren't planning to scare you to death," Jim said.

Kevin looked her over for a couple of seconds, making sure she was okay. "I'll be right back."

He came back with a fresh funnel cake. Julie smiled and thanked him. "You didn't have to do that."

Kevin shrugged.

The four of them walked a little way before stopping under a tree and sitting in the shade. Julie, her face and voice almost back to normal, introduced her friend Shannon Thompson.

"Shannon, Jim, and I all had calculus together our first semester," Julie explained. "Torture brings people together." The other two laughed at that. "Shannon's planning on going to UK's College of Engineering."

The four of them sat under the tree and talked for a while. Julie shared the funnel cake with Kevin.

The four of them spent the entire afternoon together. They watched the balloon race, played carnival games, and rode paddle boats on the lake. Kevin and Julie went in one boat while Jim and Shannon went out in another.

When the sun began to set, Kevin walked to his car to get a blanket. He carried it to where Jim and the girls were holding a spot on the dam. They settled onto the blanket and waited for it to get dark.

Kevin lay next to Julie. Even though there were several inches between them, he could feel her all along his right side. They both had their hands resting on the blanket between them; their pinkies were touching. This was the connection Paul had talked about. Kevin was almost positive Julie felt it too.

As the first bursts of red, white, and blue exploded overhead, Kevin shifted his hand in an effort to cover hers. Julie sat up. She pulled her legs to her chest, wrapped her arms around them, and rested her head on her knees. Kevin could tell from her outline in the dark that she wasn't even watching the fireworks. After a few moments,

Kevin sat up beside her. He was very careful not to even brush against her.

Very quietly he asked, "What's the matter, Julie?"

"Nothing." Then a minute later, "I'm just…" Kevin heard the sound of her taking a deep breath and letting it out. "I'm just worried about school."

Kevin knew she was lying but said nothing. More than anything, he wanted to wrap his arms around her and protect her.

Her ex-fiancé must be psychotic.

Chapter 15

Julie was miserable the week she had to work nights. Jeremy's phone call July Fourth still had her on edge. She'd never realized before how creepy the hospital parking lot was at night. Shadows loomed everywhere. She imagined hearing footsteps behind her but saw nothing when she turned to look. Curt volunteered to walk her to her car after they left each night. She gratefully accepted his offers. He probably thought she was a paranoid nut the way she looked over her shoulder and scanned the parking lot as they walked through it. If Julie hadn't been so genuinely afraid, she might have laughed at Curt's expression when she checked the inside of her car every night, said a hasty good-bye, jumped in, and locked her doors before driving off.

The worst part of the week was going nine days without seeing Kevin. He made her laugh. Everything with Kevin was more enjoyable, even something awful like history. Days were not the same without him.

Part of her hoped he would ask her out on a real date while another part was afraid for him to. It was all very confusing.

Once her stretch of working nights was over, she reached a compromise with herself by spending time with him over history. Now that she knew what Tomey expected, she really didn't need Kevin's help anymore, but she didn't want to give up that time with him. Besides, it was much easier and more fun to study the material with Kevin.

She wasn't completely sure he was attracted to her. Sometimes she convinced herself he was. Other times she was sure he was only being nice. There was the Fourth of July thing when she thought he was going to hold her hand. Looking back, she was pretty sure that had been her imagination.

Once the fall semester started, she wouldn't have time to worry about any of this stuff. She was looking forward to it. Getting lost in schoolwork was a lot easier than trying to figure out guys.

Kelly had her baby July 21. Everybody said his niece was perfect. He couldn't tell. All babies looked alike to him. His sister was happy. His mom was happy. Doug was happy. His dad didn't say much. Kevin could enjoy her when she got a little older.

He went to the hospital Friday afternoon and stayed until he thought his sister and mother were satisfied. Derrick had been there about three hours. He had Legos and some books to keep him occupied, but a kid can only stay in one room so long.

"Why don't you let Derrick leave and run around with me for a while? I'll entertain him and feed him before we come home."

Derrick's parents and Kevin's mom agreed. Derrick was thrilled. Kevin had to remind him three times to quiet down as they walked through the halls of the hospital on their way out. Kevin wanted to drop by the pharmacy and see Julie, but it was already after three o'clock. Besides, Derrick needed to burn off some energy before Kevin let him meet her.

Kevin took him to Baskin Robbins for ice cream before taking him to Freeman Lake Park to play on the playground. They actually started at the entrance and hit several playgrounds. Kevin would park near one, they would play for a few minutes, and then, when Derrick was ready, they would drive around to the next set of playground equipment. Each play area was different. Kevin didn't mind giving his nephew a chance to try out everything.

The day was a little overcast, and the park wasn't as crowded as Kevin figured it usually was. There weren't many other kids around for Derrick to play with.

"Let's go over there," he said pointing across a grassy area where other children were playing.

Kevin gave him a thumbs-up, and Derrick took off running. Kevin scanned the area, saw no hazards, and let him keep going. By the time Kevin got to the playground, Derrick was climbing on the monkey bars, talking to another child.

"We're having a contest," the little girl, who looked to be a couple years older than Derrick, was explaining.

"Whoever can hang upside down the longest wins. I already lost. It makes my head hurt."

Kevin's eyes moved to the two remaining competitors. One was a boy about Derrick's size. The other was a grown woman. Like the little boy, she had her legs hooked over the bar at her knees. Her back was to Kevin. Her dark hair hung down and barely missed brushing the ground. She was using her hands to keep her shirt from falling down in front, but Kevin could see about four inches of the smooth, fair skin on her back.

"Aren't your legs getting tired yet?" the little boy asked hopefully.

"Not at all. I could do this … all … day … long." Kevin watched as she began to swing her body back and forth. "What about you, Dillon? Are your legs getting tired?"

The little boy started giggling. "Don't make me laugh! I'll fall; I'll fall."

"Don't you dare fall! Your parents will kill me if I let you get hurt."

The little boy kept laughing. Just when Kevin thought he was going to have run in and catch the kid before he landed on his head, the little boy grabbed the bar with his hands, unhooked his legs, and dropped to the ground. "You're good at this," the boy said.

The woman followed the boy to the ground. She hadn't noticed any visitors yet. She stood with her head above the interconnected bars and raised her arms up as if she were flexing her biceps. "I am the champion," she declared in a deep voice.

The kids laughed, including Derrick. The woman noticed him for the first time. "Oh. Hello. Who are you?"

"I'm Derrick."

"Is your mom here, Derrick?"

"Nope. She's at the hospital."

"How about your dad, honey?"

"He's at the hospital too."

"Who brought you to the park?"

"My uncle." Derrick pointed, and the woman turned.

She stared for a few moments. "Kevin," she said quietly.

"Hello, Julie. I watched your contest. You're very good at that."

Kevin watched her face turn red. She pulled at her shirt and ran her fingers through her hair. She didn't have a thing to worry about. She looked great.

"You didn't go to Lexington today."

"No, Kelly had her baby this morning. I'm staying here this weekend. Derrick was getting antsy staying at the hospital. I volunteered to take him out and give him time to run down." Kevin looked over at his nephew who was sitting at the top of the jungle gym with the other two children. He was talking a mile a minute. Derrick knew no strangers.

While the three children played, Kevin and Julie sat together on a bench.

"I didn't know the serious Miss McCourt took time to play."

"I know how to have a good time just like anybody else." Kevin watched as she glanced toward the playing children and looked back. "May I make a confession?"

"Sure."

She leaned toward him and quietly said, "My cousins guilted me into it."

"Into playing?"

"Yeah."

"How?"

"When I got to the house this afternoon and after my aunt and uncle left, I started reading my history. There's so much material that he doesn't cover in lecture that we're responsible for. I just feel like I need to work on it during any spare minute I have.

"So I'm reading. The two of them"—she nodded toward her cousins—"are playing in the other room. They're quiet, and I figure all is well. The next thing I know, one of them is on each side of me, leaning against me, and looking at my book. They start telling me how I used to be fun but I'm not fun anymore. 'It's wrong to study over summer vacation, especially on a Friday,' they tell me. That's when I start feeling the guilt because I know they're right. I did used to play. I used to know how to have fun."

"You still know how," Kevin said.

She looked directly at him. "You think so?"

"You sure looked like you were having a good time hanging upside down a few minutes ago."

She gave a silly grin. "Yeah, I guess I was."

He reached over and rubbed the area between her brows. She'd scrunched it while she talked about not having fun. "You only need practice—more fun and much less worrying."

Julie smiled at him, and he saw the tension leave her face.

Before Kevin knew where the time had gone, it was August. The summer was over, and he hadn't asked Julie out. Well, as long as he didn't count the lame attempt he made when he asked her to grab fast food before studying, he hadn't asked her.

In all the time they'd spent together, he still wasn't sure how she felt about him. At times, he was positive she felt the same attraction he did. Other times, like when they were watching fireworks, she shut herself off from him. He didn't know what caused her to do that. He suspected it had something to do with the ex-boyfriend, but Kevin didn't know if it was because she wanted to reconcile that relationship or because she wasn't ready to be involved with someone else.

If he could spend time completely alone with her, he might be able to have a better gauge of her feelings for him. Without asking her out, which he was hesitant to do, he didn't know how he'd have an opportunity to be alone with her. He only had a few days left before he moved to Lexington for the semester. He was running out of time.

The chance he was looking for came on the last day possible. It was a Thursday, his final day to work at Hardin Memorial Hospital. Almost all the pharmacy was taking part in a night out in his honor. Well, that's what they told him anyway. He suspected he was the excuse they were using this time.

They were going to Otter Creek Tavern. It was a redneck, hillbilly restaurant and bar in Meade County.

Elizabethtown was in a dry county. When the pharmacy employees went out together, they went to Otter Creek.

At lunch Kevin asked Julie if she was going. He knew her summer classes were over and hoped she didn't have another reason not to go.

"Oh, I don't know. I've never gone with them before. I'm not even twenty-one yet."

"You don't have to be twenty-one," Lisa said. "It's not just a bar. They serve food. Some people even take their kids there. Besides, it would really help me out if you would go. My husband is planning to come by after work. If you let me ride over with you, we won't have two cars to drive home."

Kevin could tell Julie was thinking about it. He stole a glance at Lisa. She gave him one of her winks.

"I'll go, but I don't know how to get there."

"I know how to get there. My house will be on the way from your grandmother's. You can pick me up, and I'll get you there," Lisa told her.

Lisa pulled some scrap paper and a pen out of her pocket. She wrote out her phone number and directions from Julie's house to hers. Kevin felt like hugging Lisa.

After Julie clocked out at three thirty, she filled up her car with gas and headed home to get ready for the evening. Julie was excited about going out, but she wasn't sure why. She was glad Grams didn't mind. Actually, Grams seemed to be excited for her. She dressed in comfortable shorts and a T-shirt, brushed her hair, freshened up her makeup, and headed out the door to Lisa's.

Even with directions, Julie would never have been able to find the way to the tavern on the twisting, back country roads without Lisa in the car with her. She was relieved when they pulled into the crowded gravel parking lot beside a somewhat rundown-looking building.

As Julie and Lisa made their way through the mass of cars, Julie could hear country music blaring. Inside she could barely hear herself think. Lisa directed Julie through the smoke-filled room. She guided Julie over to a group of tables that had been pushed together to accommodate everybody.

The first person Julie noticed was Kevin. Feeling self-conscious for noticing him, she slid into a seat at the opposite end of the tables. Julie watched as Lisa made her way around the tables and chairs, stopping to talk to everyone in the group. Julie saw her lean close to speak to Kevin. She worried that Lisa was up to some kind of match-making scheme, but when neither of them looked in her direction, she figured she was safe.

Several people waved hello as Julie scanned the faces around her. She smiled and waved back. She felt some-one lean over her shoulder from behind. She turned to see Curt's face close to hers. He said something, but Julie had no idea what. She smiled and shrugged her shoulders. A waitress moved from Lisa to Julie.

When Julie turned from giving her order, Curt was gone. She was beginning to feel out of place and was relieved to see Kevin moving toward her. He said something as he sat in the chair across from her, but she couldn't hear him.

Julie shook her head and pointed to her ears. Kevin moved his chair around to the end of the table so that he was right next to her. They were almost touching. She felt a surge of anticipation.

"I'm glad you came," he said, leaning even closer to be heard.

Julie looked straight at him. She noticed the partially filled beer bottle in his hand. His eyes didn't look like someone's who had had too much to drink, and his speech wasn't slurred. His tone sounded almost flirtatious, though, and he'd never flirted with her.

"Are you drunk?" she asked.

"No, I've been nursing this"—he lifted the bottle about an inch off the table before setting it back down—"for the last hour."

He sounded like he was telling the truth. He was still wearing his dress clothes from work today. The only difference was the absence of his tie. "Hey, how did you get here? Are you driving?"

"Why? Worried about me?" Kevin said, dropping his voice an octave.

Julie gave him a you've-got-to-be-kidding-me look, her right eyebrow arching up higher than her left one.

"Sorry," he said, somewhat apologetically. "I rode over with Curt in his new SUV. He brought a bunch of us straight from the hospital. Besides, I don't drive if I have more than a couple beers."

When her hamburger and fries arrived, she asked for a refill on her Coke. Kevin ordered a Coke too.

"Aren't you eating?"

"I already had something. We've been here awhile, just waiting for you."

Julie cocked her eyebrow again and watched as he finished off the rest of his beer. He laughed and then said, "Your fries look good though."

"Have some," she said as she squirted mustard onto her plate. "I won't be able to eat all of them."

"You eat mustard on your French fries?"

"I like mustard. Pour some ketchup on the plate if you want it. Besides, I like to double dip. If you have your own ketchup, you won't have to worry about getting any of my germs." She smiled and dipped a fry into the mustard before eating it.

"Are you looking forward to being back in Lexington?" she asked as they both munched from the same plate.

"Yeah. I enjoy Lexington."

"Tell me about it. I've never been."

Julie listened as Kevin told her about Lexington, about his roommate Paul, and their apartment. She asked about pharmacy school, his schedule, and his classes. She wanted to know what he liked best about pharmacy school and Lexington.

He described classes that he said were easy, and he described classes that sounded impossible to Julie. He described all kinds of places around Lexington—parks, restaurants, stuff on campus, even bars. He told her about people he'd met in the dorm when he'd lived there, crazy things he and his roommate had done, different professors, and some of his classmates. Julie laughed so hard at some of his stories that she nearly cried.

After a while, they talked about more personal things, their families and hobbies. She didn't say anything specific about Jeremy, but she mentioned that she'd been engaged once. When Kevin asked her what happened, she told him it didn't work out and left it at that.

As Julie finished off her hamburger, the conversation lulled. She glanced at Kevin and noticed he was staring at something or someone at the other end of the table. She looked to her right and saw Curt watching them. She picked up her Coke and sipped through the straw, trying to figure out what the staring match was about. She heard Kevin's voice in her left ear.

"How 'bout a game of pool?" He motioned toward the pool tables with his hand.

"I don't really know how to play."

"That's okay. I'll show you," Kevin said encouragingly. "Come on."

"All right, but you might be sorry."

They carried their drinks over to the billiard area of the tavern. Kevin set his Coke on the edge of one of the tables and took two cue sticks from the rack on the wall. He put a dollar's worth of quarters into the slot on the side of the table to release the balls. He handed Julie a stick before he set up the balls.

"Do you want to break?" he asked.

She gave him a blank look. "I don't even know what that means."

"You have led a sheltered life," Kevin told her teasingly.

"You're probably correct about that. This is the first time I've ever been to a tavern. You are enriching my experience tremendously with a lesson in billiards."

"Well, watch, and I'll show you how to break. We'll play eight ball." He removed the plastic triangle he had used to set up the balls. He took his cue stick in his right hand and, using his left hand to steady the stick, expertly hit the cue ball. All the other balls went flying. He explained everything as he went.

Julie watched as the balls rolled in all directions, and a striped ball fell into one of the corner pockets. Her eyes were wide, and her mouth gaped open slightly. "I can't do that."

He smiled. "You don't have to. I already did." He explained that his balls would be the striped ones and hers would be the solid ones and that the black eight ball would be the last one to hit in. "I get another shot because one of my balls went in. Once I miss, it will be your turn." He moved around the table to get ready for his next shot. He took aim but missed. It was close but didn't fall in.

Julie was impressed. She could tell he was good at this. He really seemed to know what he was doing. She, on the other hand, had no idea what she was doing.

Hoping Kevin would take advantage of the opportunity to put his arms around her, she asked, "Can you show me how to hold the cue stick?"

For a moment, Kevin stared at her as if he wasn't sure what to do. Julie felt her cheeks warm, and she knew she was blushing. Either she was really bad at flirting or he just wanted to be friends. Thankfully, he stopped staring, took his cue stick in hand, leaned over the table, and explained verbally how to shoot. He looked over his shoulder at her as he talked through the steps.

She leaned over the table like she'd had no ulterior motive and tried to mimic what Kevin showed her. Their game continued. He showed her how to choose shots and made suggestions as they went. She even managed to hit some balls in. Her earlier embarrassment disappeared, and she started laughing. She was really enjoying herself.

After Kevin beat her at the first game, he set the table up for another game. After Kevin beat her at the second game, they put their cue sticks back and walked toward the other side of the room.

As they approached their co-workers, Julie noticed that Lisa's husband had arrived. Lisa absolutely glowed in his presence. Julie envied such happiness. She was sure she would never have anything like Lisa had. She stopped herself from being melancholy. She had been having too good a time to get down.

Lisa introduced Kevin to her husband Jerry. Julie told Jerry hello, and the four of them talked for a while. Julie noticed couples making their way to a dance floor. She hadn't danced in so long. She loved to dance.

When a security guard from the hospital—the one Kevin called Barney—asked her to dance, she said yes. As she followed him onto the dance floor, she almost laughed when she remembered what Kevin had said about him. She told herself that he didn't look as much like Barney Fife in blue jeans and a T-shirt and was able to smile at him instead of laughing out loud. She put her arms up on his shoulders, keeping her lower arms against his chest.

She wanted to be able to keep her distance in case he got grabby. When his hands slid down to her rear end, she politely lifted them back to their proper position. The second time he put his hands on her butt, she pulled away. She walked right off the dance floor and back to the tables where Lisa was, leaving him standing there gawking after her. That's what she got for dancing with some drunken guy in a tavern! Curt asked her to dance when the next slow song started. Julie told him, "No, thank you." He looked like he'd had a few drinks too. She sure didn't want to deal with someone she had to work with groping her. Even if he was drunk and wouldn't remember, she would.

Part of her wanted Kevin to ask her to dance. He didn't, but he sat close beside her as they talked with Lisa and Jerry. Julie wasn't sure how long they laughed and talked together and was surprised when she looked around to see that she was the only one of their group left that had to work early tomorrow. She checked her watch. It was already ten o'clock.

"Man, I've got to go. I have to be at the hospital at seven in the morning," she said, still looking at her watch. She looked up, suddenly realizing she had a problem, "But I don't know how to get home. Lisa, can I follow you guys?"

"Oh, honey, Jerry just got his food. You don't want to wait for us," Lisa said sweetly. "I understand Kevin rode with Curt. Why don't you let him ride with you back to town? He has to get his car anyway. You'll know your way home from the hospital." Lisa looked like the cat that had eaten the canary.

Julie felt her eyes grow as big as half dollars.

"I don't mind riding back with you," she heard Kevin say. "I know how to get back to the hospital from here. I would appreciate you taking me to my car, anyway. I think it might be a while before Curt's ready to go."

"Well, if you're sure you don't mind," Julie said as she glared daggers into Lisa.

Lisa smiled sweetly and said, "You two be careful."

Kevin congratulated himself as he and Julie made their way to her car. He really owed Lisa. He could kiss her for arranging this.

He worked hard to contain his smile as Julie unlocked her door with her key then reached over to open the passenger door. Kevin slid in and fastened his seatbelt. Julie did the same and then started the car. She drove through the parking lot toward the road.

"Which way?" she asked.

"Go left," he directed. "You shouldn't drive too fast. These roads are really curvy. With it being dark and since you're not familiar with the roads, it would be easy to have an accident." He tried to sound sincere, but he really wanted this drive to take as long as possible.

Kevin was so nervous, he babbled. He never babbled. This was the first time he'd been completely alone with Julie, and it was really affecting him.

"Kevin, are you sure you didn't have more beer than you think you did? Are you sure you're gonna be okay to drive home? Do you want me to take you to your house?"

He wanted to say yes just so he could spend more time with her, but he couldn't ask her to drive all the way to Hodgenville. Besides, alcohol had nothing to do with the way he was acting. He didn't figure she would be comfortable with the real reason, so he said, "I'm fine. Really. I only had that one beer." He kept babbling though.

In Kevin's opinion, they made it back to the hospital way too quickly. He directed her to the spot where he had parked his Mustang that morning. He did not want to get out of her car. This may be the last time he ever saw her. He wished now he had put his arms around her while they played pool. He wished they had danced. As badly as he wanted to, he knew he couldn't kiss her. She'd probably bust him up side the head if he tried. *Think, Kevin, think!*

"If you're ever in Lexington, look me up, and I can show you around. I could even take you by the pharmacy building if you like." He sat there smiling at her as he spoke.

Because of the lights in the hospital parking lot, he could easily see the concerned expression on Julie's face. He thought she must really be worried about him driving. He felt guilty but thought it was better for her to think he'd had more than he said he had to drink than to tell her that she was the reason he was acting weird.

"I don't know your number."

"Do you have paper and a pen?"

"I've got paper in the glove compartment. Let me look for a pen." She dug through her purse until she found one.

Kevin opened the perfectly organized glove box and pulled out a small pad of paper. He took the pen she offered, wrote down his name and the phone number to his apartment, tore off the sheet, replaced the pad, and shut the door to her glove compartment. He handed the slip of paper and the pen to her and smiled. She looked at it for a moment, folded it, and tucked it into her wallet inside her purse. Kevin hoped that was for safekeeping.

"Thanks for the ride," he said and opened the door of the car.

"You're welcome," she said. "Are you positive you're okay to drive?"

"I'm fine. I promise. Good night. Thanks, again." He shut the door and dug out his keys. He noticed she sat in her car and waited while he unlocked his car and started his engine. When he turned on his lights, she started to pull out of her parking spot next to his. He waved to her and watched as her taillights disappeared.

"The ball's in your court now, Julie," he said aloud to himself.

Chapter 16

Classes started August 23. Julie was glad to get back into it. She had a tough semester ahead of her. Organic chemistry and Physics 211 were going to be tough classes. This semester would make or break her. By January she had to have her application submitted. She'd be taking the PCAT in October. Those scores had to be included in her application. There was so much to stress about.

Shannon suggested they attend a UK football game to relax a little and have some fun. Kevin had told her that she needed to practice having fun. The football game would be good practice. Shannon, Julie, and Karen, another girl in pre-pharmacy, checked the football schedule, found a date that worked for all three of them, and made arrangements to go.

The same day they ordered their tickets, Julie found Kevin's number in her wallet. *If you're ever in Lexington…*

She asked Shannon and Karen what they thought about her meeting Kevin at the game.

"You mean history tutor, tennis-playing, Fourth-of-July Kevin?" Shannon asked her as she waggled her eyebrows.

Julie rolled her eyes.

"He's there on main campus," Shannon said. "His tickets would be better than ours. Maybe we could sit with him and have better seats."

Karen agreed.

Julie planned to call him that night. She made it through the rest of her day without much thought of Kevin. As she drove home, she thought about what she would say to him. She wasn't even sure he would remember her. It'd been almost a month since they last spoke to each other.

She went for a walk after she got home. It cleared her mind. She worked on some physics problems. She ate dinner with her grandmother in front of the television.

When Grams went upstairs at eight o'clock, Julie dug Kevin's number out of her wallet. She sat down by the phone and dialed. She heard the call go through and ring on the other end. It rang once, twice, six times. She would give it eight rings. Wasn't that the polite number? She knew she had heard that somewhere, probably in elementary school. She was about to hang up the phone when she heard a warm male voice on the other end.

"Hello?"

She didn't think it was Kevin. She remembered he had talked about a roommate. Maybe it was him. She could not remember his name.

She shook her head. It didn't matter right now. "Hi. Is Kevin there?" she asked.

"No, he's not here right now."

He didn't sound surprised at all that a female was calling his roommate. She figured Kevin had girls calling him all the time. He was probably on a date right now.

"Could I take a message and have him call you later?"

"Sure. That would be great," Julie said, sounding disappointed even as she told herself she wasn't. "This is Julie. Julie McCourt. I worked with Kevin this summer. He may not remember me…"

She heard the person on the other end chuckle and say something she didn't quite make out. When he spoke again, his voice was perfectly clear.

"Okay, Julie, let me have that number. I'll have Kevin call you when he gets in."

Julie recited her number, listened as he read it back to her, thanked him, and hung up.

She sat in the chair with her legs folded under her for a long while after she hung up the phone. The comment Kevin's roommate had made finally became clear to her. He had said he was sure Kevin more than remembered her, but that didn't make sense. Kevin was probably too busy to give her a second thought. He had surely forgotten about giving his number to her.

She finally got up, got ready for bed, and picked up a book. She sat and read in the chair by the phone. *Just in case he does call back.*

———

In Lexington, Kevin was at the Medical Center Library studying and doing some research with Mitch and Dave. Dave had been sharing his new insights into parenthood. Kevin wondered how in the world someone could look so totally exhausted and happy at the same time. Mitch was dazzling them with his newest conquest, a new third-year student. Kevin could not believe that after less than two weeks of class, Mitch was already at it.

After they left the library, Kevin dropped Mitch off at his apartment and headed home. It was nearly ten o'clock when Kevin unlocked the door. Paul was standing in the hall waiting for him. Kevin noticed a piece of paper in his hands. He was smiling ridiculously, so Kevin couldn't help but ask, "What's got you so happy?" Kevin couldn't help being irritable. He had expected Julie to call by now if she was going to. He was about to give up hope, and that made him cranky.

Paul followed Kevin into the kitchen and watched him fix a glass of ice water.

"You got a call while you were out," Paul said.

"So?"

"It was a girl," Paul added.

"So?"

With a smug look on his face, Paul studied the piece of paper in his hands. After a moment, Paul looked Kevin straight in the eye. "This girl's name was Julie."

"What?" Kevin screamed, splashing water all over the counter as he put down his glass. He practically ripped the paper from Paul's hand. "Why didn't you say so? When did she call? What time is it?"

"Man, calm down. Take a deep breath. You've got to get a grip before you call her. She'll think you're some kind of lunatic ranting like this."

Kevin paced back and forth in the kitchen. Paul was right. He had to calm down before he called. He took a few deep breaths and looked at his watch. It was after ten. He hoped it wasn't too late to call her because there was no way he could wait until tomorrow. Kevin made his way to the living room. He took another deep breath as he sat down next to the phone.

"Hello," he heard Julie say after the call went through.

"Could I speak to Julie, please? This is Kevin Sanders." Kevin didn't want her to know he knew her voice.

"This is Julie."

"So, what's up? Paul told me you called earlier," Kevin was amazed at how calm he sounded.

"Well, do you remember giving me your phone number your last day at the hospital?"

"I remember," he said, trying to keep his voice light while his pulse was pounding in his ears.

"You told me to call if I was coming to Lexington. Two of my friends and I are coming to town for the football game on September ninth. I thought if you were going to the game, we could meet you there."

Kevin wanted to scream. Instead, he calmly said, "Oh, I go to all the home games. In fact, that Saturday after the game we're having a party at our apartment. You and your friends could come over after the game and crash here for the night." He hadn't really thought that last part through before he said it, but he hoped she would stay.

"A party? That sounds good. But stay at your apartment? Where would we sleep?"

"Don't worry. You'll be safe here with me."

"Okay, Kevin. Let me check with my friends. Can I call you back tomorrow night?"

"That'd be fine."

"What time would be good to call?" she asked.

"How about seven? I should be around the apartment then."

"Seven. Okay. Well, I'll talk to you then. Good-bye."

"Good-bye."

Kevin hung up the phone, turned out the lights, and went upstairs. He stuck his head in Paul's open doorway.

"How would you like to have a party next Saturday after the football game? A party and some overnight guests?" Kevin asked hopefully.

"Overnight guests, huh? It's all right with me. You know I'm always in the mood for a party."

It was a long time before Kevin fell asleep that night.

Chapter 17

When Julie called to let Kevin know that she and only one of her friends would be coming to his apartment after the ball game, he was sitting by the phone. He had been staring at it for the last fifteen minutes, willing it to ring. When he finally heard the piercing sound, he jumped six inches off the couch.

They made arrangements to meet outside the front of Commonwealth Stadium, twenty minutes prior to kick-off. He gave her directions to Lexington and told her how to make her way to the stadium. He told her parking would be difficult and for her to expect a hike from the parking area to the stadium. Traffic would be bad on game day too, he explained.

Kevin could hardly wait for the ninth to arrive. He floated through the next few days. Mitch was having a hay day teasing him, but he didn't care. He was just glad Julie was coming. This was his chance to make his move. He was not going to blow this.

That Saturday Julie hit the Bluegrass Parkway with plenty of time to make it to the stadium at the appointed time. She did not want to be late. She exited in Bardstown and drove to Shannon's house. Shannon was going to ride with Julie while Karen followed in her own car. Shannon was staying at Kevin's, but Karen was just going up for the game.

Julie added Shannon's luggage and sleeping bag, which Kevin suggested they bring, to her things already in the backseat. She looked at her watch. Karen was late. Shannon's mom came out of the house to tell them that Karen had called. She was running late, but she was still coming. They waited. Then they waited some more.

Once Karen arrived and they were on their way, the extra time Julie had allotted herself was gone. She found herself booking it on the BG, driving well over the speed limit. She was trying to make up for lost time but had to keep slowing down for Karen to catch up. Julie was ready to choke her. She was never going to get to the game in time to meet Kevin.

Once they got to Lexington, they hit heavy traffic going into town. It was bumper to bumper nearly the entire way to the stadium. As Kevin predicted, they had to park a thousand miles away and hike. Well, it wasn't quite a thousand, but it felt like it as she tried to run and hurry her friends along. She looked at her watch. She was well over thirty minutes late. She could hear fans screaming from inside the stadium. The game had probably been going on for a while now. Would he have waited for her?

———————

At the stadium, Kevin stood with Paul waiting for Julie to show up. He'd arrived a few minutes early. He was anxious to see her. The appointed time came and passed. Kevin heard the sounds of the kick off as the game began. Paul looked at his watch then at him.

"Why don't you go on in? I'm going to hang out a few more minutes." Kevin hated for his friend to miss the game. Mindy and Nina were already in there waiting for them. Paul left him to wait alone.

Kevin couldn't believe he had let himself get so pumped up for this, and she wasn't even going to show. He'd never been stood up before. Then he started thinking. Maybe something happened to her. She could've had a flat tire—or an accident. She could be lying dead on Bluegrass Parkway. *Get a grip, Kevin!* She probably changed her mind and was too embarrassed to call. It was more than likely the invitation to stay at his apartment for the night. He probably freaked her out with that idea.

He waited for several more minutes, turning over in his mind all the horrible things that could've happened to make her not show up. Then he convinced himself she wasn't interested in him and had decided not to come. He took one more sweeping look around the area before he turned and trudged to the gate leading to the student section.

———————

When Julie finally dragged Shannon and Karen to the front of the stadium, there were only a few stragglers in the area. Kevin was not one of them. Julie looked around as she tried to catch her breath. She didn't see him anywhere. He hadn't waited. She didn't blame him.

"We'll never find him in all these people," Shannon said as she waved a hand toward the stadium, "unless you know where his seat is."

"I don't," admitted Julie.

"Well, let's find our seats and watch what's left of the game. After it's over, you and I will find a phone and call his apartment. You brought his number, didn't you?"

"I did. Thanks, Shannon."

Karen tried to brush the whole thing off like it was no big deal. Julie really, really wanted to strangle her.

They made their way to their seats. The second quarter had already started. The stands were packed.

It was hard not to enjoy herself a little. The atmosphere was exciting. She didn't know the ins and outs of football, but she knew enough to cheer when they made a touchdown. She found herself craning her neck every which way, looking for Kevin among the hundreds in the student section.

After the game, Julie insisted they wait until the crowds around them thinned before leaving. Giving up finding Kevin in the crowd, Julie finally followed her friends down the bleachers. They trekked back to their cars. Julie and Shannon said good-bye to Karen and joined the long line of vehicles exiting the area.

Not knowing her way around Lexington, Julie went along with the flow of traffic and drove until they were on Nicholasville Road. She spotted a mall ahead on the right and made her way through the traffic to turn into the parking lot. Inside the mall, Shannon helped her find a pay phone. She dialed the number, and waited for an answer.

When Kevin, Paul, Mindy, and Nina got back to the apartment, Kevin headed straight for the refrigerator and grabbed a beer. He downed it in a matter of minutes. He noticed Nina, Mindy, and Paul looking at each other and watching him. Not one of them said a word to him. They were probably afraid to. Kevin was almost done with his second beer when the phone rang.

"I'll get it," Paul said.

Kevin didn't care. He heard Paul's voice in the living room but didn't pay any attention to what he said. Then he heard Paul calling for him.

Kevin walked into the living room to find Paul holding the phone against his chest. "I think it's her," he whispered.

Kevin did care. He stared blankly at the phone in Paul's hand.

"Do you want to talk to her?" Paul finally asked.

Kevin nodded dumbly and took the phone from Paul. "Hello?" he said, trying to sound normal.

Julie's words tumbled out of her mouth. Kevin made out something about Karen somebody making them late … driving eighty miles an hour … hiking a thousand miles … the first quarter already over … she looked and looked for him. Finally she took a deep breath and asked, "Can we still come to your apartment?"

She was here. She wanted to come over. He was going to see her. He couldn't believe it. "Sure you can still come," he said. His three friends who were watching him, trying to look like they weren't watching him, smiled. "Where are you now? I'll give you directions to get here."

About twenty minutes later, Kevin heard a knock on the door. Paul, Mindy, and Nina huddled around him as he moved to answer it. He pushed the three of them back down the hall.

"You three are going to scare her to death. Now back up."

Once Kevin had the door opened, he stood facing Julie across his threshold. Neither spoke; they just stood there looking and smiling at each other. Remembering they had an audience, Kevin grabbed her by the hand and pulled her into the apartment. A laughing Shannon followed and closed the door. Kevin continued to hold Julie's hand as he led her into the living room. Paul, Mindy, and Nina, who had been hovering in the hall, now crowded into the room, followed by Shannon. Everyone seemed to be talking and laughing at once.

Somehow, introductions were made, and then Kevin went out with Shannon and Julie to help them bring in their stuff. He led them to his room so they could store it until the party was over. He gave them a quick tour of the small apartment, ending in the kitchen where he got drinks for both of them.

Even though he already had a pretty good buzz going, Kevin grabbed another beer from the fridge. He was pretty sure his euphoric feeling could not be attributed completely to the alcohol. Julie being here had a lot to do with it. She was prettier than he even remembered. Oh, and the way she smelled. He found himself getting as close as he could, leaning near her to catch a hint of her perfume. He'd never noticed her wearing any perfume during the summer.

The party wasn't a large one, especially compared to some Paul and Kevin had thrown. Mitch came by. Kevin knew he wanted to see Julie for himself—that and to harass Kevin mercilessly about her being *the one* and falling hard for her.

The size of the party was perfect. There weren't so many people that he couldn't carry on a conversation. He missed the conversations he and Julie had practically every day over the summer. The entire group gathered around the table eating pizza and playing drinking games. Because of the lack of chairs, Kevin was able to orchestrate Julie sharing a chair with him. They sat next to each other; both of them part way on and part way off the seat. After a while, Kevin couldn't stand it anymore. He had to touch her.

"Sitting like this is killing my butt!" Kevin declared.

"Oh, I'm sorry," Julie said as she started to stand.

In one swift motion, Kevin shifted to the middle of the chair and grabbed Julie around the waist, pulling her down so she sat on the chair between his legs. "You don't need to leave," he told her. "We just need to rearrange."

"This won't be comfortable for you."

Kevin shifted slightly forward so that his chest barely brushed Julie's back. With his chin on her shoulder, he whispered, "I'm very comfortable. I want you to sit here with me. Are you uncomfortable? If you are, I'll let you have the chair to yourself, but I'd like us to sit together."

Julie blushed. "No, I'm fine as long as I'm not hurting you."

Kevin kept her close for the next hour. He had dreamed of this, but actually holding her far surpassed his expectations. The closer he was to her, the closer he wanted to be.

After the drinking games wound down, Paul suggested that the group move into the living room to watch a movie. Kevin reluctantly let Julie stand up out of his embrace. People milled about to separate parts of the apartment—some to one of the bathrooms, some to the kitchen to get more drinks, and some headed into the living room. Kevin walked with Julie into the kitchen.

"Can I get you something else to drink?" Kevin asked her.

"Could I have a glass of water?"

Kevin grabbed himself another beer and fixed Julie a glass of ice water. When he handed her the glass, their fingers brushed together and their eyes locked. He could get lost in those gorgeous, deep, dark eyes.

He didn't know how long they stood there, oblivious to all around them, gazing at each other. Finally, Julie broke the spell, muttering something about the little girls' room as she walked out of the kitchen. Kevin made his way into the living room where the others were already settling in for the movie. Paul was sticking the tape into the VCR. It was a classic, *The Attack of the Killer Tomatoes*. It was a completely stupid B movie that he and Paul loved, although Kevin didn't know why.

Kevin made himself comfortable on the end of the sofa nearest the hallway where Julie would enter. As she walked in the room, all Kevin could do was stare at her. She looked so beautiful.

Not spotting a place to sit right away, Julie stood just inside the entry to the living room. She set her glass she had retrieved from the kitchen on the end table near where Kevin sat looking at her. As she released her hold on the glass, Kevin caught her wrist and tugged her toward him. She lost her balance and practically tumbled on top of him, her momentum causing her to land part way on his lap, her behind on the sofa and her legs dangling across his thighs.

Kevin had his right arm at her back, supporting her. His left arm lay over her legs, his left hand rested warmly against her right thigh. They both laughed as he pulled her down over him, but when their eyes met, their laughter suddenly stopped.

As he gazed intently at her, Julie noticed flecks of green in his eyes that she'd never noticed before. Time seemed to stand still. *He's going to kiss me.* She hadn't kissed anyone in months. She hadn't had a first kiss in years. She was suddenly filled with anticipation ... and fear.

As Kevin's warm, firm, full lips settled on hers, Julie lost all fear. In fact, she lost all touch with reality. The movie and the voices of their friends seemed to float away. All that remained was the two of them. Julie had been kissed before, lots of times. She'd had good kisses and not so good kisses, but Kevin's kiss … Kevin's kiss was … perfect, absolutely perfect. Julie felt herself melting into him.

When the kiss, which felt like it lasted forever yet wasn't long enough, ended, Kevin leaned his forehead against hers. Julie could hear him breathing.

After sitting there for several minutes, her eyes closed and her forehead against Kevin's, Julie finally broke away. She excused herself and headed to the bathroom.

Nothing had ever made her feel like this. Her heart was pounding like it would never slow down. As she looked at herself in the mirror, she noticed her face was flushed. She finally got her heart and breathing under control and splashed cold water on her face several times. Drying her face on the hand towel by the sink, she took one more deep breath and walked out of the bathroom and back toward the living room, back toward Kevin.

Kevin had picked up his beer and was drinking it. He didn't pull her back onto his lap, but, when she sat down next to him, he pulled her close to his side and kept his right arm snuggly around her.

"You okay?" he murmured looking at her with those sweet, warm eyes.

"Yeah, I'm okay." And she realized she was. She really was.

After soaking up Kevin's warmth for several moments, Julie finally turned her attention to the movie. "Kevin, what is this?" she asked, gazing at the television where people in tomato costumes were racing across the screen.

"This," Kevin said, motioning toward the screen with the hand grasping his beer bottle, "is a classic. It's *The*

Attack of the Killer Tomatoes. It is my and Paul's favorite movie."

Paul gave a huge cackle at that and said, "Right on!"

"I don't get it. It seems … well, it seems … stupid."

"That, my dear," Kevin said, grinning drunkenly, "means you haven't had nearly enough alcohol."

Julie laughed. She looked skeptically at the screen. There wasn't enough alcohol in the world for her to appreciate this movie. Somehow, it didn't matter. Being here, warm and comfortable, next to Kevin felt right.

Chapter 18

With the movie over, the party finally broke up. Paul left to walk Mindy and Nina back to their apartment. Julie and Shannon went upstairs to change and get their sleeping bags.

Mitch followed Kevin into the kitchen. "So Julie and Shannon are spending the night here, huh?"

"Yeah," Kevin replied.

"I guess you'll finally break down and get lucky, won't ya, big guy?"

Kevin glared at Mitch. When he spoke his voice was even and controlled. "She's not like that, Mitch. She's not that kind of person. She and her friend Shannon are sleeping down here in their sleeping bags—just the two of them. I'll be upstairs in my bed. Alone. Julie is not some nobody I just want to have a fling with."

"Hey, man," Mitch said sincerely, "I'm sorry. I didn't mean anything by it. You know me." He smiled weakly.

"Yeah, I know you. You go from one easy conquest to the next with no thought of what you're doing to them— or yourself." Kevin surprised himself with his reply.

Mitch stared blankly at the kitchen floor for several long minutes before he said anything. "You're right. I…I've been thinking. Well, Julie's friend Shannon…she's seems like a nice girl. She's really pretty too. You know how I have a weakness for blonde hair and blue eyes—"

"Mitch," Kevin cut him off, "she is not like your usual dates. I don't think you're gonna get a quick thrill out of her. She doesn't seem the type."

"I know," Mitch said. "She totally brushed me off tonight, and I was using all my smoothest moves. Are they going to hang out in Lexington for a while tomorrow, or are they leaving early? Maybe if they're going to be around tomorrow, I could go with you to show them around campus." Mitch's expression was hopeful.

"We haven't actually made any plans for tomorrow. When they come down, we can talk to them about it."

Just then, Julie and Shannon walked into the room. Kevin noticed Julie had washed her face, and even though her skin was free of makeup, she glowed. She had the kind of looks that were beautiful with or without makeup. She looked fresh and young, even younger than her nineteen years. She had changed her clothes. Kevin never guessed an oversized T-shirt and boxer shorts could look so good.

He and Mitch asked the girls about their plans for the following day. Shannon looked skeptically at Mitch but didn't say anything against his going with them. The girls said they could kill some time in Lexington tomorrow and would love to look around campus. They made plans to call Mitch when they were up and about.

Kevin walked Mitch to the door while Julie and Shannon spread their sleeping bags out in the living room. Kevin stood by the door and watched as Julie walked down the hall toward him.

He folded her in his embrace, and she wrapped her arms around his waist. She felt so good next to him.

He kissed her—just a soft brush of the lips. He pulled back, studying her face. His pulse quickened. He gently brought her head to his chest and ran his hand over her thick, dark hair.

For several minutes they stood there, holding each other in the dim light of the hall. When they heard a sound at the door, they pulled apart. Both of them smiled and said good night as Paul came in and went up the stairs to his room.

Kevin pulled her back to him. "I am so glad you're here, Julie. You just don't know how glad I am that you're here."

Julie had her eyes closed. She could feel Kevin's heart beating against her cheek. She felt like she was in a wonderful dream. "I'm glad I'm here too," she finally said softly.

Kevin released her and nudged her toward the living room. After she crawled into her sleeping bag, he knelt down and kissed her on the forehead.

"Good night," Julie heard him say, his voice floating through the darkness from the foot of the stairs.

"Good night," Julie and Shannon said together.

After the sound of Kevin's steps faded up the stairs, Shannon and Julie talked for a while.

D.A. Lawson

"Why do you think Mitch wants to go with us tomorrow?" Shannon asked.

"Because you're hot," Julie didn't hesitate to say.

"Sure," Shannon said sarcastically. "He's a player. I can tell. He's not really my type."

Julie didn't say anything. For a few minutes they were both quiet.

"Julie?"

"Yeah?"

"I think you should go for it. I think you should take a chance with Kevin."

"I think I might."

After a short time, Julie heard Shannon's soft and steady breathing. Julie lay there for a long time, thinking about Kevin. She could hear movement above her and caught herself trying to picture him moving around his bedroom, getting ready for bed. She could still feel his kisses. She began to think, too, that the alcohol had affected him. Kevin would probably have a different view of her in the morning. She asked herself what her view would be in the morning and wondered if she was ready to trust someone again. After a long time thinking, Julie finally slept.

When Kevin got upstairs, he took a shower, a cold one. He'd never had reason to take a cold shower before. And for all the talk about cold showers, they sure didn't seem to help much.

Lying in bed, he was unable to sleep. He stared into the darkness toward the ceiling. He should have slept on the couch and let them have his bed. It was a queen size, big enough for two people. *Big enough for two people.* The thought of Julie sleeping in his bed about did him in. He twisted around under his sheet and punched his pillow several times. It was a long, long time before Kevin went to sleep.

The next morning Kevin awoke to sunlight filtering in through the plain white mini-blinds in his window. According to his bedside clock, it was already ten thirty. He lay still in his bed, listening. The apartment was quiet. He guessed everyone else was still asleep. He got up, showered, and went to the kitchen to fix a cup of coffee.

He tiptoed into the living room, coffee in hand. He glanced first at Julie and then at Shannon. Noting they were both still asleep, his eyes came back to Julie's face. She looked like an angel snuggled up in her sleeping bag. She was lying on her side, facing him. Her russet hair spread behind her on the pillow. By the way the quilted fabric lay over her, Kevin could tell her knees were pulled up toward her chest. Her dark lashes contrasted with her fair, freckled cheeks. Her lips were slightly parted and appeared so very kissable even as she slept.

Kevin remembered the taste of Julie's lips from their kissing last night. She had tasted rummy and fruity and something else that must have just been Julie.

He heard Shannon quietly clear her throat. Kevin's eyes moved toward her. She was looking at him, a knowing grin playing across her lips.

"Good morning, Kevin," she said quietly but cheerfully.

"Morning, Shannon," he murmured, looking away from her. He cleared his throat. "Would you like a shower this morning? I think the bathroom is empty."

"Sounds great," she replied and padded quietly through the hall and up the stairs.

Julie turned to her back at that moment and stretched her legs and arms as far as she could. The sleeping bag shifted to the level of her abdomen.

She opened her eyes and blinked several times as if she were trying to focus. Kevin watched as her eyes met his and a warm, sleepy smile spread across her features. He knelt beside her on the floor, setting his coffee cup next to them on the carpet. He placed his hand against the side of her face and caressed her cheek with his thumb. Her smile deepened as she pressed her face against his hand.

He leaned over her, placing his other hand on the right side of her face. He kissed her softly. "Good morning," he whispered against her lips.

"Good morning," she answered huskily.

He took his hands from her face and stood, retrieving his mug with his left hand. With his right hand, he clasped both her hands in his and pulled her to her feet next to him. He snaked his arm around her so that he could run his hand slowly up and down her warm back.

"You know, you look great in the morning," Kevin said sincerely.

Julie blushed and self-consciously raised a hand to brush at her mussed hair.

"I'm serious, Julie. You look fantastic."

She didn't say anything, just blushed more deeply. Kevin loved the way she looked when she blushed. Reluctantly he dropped his arm and stepped away to put his coffee on the table next to the sofa. He helped Julie fold up the sleeping bags.

Shannon came downstairs shortly after Kevin and Julie finished piling the sleeping bags and pillows by the door. She had her bag with her and added it to the pile. Julie trotted up the stairs to take her shower.

Kevin asked Shannon if she'd like coffee. When she said yes, he led her into the kitchen. As he collected sugar, milk, a mug of hot water, the instant coffee, and a spoon, he asked her again if it would be okay to take Mitch along with them today.

She seemed to be terribly focused on preparing her coffee, and Kevin thought she hadn't heard him ask about Mitch. When Kevin was about to repeat his question, Shannon spoke. "He's quite a ladies' man, isn't he?"

Kevin thought before he spoke. Finally, he said, "I'm not going to lie to you. Mitch has been with a lot of different girls since I've known him. I think he does it for his own protection. He purposely chooses to date people who are not interested in a lasting relationship. Before I knew Mitch, he was burned badly. I don't know all the details; he's only spoken about it a couple of times."

"Are you trying to warn me away from him?" she asked, looking at Kevin over her steaming mug.

"I'm not sure. I felt like I should let you know something about him. I would hate for you or him to be hurt."

"Well," Shannon said smiling, "it's just a day out and a tour of campus. It's not even like it's a date or anything."

So Kevin called Mitch. He picked it up on the first ring and started talking. "It's about time you called. I've been waiting all morning. I'll be over in five minutes."

He barely gave Kevin a chance to respond before he hung up. Kevin couldn't help laughing out loud as he replaced the handset. As good as his word, Mitch was knocking on the door five minutes later. When Julie was ready, each of them grabbed something from the pile next to the door. When all was loaded and Julie's car was locked, the group climbed into Kevin's Mustang. Julie sat up front next to Kevin, and Shannon and Mitch sat in the back. Kevin took Julie's left hand in his right as he drove out of the parking lot.

The sun was shining brightly, and the day was warm. They drove around Lexington and stopped at a Mexican restaurant for lunch. Both guys insisted on paying for lunch no matter how much Shannon and Julie argued. After eating, Kevin took them all over campus, pointing out the pharmacy building, the College of Engineering, the tennis courts, the Aquatic Center, and the dorms where he lived last year. He showed Julie White Hall and told her that was the location for the PCAT.

"When you come to take it, you can stay with me. I'll drive you down here and come pick you up after you're finished. We can spend the rest of Saturday and Sunday together."

When they returned to the apartment, Paul and Mindy were working on some kind of schoolwork at the dining room table. The six of them had a supper of leftover pizza and soft drinks. After eating and talking for about thirty minutes, Kevin motioned for Julie to follow him. He led her up to his room and closed the door.

Looking directly into her eyes he said, "I had a really good time, Julie. I'd like to see you again. Are you going to be around next weekend? Would it be okay if I call you?"

"I have to work Saturday and Sunday, but I don't have anything else planned."

"I'm playing in a tennis match Friday evening in Louisville. I know that's not much of an exciting date, but the match has been scheduled for a few weeks now. I'd love it if you'd go with me and watch me play. I'll buy you dinner afterward. I'd like to see you Saturday too, if you don't mind."

Julie opened her mouth as if she was going to say something, but nothing came out. She shut it again.

Kevin was afraid he had screwed up. He didn't want her to sense his frustration. He really didn't want to pressure her into doing something she didn't want to do. "You don't have to tell me now. I'll call you later this week. Is that okay?"

"That would be great, Kevin."

Chapter 19

The inside of Julie's car was quiet as she made her way out of Lexington traffic and onto Bluegrass Parkway. Julie used maneuvering through traffic as an excuse not to talk. Shannon seemed to be lost in her own thoughts anyway.

Julie didn't know what to do about Kevin. He seemed so great, but her plan was to stay out of any kind of serious relationship. She was pretty sure Kevin was an all-or-nothing kind of guy. He would not be satisfied with an on-again, off-again relationship. She wasn't sure she was ready for this kind of intensity. She also had the feeling that if she let him go, she would miss out on the best relationship of her life. Lisa's words of Kevin being *the one* for her popped into her head. She came to a decision. She would go out with Kevin next weekend and see what happened.

With her mind made up, Julie pulled onto the practically deserted westbound lanes of the parkway. She stole a glance at Shannon, who was gazing toward the horizon, where the sun had just disappeared.

Julie finally broke the silence. "How did your good-bye go with Mitch?"

Shannon turned and looked at her. "Oh, he tried to kiss me, but at the last minute I turned my head and took it on the cheek. You know the trick. It keeps you from getting a slobbery, mushy kiss that you don't want."

"Hmm. I'm not really sure Mitch would give slobbery, mushy kisses."

"No," Shannon admitted. "I'm pretty sure he wouldn't. I honestly think, though, that he's the kind of guy who chases after a girl until he catches her and has his way. Since I'm not about to sleep with him, I didn't see any reason to let him kiss me. I did give him my phone number when he asked for it."

Julie was quiet for a moment while thinking. "Did he ask for your number before or after you evaded his kiss?"

"After."

"He'll call you," Julie said. "What are you going to do when he asks you out?"

"You think he's going to drive from Lexington to Bardstown to take me out on a date?"

"Why not?"

"I don't see it happening. What is there to do in Bardstown anyway? Maybe I'll see him when I go back to Lexington with you to see Kevin."

Julie grunted.

"Kevin's the real deal."

"I think you're right." Julie told Shannon about Kevin wanting to see her again and the decision she had made.

"You deserve a good guy, Julie, especially after psycho Jeremy."

Julie grunted again.

The girls didn't talk about guys anymore the rest of the way home. They chatted about classes, music, and where they would go for lunch tomorrow. After Julie left Shannon off at her house, the last part of her time on the parkway seemed lonely. She didn't see another car until she got to Elizabethtown.

Because Julie had made up her mind about seeing Kevin next weekend, she started wondering when he would call. She couldn't remember him telling her a day to expect his call. At the time, she had been a bit overwhelmed. Now she was eager to hear from him. She shook her head and smiled to herself.

Traffic was heavier once she reached Highway 62 in E-town. Julie stopped at a red light, and a truck pulled up close behind her. The grill of the truck filled the entire view in her rearview mirror. She began to feel uneasy when the same truck stayed behind her all the way through town. When she turned off onto Highway 86, the truck did too. She felt even more uneasy. When she got through the little town of Cecilia and the truck was still behind her, she wanted to stomp on the gas but didn't. She wouldn't be able to outrun anyone in her little three-cylinder car. She sent up a silent prayer and tried to keep from staring into her rearview mirror.

As she turned onto smaller and smaller roads, making her way home, she became more and more wary. The truck was still behind her. She hadn't seen another vehicle except this truck for several miles. People didn't come out here unless they lived here or were visiting someone who did. It was too late for a visit, and Julie didn't recognize this truck as one that belonged to any of her grandmother's neighbors.

When she finally reached her road, she gunned her little car before the truck turned. She pulled into her grandmother's driveway and cut her engine and lights. She crouched down in her seat and watched in her side mirror for the truck to pass. When the truck appeared in front of her grandmother's house, she could make out the color by the security light near the road. It was a charcoal gray truck with red striping down the side. It didn't pull into the driveway, but it moved so slowly on the road that Julie thought it would come to a complete stop.

Eventually, the truck moved past the drive. She heard the noise of the engine as it picked up speed. She let out a breath she didn't realize she was holding. For a split second, she considered going out to the road to see if she could get a look at the license plate. She thought the driver might see her and come back, so she decided against it. Once the sound of the engine faded, she got out of the car, grabbed her stuff as quickly as possible, and ran up onto the lit porch. Keys already in hand, she unlocked the door and rushed inside. Hurriedly she shut and locked the door then turned off the porch light.

Standing in her grandmother's kitchen with her back against the door, she took deep breaths and closed her eyes to calm herself. Suddenly, an uninvited image popped into her mind. *Jeremy.* Her eyes flew open. She told herself she was being ridiculous. She hadn't heard from him in weeks. He had no way of knowing where she'd be or when.

Her grandmother was calling to her from her bedroom. Julie made her way through the house to her grandmother's bedside.

"Did you have a good time at the game and with your friends?"

Julie felt a little guilty. She told Grams she and Shannon were going to the football game and would be staying with friends. She hadn't told her the friend was male. Julie was pretty sure Kevin would not technically be counted as a friend. She'd never had a friend kiss like that before!

"We had a very nice time," Julie answered. She went on to tell Grams how Karen made them miss most of the first half of the game. She told her about seeing the pharmacy building and the other things on campus. She omitted the alcohol and kissing. Grams was a staunch Southern Baptist and opposed to alcohol of any kind. Julie doubted Grams had ever consumed a drop, even for medicinal purposes. And the kissing…well, Julie wasn't ready to talk about that with Grams and probably never would be.

They talked for a few more minutes, but Julie did not mention the truck. After a while, Julie walked back to the hall and grabbed her toiletry bag. She unpacked it in the bathroom, brushed her teeth, and washed her face. She carried the rest of her belongings down to her room. She put off unpacking until tomorrow and got ready for bed. She set her alarm to wake her in the morning, grabbed her book, and crawled into bed.

She read a couple of chapters before growing sleepy. She put down the book and turned off her lamp. As she began drifting off to sleep, she heard the neighbor's dog barking. He usually didn't bark.

Chapter 20

Not wanting Julie to feel pressured, Kevin forced himself to wait until Wednesday before calling. Those three days felt like an eternity. When Wednesday finally arrived, he was filled with nervous anticipation. He wondered what he would do if she told him she didn't want to see him again. He convinced himself not to think about that until he had to. For now, he was going to have a positive attitude. Besides, if her response to his kisses was any indication of how she felt about him, he felt pretty confident he could win her over.

He started thinking about the phone call first thing Wednesday morning. He was getting used to thinking about Julie. She filled his every waking thought. No, revise that. She was in his dreams too. Essentially, the woman was always on his mind, one way or another.

He wanted to wait until evening to call to be sure she was home and done with her schoolwork. To distract himself, he went along with Paul to the mall after class. Paul wanted new dress clothes. He had started going to church with Mindy on Sundays.

As the two men perused the ties, Paul said, "My mother is amazed that I'm actually going to church. She loves Mindy."

"Do *you* love Mindy?" Kevin teased.

Paul's expression grew serious. "I do, Kevin. I really do."

"Wow." After a moment he said, "Have you told her? I mean have you said the words?"

"No," Paul admitted. "I'm kinda scared. We haven't dated all that long. What if she thinks I don't mean it? Even worse, what if she doesn't feel the same about me?"

"Well, like I told you before, things have a way of working out. You'll know when the time is right to tell her." Kevin sounded much more confident than he actually was. Not about Paul and Mindy. He was pretty sure that Paul's feelings were reciprocated. It was easy to see it in someone else. He wondered if he would know when the time was right to say the words.

Paul made his selections and paid for them. The next stop was a shoe store. On their way back out to the parking lot, they ran in and talked with Nina for a while. She wasn't very busy since it was the middle of the week. When Paul told her what he had been shopping for, she mentioned Kevin joining them on Sundays. She told them what a wonderful youth pastor the church had, blushing while she said it.

"Aren't you a little old for the youth program?" Paul asked.

"Too old for the youth program but not too old for the new youth pastor," she answered, her cheeks growing rosier.

"Ah...." Kevin and Paul said, looking at each other.

Then Paul said, "So how 'bout it, Kevin? Join us some Sunday?"

"Oh, I don't know, maybe."

Truth be told, he wasn't all that keen on going to church. He believed in God and the Bible. It was people he had the problem with. Too many times he had seen church people come into the pharmacy and act anything but Christlike when they had to wait longer than they thought they should, their co-pay was higher than they thought it should be, or they couldn't get an early refill on their controlled substances. Several of these church people had even been self-righteous pastors who acted all holier than thou but were the first to raise a big stink if something didn't suit them. So no, he wasn't interested in going to church with his friends. He was glad they enjoyed it, so he kept his opinions to himself.

After talking to Nina for a few more minutes, Paul and Kevin returned to their apartment. When Paul had put all of his new clothes and shoes away, Kevin walked with him to Mindy's. The three of them ate dinner together. Mindy liked to cook and insisted it was easier to cook for three or four people than it was for just two. Kevin was frequently a dinner guest along with Paul at Mindy and Nina's.

After eating, Kevin went home, giving Paul and Mindy some privacy. He did some studying, preparing for the regular Thursday battery of tests. He caught himself checking the clock every five minutes and at eight o'clock he called. The phone rang about fifteen times. No answer. No answering machine, either, not that he wanted to leave a message. He wanted to talk to her.

He went back to studying, but he kept losing his place and reading the same material over and over again. He made himself focus, reading his notes out loud. He was glad he was alone in the apartment. He didn't want everybody to know he'd completely lost his mind.

At eight thirty, he tried calling again. No answer. He was beginning to get nervous, but he wasn't sure why. It's not like he had expected her to be sitting by the phone waiting for him. Although, on second thought, that would have been nice. He called again at nine. No answer. He wondered if she could be on a date. That idea made his stomach ache. He called again at nine thirty. As he waited for an answer, he told himself this was the last time he would try tonight. He could try again tomorrow. Someone answered the phone, but it wasn't Julie.

"Hello?" The voice sounded older but pleasant. Kevin remembered Julie lived with her grandmother.

"Is Julie around?" Kevin asked politely.

There was a pause. "Julie?" the woman's voice repeated.

"Yes, ma'am. Julie McCourt. May I speak with her?"

Kevin had decided the woman wasn't going to allow him to talk to Julie when she finally said, "Just a minute."

Kevin could hear rustling and then muffled voices. Finally, he heard a click on the line and Julie's subdued voice. "Hello?"

He heard the sound of a phone being disconnected and thought maybe she had hung up. "Julie?" Kevin said.

"Kevin? Is that you?"

Her voice sounded like she was relieved, and he was pleased that she recognized his. He smiled.

"It's me. How are you?" he said.

"I'm good. I had decided you weren't going to call me."

"Why? I told you I would. I tried to call earlier today, but I didn't get an answer." He definitely wasn't going to share the fact that this was actually the fourth time he had called.

"I'm sorry I missed your call."

"Me too," Kevin replied, "but we're talking now, and that's all that matters."

There was a pause before Julie spoke again. "I was at church this evening," she said. "I teach a group of pre-schoolers on Wednesday nights. While the adults have Bible study classes, I take care of the young kids. We do crafts, have snacks, and I teach them about missionaries. Class is over by eight thirty, but Grams likes to stay and talk. We just got home right before you called."

Kevin was glad she hadn't been out with someone else. The Wednesday night class was probably why she hadn't been able to go with him when he'd asked this summer. He felt a wave of confidence.

"Have you had time to think about this weekend—if you'll go out with me?" Kevin so wanted her to say she would go and at the same time was terrified she would say no.

"I'd love to go with you to the tennis match Friday."

"And Saturday? What about Saturday?"

Julie laughed. "You want to see me on Saturday too? Don't you think you might get sick of me after just seeing me last weekend?"

"Not a chance," Kevin said promptly. "That could never happen."

"Okay, then, Friday and Saturday. I'm all yours, Kevin. Ah … I mean … um," Julie stammered.

"Oh, no," Kevin said, laughing. "You've already said it, and you can't take it back." He was only half kidding.

He smoothed over her embarrassment by making arrangements for Friday, setting up a time to pick her up and getting directions to her house. "Be thinking about what you would like to do on Saturday. I can even pick you up at the hospital right after work if you'd like."

They talked for a long time—about everything and nothing at all. When Kevin hung up the phone and glanced at his watch, he was surprised to see that over an hour had passed.

Kevin called his parents to let them know he would be home this weekend.

"Hey, Mom. Sorry it's so late, but I wanted to let you know I'd be home some time Friday afternoon."

"Why? You can't already be out of clothes."

Kevin chuckled at his mother's reaction. He'd probably really shocked her. The semester had barely started, and he was already going home. "No, my clothes are fine. I'm playing tennis in Louisville Friday night and thought I'd stay at home this weekend."

"Okay," she said slowly. She was quiet for a moment and then asked, "Kevin, what's going on?"

"Nothing."

"But you don't usually stay at home when you play in Louisville."

"Well, I want to this time. What's wrong? Don't you want me there?" he teased.

"Of course we want you here. It's just strange, that's all."

After a few more questions that he avoided answering, Kevin said good-bye and hung up the phone.

Chapter 21

When Julie got home from ECC Friday around three, she took her second shower of the day. She was so nervous she changed outfits at least three times before finally deciding on one. She couldn't remember being this nervous since she had her first date at fifteen.

That date was prom with a junior who was, to her at least, just a friend. Her biggest fear that night had been that her date would want to kiss her good night. She remembered getting out of the car and running up to the porch before her date could even get his car parked in her parents' driveway. She waved, told him good night, and ran in the house. He didn't ask her on any more dates.

She laughed at the memory. She'd been such a chicken. She wasn't exactly sure why she was so nervous about this date. She and Kevin had already kissed, and sharing more kisses with him was not going to be a problem as far as she was concerned. Memories of Jeremy still haunted her—how he had treated her and, in her mind, how he had betrayed her. The worst was the intimacy she had shared with him. Her virginity was gone and was something she could never get back. Neither could she give it away twice.

She had told herself that she didn't need anyone else after Jeremy, that she could live her life for herself and her future career. Somehow, she could not bring herself not to go out with Kevin. She took a deep breath and told herself to take one step at a time. She sent up a prayer asking for guidance and direction and felt better.

As Kevin made his way from Hodgenville to the other side of Cecilia, it occurred to him that he had never gone this far out of his way for anyone. Julie lived out in the absolute middle of nowhere. When he thought he had taken a wrong turn somewhere and reached the end of the earth, he saw the sign for Julie's road. He turned right and eventually saw the house she had described as her grandmother's. He saw Julie's little white car in the driveway. He was finally here. The girl gave good directions.

If Kevin had let himself, he would have sprinted up to the door. He held himself back and merely walked. He knocked on the front door and was greeted by a woman who looked to be in her late fifties. She had a pleasant face, and Kevin figured she must be Julie's grandmother even though she looked nothing like Julie.

"Hi. I'm Kevin. I'm here to pick up Julie."

"Hello, young man. Come in. Julie's ready."

Walking through the door, he saw Julie stand from the chair across the room where she had been sitting. She looked great. She was wearing a pair of dark slacks and a bright blouse. The front and sides of her hair were pulled back while the rest of it hung loosely at her shoulders.

She walked toward him. "Hi, Kevin. I guess my directions were okay? I know it's a long way out here. Sorry about that."

"I had no trouble finding you," Kevin said. He wanted to tell her that no distance would be too great to get to her, but he thought that would sound a bit dramatic. Instead he said, "It's not too far."

"Kevin, this is my grandmother Ann Young. I call her Grams. Grams, this is Kevin Sanders. Kevin's the UK pharmacy student that I worked with this summer."

"It's nice to meet you, Mrs. Young," said Kevin politely.

"It's nice to meet you too. Please call me Ann."

"Yes, ma'am," Kevin replied. Then to Julie he said, "We better get on our way so I won't be late for my match."

Julie gave her grandmother a kiss good-bye.

"Take care of my girl," Ann said as they walked out the door.

"I will. I promise," Kevin replied over his shoulder.

When they were in the car, Kevin leaned over and kissed Julie. "I missed you," he said.

Julie blushed. "You did?"

Kevin smiled and nodded as he looked over his shoulder to back out onto the road. Once he was on the road, he took her hand in his. It was small and fit perfectly within his larger one. He let their hands rest entwined on the console between the seats.

"How was your week?" Kevin asked.

"It was good," Julie said.

She talked about her week, and he talked about his. They talked back and forth the whole way to Louisville. Before he knew it, they had arrived at the indoor tennis courts where the match was scheduled. Julie stood near him while he took his tennis bag from the trunk. He took her hand in his, and she walked with him into the large metal building.

"Have you ever watched a tennis match?" Kevin asked as he led Julie to the spectator area that overlooked the courts below.

"Only on television."

"This will be a bit different, but the rules of the game are the same."

He watched her face as she looked around. She frowned. "Everything all right?" he asked.

"Oh, everything's fine." She smiled, and he felt better.

"Can I get you something to drink before I go down?"

"No, thanks. I'm good."

Kevin pointed out the ladies' locker room where the restrooms were. He squeezed her hand then walked toward the men's locker room door.

"Good luck," Julie called after him.

He looked back over his shoulder, smiled, and said, "Thanks!"

Kevin knew immediately that he was not on his game. He hadn't played this badly since ... well ... since ever. He knew Julie was watching him. He could *feel* her watching him. He didn't look at her. He couldn't look at her. If he did, he would probably forget what a tennis ball was and what he was doing out here. The man he was playing against had never beaten him. It should've been an easy match, but Kevin couldn't focus. He gave up nearly every break point; if his opponent went cross-court on him, he didn't even try to reach the ball; and he only served about half speed of what he was capable. He wanted to get this over with so he could be with Julie. It had been foolish of him to think he could play tennis on their first real date with her up there waiting for him.

Kevin was so glad when it was over. He honestly didn't care at all that he lost this match. It didn't matter; now he was free to enjoy his evening with Julie. He didn't walk to the net to shake his opponent's hand. He didn't jog to the net. He flat out ran to the net. He had never smiled so much after a loss. The guy probably thought he was crazy. Kevin didn't care.

After the handshake, Kevin made a beeline for the locker room. He got what he needed out of his tennis bag and showered quickly. He toweled off, leaving his hair damp. He dressed in the jeans, red Polo shirt, and leather loafers he had packed in his bag. He did take time to put on a little cologne and comb his hair. When he had himself presentable, he threw his sweaty clothes and his gear in his bag and bolted out of the locker room.

Julie smiled and stood as he walked through the door. Kevin felt like the luckiest man in the world to be on the receiving end of one of her heart-stopping smiles.

"Hungry?" Kevin asked as he took her hand and led her out the door and to his car.

"Sure," she answered.

Kevin remembered that she liked Italian and knew a good place on Hurstbourne. He hoped he could figure out the way from the tennis center. He wasn't nearly as familiar with Louisville as he was with Lexington, but he was determined to find her Italian.

"Your match went well?" she asked.

"Well, it's over." Kevin laughed.

"Did you win?"

"You don't know?" Kevin asked, laughing again.

"No," she admitted. "I don't know much at all about tennis."

"I'm sorry," Kevin said. He was no longer laughing. "You must have been bored to death sitting up there, having no idea what was going on."

"It's okay. I really enjoyed watching you play."

He glanced at her as he waited for the light to change. She looked like she meant what she said. "Would you like to learn how to play? I could teach you."

"That would be great. My own private tennis coach."

Kevin found the Italian place he had in mind. The food was really good, the lights were low, and they served the food family style so they could share. The atmosphere was intimate and romantic, just what he wanted.

Kevin parked in the lot that surrounded the restaurant and turned off the engine. "Have you ever eaten here?"

"No, I haven't."

"Good. I think you'll like it."

Dinner was good. Their table was fantastic. Kevin could not have picked a better spot himself. It was a small table, tucked in a corner. Once he and Julie were seated, it was as if they were the only two people in the place. A candle burned on the table. Her dark eyes reflected light from it. There was a glow in her cheeks. Kevin could tell she was having a good time. He was glad. He wanted her to be having the best date she'd ever had. He certainly was.

The ride back to Julie's was quiet but not uncomfortably so. He had a Genesis CD playing, and the music flowed softly around them. Kevin continued to hold her hand. He couldn't help touching her.

When Kevin pulled into the driveway at Julie's house, it was nearly ten o'clock. He hoped she would ask him in. He hadn't had enough time with her.

Chapter 22

Kevin slept late Saturday. In fact, it was nearly noon when he finally awoke. He was surprised his mother had let him sleep so long. Both his parents were early risers and morning people. Kevin had never been a morning person. He hoped Julie wasn't a morning person. There was so much still to learn about her.

He let the events of last night roll through his mind. When he'd gone inside with her, he really hadn't meant to stay so long. He knew she had to get up early today for work. They started talking and laughing. Julie even showed him pictures of her as a baby and young girl.

They had both been talking about what they were like as children. When she told him she had been overweight until she was a teenager, he didn't believe her. To prove her point, she'd brought out several photo albums her grandmother had filled with pictures of Julie at every age. She had been on the chunky side, but she had still been pretty. Those eyes were the same. They seemed to sparkle with some sort of internal light, even in the photographs.

Kevin had learned more about her parents and her grandfather who had died. She wasn't particularly close to her parents, but Kevin could tell she thought the world of her grandmother. He was glad Julie had moved down here to live with her.

He shared some stories about his family too. He described his parents, his sister and her family, and his crazy aunts and uncle. He was fortunate enough to have all four of his grandparents still living. He told her about them too.

In all his twenty-one years, he had never told anyone as much about himself as he had told Julie. He felt this undeniable urge to tell her everything. He wanted her to know all about him, and he wanted to know all there was to know about her.

When he finally got out of bed, he pulled on a T-shirt and a pair of sweatpants. He made his way to the kitchen where his mom was fixing lunch.

"You finally decided to get up," his mom said, smiling. "Hungry? I'm making hamburgers, baked beans, and macaroni and cheese."

"That sounds great," Kevin said as he reached into the fridge for a Coke.

"You got in late last night."

Kevin said nothing. His mom was usually pretty good not to nag him about where he went or about how late he was out. She was even like that when he lived at home during high school. He suspected she knew something different was going on, but he didn't want to tell her about Julie yet. He didn't want his mom seeking her out at work. He could see his mom doing just that, and he was afraid it might embarrass Julie or scare her away. He didn't want either to happen. For now he was going to stay tight lipped.

"How was your tennis match?" Joann continued questioning as she worked on lunch.

"I lost. I had a bad match."

"Well, everybody has a bad match from time to time. You'll get 'em next time."

He gave his mom a peck on the check and walked into the living room, where his dad was watching college football.

Kentucky had an away game today. It would be televised, but Kevin was going to miss the end of it. He didn't care. Julie got off work at three thirty, and Kevin planned to be there waiting for her.

When Joann had lunch ready, she brought plates into the living room for John and Kevin. She brought her food in and sat down to watch the game with them. Kevin's mom enjoyed watching sports as much as he and his father did. The three of them watched the game, talking together and commenting on various plays and players.

At halftime, Kevin stood and gathered everyone's dishes. His mom looked shocked. She walked after him into the kitchen.

"I'll clean this up after the game," she told him. "Just stack everything in the sink."

After rinsing and stacking the dishes, Kevin walked back down the hallway, stopping at the entry of the living room.

"I'm going to take a quick shower," he announced.

"The game's getting ready to come back on," his dad said.

"That's okay," Kevin said as he proceeded down the hall to his room.

After showering and dressing, he walked back toward the living room. "I'm going out for a while. I'll be back later tonight. Don't wait up for me."

Together, his parents said, "You'll miss the game."

"That's okay," Kevin said again. "I have other plans."

At three thirty Julie clocked out and went back to the pharmacy to change. She'd worn a casual dress to work. Because she'd been wearing it since six that morning, it felt good to put on jeans and a sweater. She liked looking nice, but she liked being comfortable even more.

She combed through her hair, brushed her teeth, freshened up her makeup, and put everything back in the bag she had brought that morning. At the last minute, she remembered the little bottle of perfume she had packed and dabbed some behind her ears and on her wrists. The perfume had been a gift from her aunt and uncle. Otherwise, she wouldn't have it. It was beyond her budget. They had given it to her as a thank you for free babysitting. She used it sparingly to make it last as long as possible.

Julie wasn't surprised to hear Kevin's voice as she walked toward the front of the pharmacy. She felt a smile spreading across her face. As she stepped into the room, she had eyes for no one but Kevin. She knew there were others there—Curt, the pharmacist working that night, and Joan, the night tech, but she didn't really look at them.

Julie watched as Kevin flashed Curt a friendly smile, gave a cheerful, "See ya later," and opened the door for her.

Julie gave a wave and said, "Bye, guys," as she walked out.

Kevin took her hand and brought it to his lips for a quick kiss as they made their way to the back door of the hospital. "I missed you," he whispered.

"I missed you too," Julie said without thinking. She could feel her face growing warmer. It was true. She had thought about him all day.

"I'm glad you missed me," Kevin told her quietly as he leaned down close to her ear. He opened the back door, and they stepped out into the sunny September afternoon. "I parked by your car. Do you want to put your bag in it?"

Julie nodded as he went on. "We can take my car. I'll bring you back to your car later and follow you home, if that's all right. The movie we talked about last night doesn't start until seven. I thought we could grab some pizza before the show, but that leaves us some time to kill. What would you like to do?"

Julie thought about it while she put her bag in her car and locked her door. "We could go to the mall and look around."

"Works for me," Kevin replied.

They got in Kevin's car, buckled up, and were on their way down Dixie Highway. They walked through the mall holding hands and talking. They looked through several stores. Kevin bought a new CD. Julie didn't buy anything but had a good time. Julie enjoyed whatever she did with Kevin.

They went for pizza and then to the movie. They held hands all through the show. Julie had trouble concentrating on the screen because Kevin kept rubbing the back of her hand with his thumb.

No one had ever made her feel like Kevin did. She felt comfortable with him, yet he could make her insides flutter with a look or the brush of his thumb on her hand. And when he kissed her, well, there were not words to describe how great that felt. He didn't make her feel like she had to be on guard either. With Jeremy, she had felt constantly assaulted. Kevin didn't make her feel that way. She could tell he found her attractive, but he never even tried to put his hand up her shirt or on her butt when they kissed. Ah, he was perfect, she thought as she watched him following her through her rearview mirror of her car. She asked herself if it was possible for a guy to be that good or was he too good to be true. Julie prayed he was that good.

Kevin scanned the moonlit field across the road as Julie unlocked the door of her grandmother's house. He waited for her in the hall as she went to speak to her grandmother and followed her down the steps to the basement when she was finished.

Julie turned on the television and joined him on the sofa. They talked for a while. They kissed for a while.

They sat close and Julie's head rested against his chest. He had his arms around her. To Kevin, she felt warm and soft and like she was right where she belonged. After a while, Julie grew quiet. Her breathing was deep and even. Kevin realized she was asleep. She had to be tired. He kept her up late last night, she was up early this morning, plus she had worked all day. He just let her sleep. He wasn't sure how long, but she must've slept hard. When she finally raised her head and looked at him, she looked dazed and disoriented. A sudden look of mortification replaced the look of disorientation as she realized she had drooled on his shirt. Her eyes grew wide, and her hand flew up to cover her gaping mouth. Realizing her chin was also wet, she looked even more humiliated. She wiped at her mouth frantically and jumped up off of the couch.

"Oh, Kevin, I am so, so sorry! Let me get a towel," she said, running off to another room. She returned shortly and began rubbing at the damp spot on his shirt as she stood over him.

"I am so embarrassed."

"Please don't worry about it," he said, catching her eyes with his. "It's okay. Really."

She dropped her gaze as she pressed the towel with her palm. Kevin could feel the warmth of her hand on his chest even through the towel and his shirt. She was scrunching her eyebrows like she did when she concentrated or worried. With his thumb, he reached up to gently massage the tension away. She looked into his eyes.

With both hands he caressed her face. Her hand fell away from his chest, and she eased onto the floor in front of the sofa where he sat. He leaned forward so that her face was just below his. His fingertips traced the lines of her face, along her jaw line, across her forehead, over her brows, down her freckled nose, over her high cheek bones. Her skin was smooth and soft. Her face relaxed, and her eyes softened. He had never seen what he saw in her eyes when he looked at anybody else. Their eyes held as he continued to move his fingers over her features.

He began placing kisses where his fingers had traced. She closed her eyes, and he kissed her eyelids too. Rising up on her knees, she brought herself closer to him. He wanted to touch her everywhere.

"Julie, I…" Kevin stopped. He pulled her tight against him and kissed her with everything he had. He felt her touching his face and running her fingers through his hair. She returned the kiss.

When it ended, they both were breathing hard. Kevin continued to hold her against him like he never wanted to let her go.

"Come to Lexington next weekend, Julie," Kevin said, his words coming out in a rush. "Come and stay with me. Please. Paul's going to be gone. He's going to Tennessee with Mindy and Nina. He's going to meet Mindy's parents. They'll all be gone. It will just be the two of us, you and me."

Julie pulled away and opened her mouth, but no words came out. She only stared at him with her heart in her eyes.

Hurriedly he added, "I won't try anything. I swear to you. You will be safe with me." As he spoke the last words, he solemnly placed a hand over his heart.

Because she still didn't speak, Kevin continued, "There's a football game Saturday. I'll get tickets. Please come."

"Okay," she answered, her voice barely above a whisper, "I'll come."

Chapter 23

Julie watched until Kevin's taillights vanished; then she turned out the porch light and locked the door. She noticed Grams's door was shut and no light was visible under it. Julie quietly got ready for bed. She had just lain down when the phone rang. She hurried out of her bedroom. She checked the clock. It was after midnight. Kevin had been gone for only thirty minutes. She didn't think he would have had enough time to get home yet, but she didn't know who else could possibly be calling this late.

"Hello?" she said, a little breathlessly.

"Hello, Julie. How are you?"

"Who is this?" she said, pretending not to know his voice.

"It is so sad that you have forgotten the sound of your lover's voice. It's Jeremy, darling, your one true love."

Julie could taste the vomit coming up into her mouth. "Look, Jeremy, you are not my lover. You were not my first true love. In fact, I don't think I ever loved you."

"You know you don't mean that. You're just trying to hurt me. You hate me, don't you?"

"I do not hate you. Hate would require feeling on my part. I have no feelings for you at all, Jeremy. None. All I want is for you to leave me alone." With each word her voice grew louder. She was angry, extremely angry. He had hounded her for months, and she was tired of it. She was sick of being a victim.

"Ah," he said, "Tell me about your new boyfriend."

The sudden switch threw her off. *New boyfriend? How could he...*

"He has a really nice Mustang." He laughed, and the sound was pure evil. "I've been watching you, Julie."

Julie swallowed hard to keep from throwing up. She had had enough of this, but for once she was not going to hang up on him. She was determined to make him so angry that he would hang up and never, ever call her again. She was afraid of him, but she wasn't about to let him know that.

"Who I see and what I do is none of your concern. I wish I'd never met you."

"Oh, but you did, and you can't give him what I have," he taunted. "I'll always be your first."

"That's true," Julie admitted, "but you are not the best nor will you be the last. I'm going to be honest with you, Jeremy. I never once enjoyed having sex with you. You are not good in bed."

"You are a whore, Julie, a whore. Do you hear me?"

"I hear you, Jeremy, loud and clear. When you talk like that, I know just how much I mean to you. I can hear the love in your voice."

Jeremy screamed something unintelligible and slammed down the phone.

With shaking hands she turned the ringer off on the phone before she hung it up. She quietly went upstairs and did the same to the one in the kitchen.

She set her alarm and got into bed. She didn't sleep right away despite her exhaustion. She thought for a long time. Jeremy had been the one in the gray truck following her that night. He didn't have a truck when they were together, but it had to have been him. He had seen her with Kevin. She didn't understand why in the world he was in Kentucky instead of at home in Indiana. Surely he wasn't living down here. She was going to have to be careful. She was also going to have to tell Kevin everything about Jeremy. She would never be able to forgive herself if Jeremy did something to hurt Kevin. He deserved to know. Once he did, he would more than likely never want to see her again. She didn't want to tell him on the phone. She would tell him Friday in Lexington. He would probably send her packing once he knew the truth.

Sunday was a very long day for Julie. She was so tired she couldn't see straight. She had slept less than six hours the entire weekend. Her chest felt like her heart had turned into a two-ton stone.

She was a quiet, normal, always-followed-the-rules kind of person. Things like psycho boyfriends were not supposed to happen to her. Admittedly, even in the beginning, Jeremy had not been the typical guy a girl takes home to Mom and Dad, but he hadn't shown signs of insanity. It must be the drugs. It was unfortunate that someone would throw his life away abusing drugs, but she honestly could not bring herself to feel sympathy for Jeremy. Like she told him last night (or was it this morning?) on the phone, she didn't feel anything for him. She honestly just wanted him to stay completely away from her.

Eventually, she made it through the workday. As she walked out to her car, she scanned the parking lot for any sign of Jeremy's truck. She continued to watch for it as she drove home. Once she got there, she unlocked the door, let herself in, and then locked it behind her. There was a note from her grandmother saying that she had gone to church early for a baby shower and planned to stay until the evening service was over. It was just as well. Julie was too tired to go.

She changed into her usual sleepwear, got everything ready for her classes tomorrow, and ate a bowl of cereal for supper. When she had almost finished the cereal, the phone rang. *Fantastic.* She picked up the phone in the kitchen and let out a very gruff hello.

"Julie? Is everything all right?" It was Kevin.

"Kevin. I'm sorry. I thought you were somebody else."

"No. It's just me. I wanted to talk to you before I head back to Lexington."

"I'm glad you called," Julie said and meant it. "I had a really good time with you this weekend, even though I'm completely exhausted."

"I shouldn't have stayed so late. I just couldn't help myself. I love your company."

Julie laughed awkwardly. "Julie, are you sure you're okay?"

Julie was tempted to blurt it all out right then on the phone, just to have it out in the open and over with. She would really rather tell him in person. At least that way, if he never wanted to see her again once he knew, she would have that one last time to see him.

"I'm okay. It's just that..."

"You can tell me, Julie. Whatever it is, just tell me."

"Do you remember when I told you I had been engaged?"

"Yes."

"His name is Jeremy Beavens, and he is completely obsessed. He still calls me. He called me last night after you had been gone about half an hour. He saw us together. He knows you drive a Mustang."

Kevin was silent for what seemed a very long time.

"Where does he live?"

"He's supposed to be in Indiana, but he told me he'd been watching me." She paused for a moment before continuing. "A truck followed me the other night when I drove home from Lexington. I'm pretty sure it was him."

"Julie, do you know what his truck looks like?" he finally asked.

"It was gray with red detailing on the sides."

"Are you alone?"

"Yeah."

"Are your doors locked? Do you have deadbolts on your doors?"

"Yes," she said slowly.

"Julie, I saw that truck. Last night when I followed you home, it was sitting in the field across from your grand-mother's house. I noticed it because it looked too new and flashy to be a farm truck. Maybe you should call the police."

"What would I tell the police? 'I broke up with my boyfriend six months ago, but he still calls me. He lives in Indiana, but he told me he saw me with another guy.'" Julie knew her words sounded harsh, and she was ashamed of herself.

"I want to help you, Julie. I want you to be safe. You don't have to bite my head off."

"I didn't mean it, Kevin." She rubbed her hand up and down over her face. "I'm not upset with you. It's just that..." She couldn't finish. She closed her eyes and took a deep breath, fighting the tears that were trying to come. "I can explain it easier Friday when I come to Lexington. That is, if you still want me to come."

"Of course I still want you to come to Lexington. Nothing could change that."

Julie wasn't so sure. "Kevin, be careful. Okay? He has a drug problem, and I'm pretty sure he has lost his mind. I don't want anything to happen to you."

"I'm glad you care about me," Kevin answered gently, "but you're the one who needs to be careful. Okay? I'm going to call you this week to check on you. Is that all right?"

"Of course it is. I never tire of talking to you."

"I'm glad," he said softly. "I feel the same way."

"Please be careful, Kevin."

"I'll be careful. *You* be careful."

After talking to Kevin, Julie felt even more worn out. She cleaned up her dishes and turned the ringers off on the phones. She left a note for grandmother telling her she'd already gone to bed. She brushed her teeth, washed her face, set her alarm, and got into bed. Thankfully, it didn't take long until she was sound asleep.

Chapter 24

The first thing Kevin said when Julie answered the phone Monday evening was how much better she sounded.

"I slept for twelve straight hours last night," she told him with a laugh.

They only talked for a short time, but hearing his voice made Julie feel even better than the sleep had.

Kevin called again Tuesday, and by Wednesday Julie found herself feeling more confident. The whole psycho boyfriend thing didn't seem to bother him, except that he was concerned about her safety. Maybe there was a chance for a future with Kevin, regardless of her past.

Feeling more positive, Julie bought a cookbook when she and Shannon went to the mall during their lunch break. Julie had never cooked anything on her own. As a kid she'd made cookies and brownies with Grams, but she had never cooked a meal before. She had some kind of strange urge to cook for Kevin. As long as all went okay with her confession Friday, she would try out a recipe on him. If not, she would save her receipt and return the book.

Driving back to campus from the mall, Julie asked Shannon about Mitch. She learned that they had been talking regularly and that he had even come to Bardstown last Saturday. He had spent the whole day with Shannon. He took Shannon to her little brother's baseball game, he went sightseeing around Bardstown with her, and he took her out to dinner at one of the historic taverns in town.

Julie was impressed. "Have you let him kiss you yet?"

"I did, and it was nice. Very, very nice," Shannon admitted. "He invited me to come to Lexington this weekend. Apparently he knows you're going to visit Kevin."

"Do you want to go? You're welcome to ride with me." Of course if Kevin wanted her to turn around and leave Friday after the baring of her soul, it would put Shannon in a pinch.

"I'm not ready to go stay at his apartment with him. You and Kevin are different. Kevin is different. You can trust Kevin. I'm not so sure I can trust Mitch, not as far as sex is concerned anyway. I'm not in any hurry to push a relationship. If it works out, it works out. If not, I'm not going to worry about it."

Julie wanted to offer the chance for Shannon to go with her another time but was afraid she may not be going back to see Kevin after this weekend.

When Kevin called Wednesday night, Julie told him she had a surprise for him.

"A surprise, huh? What is it?"

"A cookbook. It's very basic. I've never cooked anything before. Well, except stuff in the microwave. I plan to experiment on you this weekend. What do you say?"

"I'm not sure that's such a good idea. I don't know if my insurance will cover it if you blow up the apartment complex."

"Ha! Ha! I'll be sure to bring a fire extinguisher and leave all my explosive ingredients at home."

They talked and teased a little while longer. After Julie hung up the phone, she spent about an hour looking through her cookbook. She marked several recipes that she felt capable of tackling.

Kevin called again on Thursday. Just before the call ended, Kevin said, "Be careful driving over here tomorrow."

"I'll be careful. I promise."

Friday, Julie left ECC campus and headed toward the north end of town. She filled up with gas and drove her car onto I-65 and then took the ramp onto the Bluegrass Parkway. She had been watching for any sign of Jeremy—so far, so good.

For the entire drive, she thought about what she needed to tell Kevin. He was so different from Jeremy. Kevin was so … good. He was the kind of man women dreamed of marrying—intelligent, dependable, trustworthy, loyal. Like Lisa had told her right before Julie met him the first time, he was even hot. Maybe he was too good to be true. She might find that out today.

She felt that it would be dishonest not to tell him of her past. She knew in her heart that Kevin deserved more than she was now or could ever be again. She wanted to tell him the truth before they spent any more time together. She would tell him as soon as she got there.

She had mixed emotions as she exited the parkway and made her way around New Circle Road toward his apartment complex. Part of her was excited to be spending an entire weekend with him alone. Another part dreaded his reaction to her confession and worried if she wouldn't shortly be going back the way she had just come.

When she arrived at the apartment, she saw Kevin sitting on the front step waiting for her. He smiled as she pulled into a parking space next to his car. He stood as she got out. She removed her keys and purse but left the rest of her things in the car.

He walked toward her, smiling. She found herself wrapped in a warm embrace, and she returned it. She closed her eyes thinking how nice it would be to freeze this moment in time. No matter what he felt for her right now, Julie was sure that would change in a matter of minutes after a few words were spoken.

"Can I help you carry anything in?" Kevin asked as he pulled back from the hug.

"Not yet. We can get it in a little while. Let's talk first. Is Paul already gone?"

"He is. We are all alone."

As the two of them walked through the door arm in arm, Kevin said, "I got you something." He pulled her into the dining room, where a Kentucky blue gift bag filled with white tissue paper sat on the table.

"You shouldn't have done that," she said as she placed her purse and keys on the table and picked up the gift bag.

"I wanted to. Go ahead, open it."

Julie pulled out a T-shirt and a sweatshirt, both in blue with UK embroidered in white on the front. "That's so sweet, Kevin. Thank you."

"I wanted to get you a shirt to wear to the game tomorrow. I didn't know if it would be warm or cool. You can never tell about autumn in Kentucky. So I got one in case it's warm and the other in case it's not. Are they the right size?"

"They're perfect," she said, studying the shirts and caressing the fabric.

Kevin stepped over to her and removed the shirts from her arms. He put them back in the bag and set it on the table. He gently grasped her upper arms in his hands and pulled her toward him. He gazed down into her eyes, and she gazed back. He studied her as if he was searching for something. He kissed her, but she didn't respond in her usual way. She took a deep breath after the kiss and said, "Kevin, I have something I need to tell you."

"Okay. Let's go sit in the living room."

He held her hand and led her to the sofa. He let go of her hand as they sat down, leaving space between them.

Julie suddenly felt stupid. What if she had this all wrong? What if he didn't really care about her at all? What if he laughed at her? What if he looked at her with condemnation in his eyes after she let this out? She had never told anyone any of this. Chances were he wouldn't want to see her anymore after he heard this, regardless of how he felt about her now, but she couldn't keep it inside any longer.

She gave Kevin a sideways glance. He sat there, patiently waiting, his brown eyes kind and questioning. "Go on," he said encouragingly.

Julie took another deep breath and let it out slowly. She looked down at her fingers knotted together in her lap then fixed her gaze on the carpet.

"Kevin, I'm not a virgin," she blurted. "I think people should be virgins when they marry. I had always planned to be a virgin when or if I got married. I thought I loved him. We were going to get married."

Then she let the whole story go about Jeremy Beavens. She told Kevin everything. She talked about the jealousy, the manipulation, the drugs, the phone calls. The words tumbled out like a rockslide that had been held back a long time but had finally broken free. She was crying, tears streaming freely down her cheeks. She took several shaky breaths, trying to suppress sobs. She was afraid to look at him, afraid of what she might see in his eyes. Neither of them spoke for several minutes.

Kevin left the room and returned with a handful of tissues. Julie took the tissues and braved a look at his face. She could read nothing there. She figured the relationship with Kevin was now over.

He surprised her when he spoke. "You can't change your past, so there is no point reliving it or worrying about it. All you can do is hope to learn from your mistakes and move on." His tone was calm and matter of fact. "How do you feel about him now?"

"I certainly don't love him. I doubt now if I ever did. I don't even care enough about him to hate him. I just want him to leave me alone." She took some deep breaths. "Basically, I guess he terrifies me," she finally confessed.

Julie could see the muscles working in Kevin's jaw. He was staring at the floor. She used a tissue and then quietly asked, "Kevin, are you a virgin?"

He lifted his gaze from the carpet and looked at her. After a few moments, he said, "I am. I've never been that close to anyone."

Julie looked him straight in the eye. She felt like her heart was completely exposed. "You cannot fall in love with me, Kevin. Don't ever fall in love with me."

Chapter 25

In the bathroom, Julie wiped her eyes, blew her nose, and splashed her face with cold water. She looked at herself in the mirror. Her eyes were red and puffy, and her face was blotchy. She looked awful.

She walked out of the bathroom as Kevin walked in through the front door.

"I brought in your things."

"You still want me to stay?" she asked quietly.

"Of course I do. Why wouldn't I?"

"Well, I … it's just that … well, I thought when you found out about my past you wouldn't want to see me anymore."

Kevin moved toward her, placing his hands on her shoulders. "Julie, none of that matters to me. All that matters is that you are here with me now." His hands moved to each side of her face, and he kissed her, oh, so very gently.

When the kiss ended, she looked over at her bag and cookbook. Noticing her sleeping bag and pillow were missing, she looked back at Kevin. She took a step back away from him.

"Were you not able to get my sleeping bag and pillow in the same trip?" she asked, trying but not succeeding to keep her tone from sounding accusatory.

"You won't need them," he said. "I want you to sleep with me—in my bed."

She felt the anger flashing in her eyes, and she put her hands on her hips. Her voice was slightly louder than conversational volume when she said, "Kevin Sanders, if you think I'm some kind of … some kind of … some kind of … slut and that I'm going to … with you … "

Kevin actually laughed at her.

"I don't think this is a bit funny!" She felt tears filling her eyes again.

Kevin stopped laughing and stepped toward her. She took two more steps backward.

"I don't think you're a slut, far from it. You just told me that you dated the only guy you've been with for nearly three years before anything happened, *and* you were planning to marry him. You made a mistake with him, but that doesn't make you a slut. I respect you. I would never pressure you into a sexual relationship. Have I ever once shown any disrespect for you in the way I touch you or how I speak to you?"

"No," she answered, not meeting his gaze. "I'm sorry."

He stepped directly in front of her. He used his fingers to push up on her chin so that she would meet his eyes.

"Don't get me wrong, Julie McCourt. I very much want to make love to you, more than I've ever wanted anything. But I can, and will, wait until you are ready. I don't care how long it takes."

Julie's eyes grew huge as he spoke. She swallowed, making an audible gulping sound before she said, "I want the next time to last forever."

Still holding her chin with his fingers, he said, "Forever with you would be fine with me."

He released her chin but remained close in front of her. "Now tell me you will spend the night with me in my bed. I promise we will only talk and sleep." He gave her an innocent little boy look, complete with puppy dog eyes and pouty lower lip.

She couldn't resist. "Okay, you win," she said, smiling.

They walked together upstairs carrying her bag and new shirts. He pulled hangers out of his closet for her to use. He took her toiletry bag from her hands and told her he would hang it on the towel bar by the sink in the bathroom.

They went back downstairs, sat down next to each other on the couch, and went through the recipes Julie had marked. Kevin picked out a lasagna recipe. Julie made a list of items she would need to prepare it.

They went to the grocery together, talking and laughing as Kevin pushed the cart and she searched up and down the aisles looking for the things on her list. When they stumbled across some candles, Julie grabbed a couple of candleholders and candles and put them in the cart. Having everything on the list and more, they made their way to the checkout line. Against Kevin's protests, Julie paid for the groceries. She told him he had bought the tickets for the game tomorrow and her new shirts. The least she could do is buy the ingredients for dinner.

"Besides," she said, "if I mess it up, I won't feel as guilty if I'm the one who paid for it."

On the way back to the apartment, Kevin stopped at a liquor store and bought a bottle of wine. Julie had never tasted wine before.

Together they carried in the bags and unloaded everything onto the counters. Kevin pulled out the pots, pans, and bowls Julie would need. She wouldn't let him help, but he stayed in the kitchen and talked to her. Cooking wasn't a whole lot different than chemistry lab. She'd always done well in chemistry, so surely she could cook. The hardest part was making sure things were done at the same time. Timing was everything, and it would take some practice to get it right.

She set the candles, silverware, and napkins on the table while Kevin poured two glasses of now chilled wine. She took a sip. It was sweet with a twang to it.

Once she finished her glass of wine, she put the bread in the oven beside the pan of lasagna. Kevin poured more wine for her and for himself. They talked until the timer went off. As she took the food out of the oven, Kevin lit the candles. Julie cut the bread and the lasagna and placed some of each, along with some salad, on two plates. She carried the plates to the table then turned out the lights.

"Well, nothing blew up," Julie said, feeling relieved. "Now as long as neither of us gets sick or dies, I'll be happy."

Kevin laughed and took a bite of lasagna. "It's very good!"

During dinner they got into a discussion about church. Julie enjoyed church and thought it important to go. She asked Kevin if he went. When he told her he hadn't been in a long time, she asked him why. He told her about his experiences with condescending, hypocritical people and how it turned him off. She asked how he felt about God, Jesus, and the Bible. He told her he believed in God and Jesus and everything written in the Bible. It was people he had issues with.

"I think," she said after considering his words for a while, "that most people who go to church are trying to do the best they can. Churches, like any other group, have some people who aren't nice, but most people I've known that go to church are genuinely good people. I've gone to church my whole life. People aren't perfect. We all make mistakes. That's why we all need God."

As Julie covered the lasagna with aluminum foil, she said, "I guess I shouldn't have made the full recipe. There's a lot left over."

"Don't worry. Paul and I will eat it. We love leftovers."

When the dishwasher was loaded and running and everything else was cleaned up, Kevin and Julie went into the living room to watch a movie.

By candlelight, they watched *Where the Red Fern Grows*. They lay on the floor with a bunch of throw pillows. When she cried during the movie, Kevin held her closer to him.

After the movie ended, Kevin turned off the television. They continued to snuggle on the pillows. The only light came from the candles. He kissed her on her cheeks, her brow, her nose, her mouth.

Kevin's kisses were growing more and more intense. His hands moved over her arms, sides, and back. Julie could feel his restraint. Hers was fading. She pulled away from him. He looked down at her; his eyes were heavy-lidded.

"Kevin, what are we doing?" she murmured.

"Just kissing," he whispered, touching his lips to her neck and nuzzling behind her ear.

Julie had never felt anything that felt this good. Her entire body tingled. The weight of him felt so satisfying bearing down on her. She felt safe and protected in his arms. But when he pressed into her, she knew they had to stop. She could feel that he was very aroused, and she knew she was. If they didn't stop now, she didn't think they would be able to.

She pressed her flattened palms into his chest. He didn't seem to notice. She pushed with more force, breaking the kiss. "Kevin, we are not just kissing anymore. We have to stop."

He practically jumped off her and sat up. His eyes looked dazed and bewildered. His lips were parted, his breathing heavy. Julie was in the same state. She sat up, and for a long while they sat looking at each other.

"I'm sorry," he said finally. He picked up both wine glasses and handed Julie's to her. Once they finished off the remaining liquid in their glasses, he took them to the kitchen.

As he left the room, he handed the TV remote to her. "Find us something to watch on television."

When he returned with a large glass of ice water to share, she had moved to the sofa and had found a standup comedy show to watch. They sat together with his arm around her shoulders. She was tucked close beside him. They laughed and talked while they watched the comedians.

At twelve thirty, Julie began to yawn. "Ready for bed?" Kevin asked.

"I think so," Julie admitted.

Julie blew out the candles, and Kevin turned off the TV. Julie walked to the stairs as Kevin checked both doors to be sure they were locked. In the bathroom, she changed, brushed her teeth, and washed her face.

When Julie reentered Kevin's room, the only light came from his bedside lamp. He was in bed with the covers tucked under his arms. His chest was bare. She noticed it was dusted with dark hair. Her eyes followed the outline of his body under the covers down to his feet and then back to his face. Her face was hot. He was smiling at her.

"You don't wear pajamas?" The words barely croaked out of her mouth.

"No. Just my boxer shorts," he answered, grinning ear to ear.

"Oh," she sighed in relief, "I was afraid you slept in the nu—"

"Would you like me to?"

"No!"

He laughed and patted the bed beside him. "Come to bed, Julie. I promise I won't bite you."

She put her clothes she had removed in her bag and then crawled to her side from the foot of the bed. Julie slid beneath the covers, careful not to look under them. Kevin turned off the lamp and slid closer to her. She turned on her left side with her back to Kevin. He placed his arm over her waist and nuzzled his mouth close to her ear.

"Good night," he whispered. After a moment he added, "I'm afraid what you told me never to do is happening."

Julie was sleepy. The wine had made her feel very relaxed. The moment her brain realized what Kevin was saying, she was already drifting off to sleep.

Chapter 26

Kevin woke before Julie the next morning, but he didn't get out of bed right away. The first thing he noticed was her warm body tucked at his side. She was curled almost in a ball facing him. Kevin turned on his side toward her and watched her. She looked very vulnerable and childlike.

He brushed his lips against hers. Her lips formed a faint smile, but her eyes remained close. She was still asleep. Kevin studied her face for the longest time and then reached out to caress her hair. It was thick and wavy and messy from sleep. He pinched several strands together and used them to tickle her cheek. She made a face, moaned, and brushed him away with one of her hands. She slept on, but she shifted to her back. Her legs were stretched out now. She turned her face away from him.

He laid his hand on her belly and gently rubbed with his fingers. She moaned softly but didn't wake. She certainly was a sound sleeper. He loved learning all these little things about her. Kevin became very aware of the soft skin of her thigh against his leg. He was torturing himself.

He couldn't figure out why he kept torturing himself. All he knew was that he could not feel enough of her.

If he could, he would marry her today and spend the rest of his life loving her. But he had no way to support her. He wasn't about to get married and continue to accept financial support from his parents or hers. When they married, he would take care of her in every way. As soon as he was out of school and had a job, he wanted them to become husband and wife. He wondered if he was moving too fast, but he knew he wanted to be with her. He would always want to be with her. He was surer of it than he'd been of anything else ever before.

Kevin continued to move his hand slowly against the fabric of her T-shirt, watching to see if it would wake her. Nothing. He brought her right hand to his mouth and trailed kisses over her fingers. She slept on. He turned her hand over and kissed her palm before tickling the inside of her wrist with his lips.

She woke with a jerk.

"What are you doing?" she asked groggily. She was smiling at him.

"Nothing."

She turned toward him and laughed lightly as she said, "Your hair is wild!"

"It always looks like this in the morning," he told her.

They lay together like that for a long time. Kevin lazily rubbed her palm with his thumb, and Julie played with his hair.

"Julie, it is definitely happening." He wasn't quite sure why he didn't just come out and say it. Maybe it was for his own good. Maybe it was for hers.

Julie pulled her hand from his grasp and dropped her other hand from his hair. She turned her face toward the wall.

"Something vexes thee?" Kevin said in a light, laughing tone in an attempt to tease her into looking at him again.

"No," she answered, "just thinking."

"About me?"

That brought her out of it. She faced him and gave him a small smile. "What else?" After a moment she added seriously, "You know, I've never slept with a man before."

Kevin watched her face turn pink once the words were out of her mouth.

"I mean, well, I've never spent the night with anybody before." She looked away from him again. "I did things with . . . him, but we never spent the night together. It was never . . . intimate. It was . . . This is not making any sense, is it?" She looked back at him.

Kevin's smile faded. He looked into her eyes and saw pain there. Kevin wondered if Beavens forced himself on her. Kevin really wanted to hurt Jeremy Beavens.

Julie looked blankly at the ceiling. "What am I trying to say?" she said aloud. "It's just that it never felt like this, Kevin." She looked at him, and her heart was in her eyes. "It feels so good being here with you like this. With you I feel safe and protected. You make me happy."

Kevin wrapped his arms around her and cradled her against him. He held her for several minutes.

He kissed her playfully and then rubbed her nose with his. "I guess we better get up and get ready for the game. Do you want to shower first?" he asked as he rose from the bed and put on his robe.

"I suppose I should shower first so I can blow dry my hair while you shower."

"I'll go down and fix some coffee then. Would you like a cup?"

She made a face. "No, thanks. I don't like coffee. I usually have Coke or something in the mornings."

"I've got Coke and Diet Coke. Which would you like?"

"I'll take a Coke. Nothing like sugar and caffeine to start the day."

"I'll bring it up when I come back. Anything else, milady?"

"No." She laughed and whacked him with a pillow.

As Kevin fixed his coffee, he heard the shower come on. He stood in the kitchen listening. She was right above him at this very minute completely naked. He groaned out loud. He had had no idea how much actual physical pain being this close to her would cause him. The weird thing was he couldn't stop himself.

Just like sleeping with her last night. That had been the most wonderful feeling, having her next to him. It wasn't that he was trying to force her into a compromising position. He would never forgive himself if they did something in the heat of the moment. He was not going to let that happen. When she gave herself to him, he wanted her to give on every level—intellectually, emotionally, as well as physically. He didn't want her to have any regrets. He had every intention of making this a lifetime commitment. But still, he couldn't seem to stop himself from having as much of her as possible without taking too much.

Kevin drank one cup of coffee and fixed himself another. He heard the shower stop, grabbed a can of Coke out of the fridge, and headed up the stairs. He stood outside the door, listening. He could hear her moving around and wondered what she was doing. Suddenly the door opened.

Julie stood in front of him in nothing but a towel. She was wet. Her skin glistened, and her hair looked black. Kevin couldn't move. He stood there staring, mouth gaping. He looked from her face to the towel. A part of him willed it to fall from her body. He finally shut his mouth and looked back at her face, which had grown red. In fact, the color had spread down her neck and onto her chest. He followed the blush right down to where the towel covered her breasts. He wanted to know if a person could blush over her entire body. He shook his head.

Julie finally spoke. "I'm sorry," she croaked. "The steam had built up in here, and I was trying to clear it out. I didn't know you were out there."

"I brought your Coke," Kevin said flatly, holding out the can. "I'll wait in my room until you're finished." He turned and left, shutting his door without another look at her.

After a while, Kevin heard soft knocking. "I'm done in the bathroom," Julie said through the closed door.

Kevin found her in the bathroom gathering her things. He noticed a small bottle of perfume sitting on the vanity. He picked it up and studied it.

"Do you always wear this?"

"No, not always. It was a gift from my aunt and uncle. The bottle's not very big, so I save it for special occasions."

Kevin opened the bottle and sniffed. It wasn't quite the same as what he had noticed on her. "Are you wearing it now? Is today a special occasion?"

Julie looked at the floor, her cheeks taking on the familiar rosy tint. "Yes."

He leaned toward her, rubbing his nose against her neck. "Did you put some here?" he murmured.

Julie nodded.

He inhaled deeply. Something about the perfume and Julie's chemistry made a scent that was all hers. It was fantastic. He was absolutely positive she would never be without some of this perfume. He wanted her to always wear it, at least when he was around her.

He pulled away from her and studied the bottle. After he memorized the name and appearance of the perfume, he set the bottle in Julie's hand.

Julie told him she was going downstairs to finish getting ready. He thought about teasing her about staying here with him and then decided he had made her blush enough for one morning.

When he finished his shower and was dressed, he went downstairs and found Julie still in the bathroom getting ready. He leaned against the doorframe and watched her in the mirror. Her cheeks grew slightly pink.

"Do you mind if I watch?"

"No." She laughed. "I'm sorry I'm not ready. It takes forever to dry my hair. I've thought about cutting it super short so it would be easier."

"Don't," he said maybe a little too forcefully.

She laughed again as he moved to stand behind her and slightly to the side. He could see both their reflections in the mirror. "You're beautiful."

"Kevin," she said quietly, as if she didn't believe him. She leaned closer to the mirror brushing mascara on her already black lashes. He noticed a deepening in the color of her cheeks. He knew it had nothing to do with makeup.

She finished and gathered her things and put them in her bag. When she had everything together, they both stood for a moment looking at each other in the mirror. She was only about two, maybe three inches shorter than he was. A perfect fit as far as he was concerned.

She turned around and gave him a quick kiss on the mouth. "You're pretty good looking yourself," she said.

Kevin rolled his eyes to the ceiling. He had never thought himself handsome or ugly, but he was pleased she liked the way he looked.

"What time do we need to leave?" Julie asked.

Kevin checked his watch. "I suppose we can leave now, if you're ready. I told Mitch he could go with us. We need to go by his place and pick him up. I hope that's okay. I forgot to say anything about it earlier."

"That's fine with me," Julie replied.

Chapter 27

Julie had a great time at the football game. Shannon had been right about main campus students getting better seats. They were nearly on the fifty-yard line, the weather was perfect for football, and UK was winning.

Historically, the University of Kentucky was not known as a football school. Basketball reigned supreme in the Bluegrass State. Even Julie knew that. Kentucky competed in the SEC, the South Eastern Conference, with schools such as Florida, Georgia, and Alabama, among others, that always had top rankings in football.

This game was so much better than the last one had been. She was beginning to understand the sport. Kevin and Mitch were both really good to explain what was going on and to answer her questions. She now understood the concept of downs, the extra point or points after a touchdown, and passing versus running the ball. The guys actually got to the point where they explained what happened during the plays before she could even ask. She hoped she wasn't driving them crazy.

Mitch talked about Shannon a lot. Julie couldn't wait to tell her.

When the game was over, the three of them were starving. Kevin drove them to Tolly-Ho's. The place was packed and wild. The line ran out the door and onto the sidewalk. Julie knew by looking around that this was a major hangout for UK students.

She noticed that several people knew Mitch and Kevin. She heard people calling out to both of them as they stood in line. She began to feel a little self-conscious and very out of place. Kevin must've sensed it because he stepped closer to her and put his arm around her waist. It felt like a protective gesture. Julie looked up and smiled at him. He smiled back. For a moment they were the only two people in the place. He had a wonderful gift of making her feel that all was right in the world.

The spell was broken when Julie felt someone looking at her. She scanned the room, suddenly fearful that Jeremy had somehow found her here. When she located the source of the glare, she found a rather short but very attractive woman shooting daggers at her. Julie held her gaze for a while and then looked away. Whoever she was had perfect hair, perfect makeup—perfect everything. The girl was plenty angry too. Julie had no idea why she was giving her the evil eye. Without looking directly back at the girl, she leaned over and asked Kevin about her.

"Don't look directly over there," she whispered, "but do you know that blonde by the window? She seems to be channeling a great deal of animosity toward me, and I have never seen her before." Julie noticed the girl's eyes narrow as she leaned closer to Kevin. As Kevin scanned the room, Julie pulled away from him and asked Mitch a question about the food.

Kevin pulled Julie closer to him and nudged Mitch. "Don't look now, but one of your old flames is giving my girlfriend the stink eye."

It was odd that she was glaring at her if Mitch was the one she had dated. Julie obviously wasn't with Mitch.

Mitch looked at Kevin with an expression of innocence in his eyes. "Oh," he murmured, "which old flame?"

"How many have you had?" Julie couldn't help but ask.

"Too many, I'm afraid," Mitch told her, looking guilty. "Ah, I see her. Cindy." Mitch looked straight at her, smiled, and lifted his chin in greeting.

Julie looked at Cindy out of the corner of her eye and saw that the girl's gaze had shifted to Mitch, and she was smiling. It was not a very nice smile.

"She's coming over," Mitch said, the smile never leaving his face.

"Did you two have a bad breakup?"

"Breakup? No, there was nothing to break up. We just had sex a few times."

Julie looked at Mitch, her mouth gaping open. She could feel her face growing hot.

"I was the consolation prize," Mitch continued. "Kevin was the one she really wanted."

Julie's chin just about hit her chest. She knew her face had to be flame red.

"Shut. Up," Kevin hissed through clinched teeth.

"What?" Mitch said innocently. "It's the truth. You had to know she wanted you, Kev." Mitch brought his fingers to Julie's chin and pushed it up to close her mouth. Then he patted her cheek, gave her a wink, and said, "Don't worry, dear. Kevin never gave her the time of day."

Kevin turned when the blond tapped him on the shoulder. "Hello, Cindy," Kevin said evenly.

"Hello, Kevin," Cindy said, placing a well-manicured hand complete with bright red polish on Kevin's chest. "Did you enjoy the game today?"

"I did." He took a step back out of her reach and pulled Julie to his side.

"Hi, Cindy. How are you?" Mitch said with a little too much enthusiasm.

Julie cut a glance at Mitch. He was smiling slyly. He gave Julie a mischievous wink. Julie rolled her eyes but couldn't hold back a grin. Cindy didn't look at Mitch. Her eyes remained fixed on Kevin.

"Mitch," was all Cindy said in reply to his greeting.

Mitch's smile widened. Julie nudged his arm with her elbow.

"Cindy, this is my girlfriend, Julie McCourt. Julie, this is Cindy…I'm sorry. I can't remember your last name," Kevin said smiling.

"Smith. My last name is Smith."

Julie saw the realization hit Cindy.

"Girlfriend!" She practically screeched. Several people turned to look at them. She looked around apparently embarrassed. "I didn't know you had a girlfriend, Kevin," she said more quietly.

"We worked together this summer," Kevin said, looking down at Julie and smiling. "She'll be applying to pharmacy school in January."

Cindy finally dragged her eyes from Kevin and looked Julie up and down. Even though Cindy was several inches shorter than she was, Julie felt like an insect that Cindy was preparing to squash. Julie knew what she was thinking. *He could have me. What is he doing with you?* Julie wondered the same thing.

"How... sweet," Cindy said.

Two girls by the door called out to Cindy. She turned to look at them and called back, "Be right there!"

"Bye, Cindy," Mitch called sweetly.

"Mitch," she responded flatly.

"I'll see you Monday, Kevin," she purred.

Then Cindy did something Julie could not believe. She kissed Kevin, right smack on the mouth. She really laid one on him. He finally pushed her away. She smiled seductively, as if kissing Kevin was something she did all the time. She cut one more hate-dripping look at Julie before she turned and sauntered out the door with her friends. Julie was shocked.

"I cannot believe I slept with that," Mitch muttered, shaking his head.

"I can't either," Julie couldn't help saying.

Kevin grabbed napkins from a nearby table and swiped at the lipstick streaked across his mouth. Cindy had apparently been wearing a lot of it. Julie had to help him remove it all.

"Julie, I'm sorry," Kevin whispered to her. "I swear I've never even dated her. I've never even danced with her at a party or anything. I have never had any interest in her."

"I believe you," Julie answered, and she meant it.

Chapter 28

Somehow Mitch, Kevin, and Julie got past the drama with Cindy and enjoyed the rest of their time at the Ho. Julie ended up with the biggest hamburger she'd ever seen, a strawberry milkshake, and chili cheese fries that the three of them shared.

Mitch wanted to know what Julie was going to tell Shannon about the whole Cindy deal. The truth was she wasn't sure if she should tell Shannon about it at all, and she told him so. She thought Mitch should be the one to tell her about his previous sexual experiences.

"You know, Mitch, Shannon doesn't have the experience that you do. As far as I know, she's never had a serious boyfriend."

"Are you telling me I should stop seeing her?"

"Not at all," she said, looking Mitch in the eye. "But you need to be honest with her. I know she's afraid you're only after one thing. Shannon has no desire to become another name on your list of conquests."

"Ouch," he said softly as he studied the condensation on his beer bottle. "I want more from her than that. Way more, I'm afraid."

"Mitch," she said laying her hand over his, "your past is done. What you do with your present is what matters."

Julie felt Kevin squeeze her leg under the table. She looked at him beside her, and they exchanged smiles.

Julie felt Mitch gently grip her fingers. "Next time you come to Lexington, bring Shannon. Please."

Julie returned the pressure of Mitch's fingers before removing her hand. "I'll try."

Because both the guys had beers with their food, she insisted on driving when they left Tolly-Ho's. Mitch and Kevin laughed at her, but Kevin surrendered his keys without any resistance. Julie felt empowered driving a Mustang. This was way more car than her little Geo Metro. More than once, Kevin had to remind her to watch her speed.

"It would not be good for our designated driver to be stopped for speeding," he told her, laughing.

Before they took Mitch home, they went to Fayette Mall. Kevin wanted to get her a tennis racket.

"Tomorrow we start your lessons," he told her.

With tennis racket purchased and Mitch home, Julie and Kevin found themselves alone again in his apartment. As soon as they were in the door, Kevin grabbed her and yanked her to him. He kissed her until they were both breathless.

"I've wanted to do that all day," he told her.

"Hmm." After a moment she said, "There's something I don't understand. If you could have someone that looks like Cindy, why in the world are you here with me?"

"Do you know," he murmured as he traced her eyebrows and the space between them with an index finger, "that I have thought of you since the first time I saw you in Sam's office?"

Julie shook her head.

"Do you remember that day?"

She nodded.

"Your eyes, Julie. Your eyes are ... I get lost when I look in them. All summer I waited for you to be ready to date. All summer I waited for any hint that you were interested in me. Why do you think I kept offering to help you study?"

"I thought you were just being nice."

"I did it because I wanted to spend time with you."

"I didn't know," she whispered.

"None of that matters now. Now that I know you, all I want to do is know you more. I think you're smart, funny, beautiful, and sexy." He was quiet for a while as he gazed into her eyes. He took a deep breath and let it out. "I'm trying to tell you that I want to be with you." He took another deep breath and blew it out more slowly. "I love you, Julie."

Julie couldn't speak. She had not expected this. She felt like she might cry.

"I've never said those words to anyone," Kevin said quietly.

The thing was, she had said those words before, and it turned out to be a mess, a gigantic mess. She did not want to ruin this with Kevin. He was undoubtedly the most wonderful thing that had ever happened to her, but she was frightened.

As if he could read her mind, he said, "You don't have to say it. I understand if you don't feel the same way. It's enough right now that I love you. I had to let you know. I hope I haven't, I don't know, messed up anything."

"Oh, Kevin." She hugged him, hugged him as tightly as she could. She didn't know what else to do, and she was glad that Kevin returned the embrace.

Julie was relieved when the phone rang. She went upstairs to his room when he went to the living room to answer it. She needed time to think. She went to the window, parted the blinds and stared, unseeing, out onto the parking lot.

She took a deep breath, let it out, and walked to the bed. She sat down on the end. She thought about how long she had known Kevin. Since April. They met the first time in April. Five months. They spent the summer talking, studying, and working together. For three weeks they had been dating. Was that long enough to fall in love? Kevin apparently felt that it was. Julie had known he'd be an all-or-nothing guy.

If she were completely free of Jeremy, things would be different. Of course, that's what Jeremy was trying to do—keep her from moving on with her life. She didn't want her past mistakes to ruin her future happiness.

Kevin walked in. He sat by her on the bed, linked his fingers with hers, and brought the back of her hand to his mouth for a kiss.

"Hey," he said.

"Hey." As she looked into his warm eyes, she found herself forgetting she wasn't in love with him.

"My mom called to let me know my family is getting together next Saturday at my papaw's farm. My mom, dad, sister, niece, nephew, brother-in-law, aunts, uncle, and my grandparents will be there. Will you go with me?" He was smiling and looking hopeful.

Julie had enjoyed hearing about Kevin's family. It would be interesting to meet them. "Sure, I'll go with you. Does that mean you're coming home again next weekend?"

"Yes. Can I see you Friday and Sunday too?"

"Do you plan on spending every weekend with me?"

"Yes," he said without hesitation, "I'd spend every minute of every day with you if I could."

Julie remembered how Jeremy had taken over all of her time. She didn't want to go through that again. But she enjoyed the time she spent with Kevin. The longer she knew Kevin the more she wanted to be with him. So what was her problem?

"You okay?" Kevin asked quietly.

"I am," Julie said looking into his eyes and smiling. "Do you want to watch some TV?"

"I've got a better idea," Kevin said. "Come downstairs."

Julie followed him down the stairs and stopped behind him as he dug in the closet.

"Here it is," he said still halfway in the closet. He stood and held a board game box in his hands. "Let's play UKopoly. It's like Monopoly only the properties are places around campus. What do ya say?"

His eyes were sparkling like a little boy on Christmas morning. "Sure," Julie answered. "I have to warn you though. I'm a great Monopoly player."

"A challenge then," Kevin said as he led the way to the dining room table. "I do enjoy a challenge."

They set up the game together. Julie offered to be the banker.

"Do you cheat?"

"Absolutely not!"

They played the game for hours. They laughed and teased and accused each other of cheating. Kevin was a ruthless Monopoly player. He did not intend to lose. He didn't exactly play by the rules either. He tried to wheel and deal his way out of trouble and found ways to get the properties he wanted. They were both very competitive. Kevin ended up winning the game, but not by much.

After the game was picked up and put away, they prepared for bed much as they had the night before. When Julie came from the bathroom into Kevin's room, he was sitting on the edge of his bed untying his tennis shoes. He still wore his jeans, but had already removed his shirt.

Julie watched as he stood, kicked off his shoes, and eased his jeans over his thighs and down his legs. Julie's face grew warm, but she couldn't pull her gaze away. He bent to pick up the jeans at his feet. He saw her watching him. She felt her face become even more heated.

He picked up his pants, walked toward her, and took her clothes she had removed when she changed in the bathroom out of her arms. He dropped it all into a mixed-up pile on the floor. He pulled her to him and kissed her. She kissed him back. After a while Kevin eased her away from him.

"Go ahead and get into bed. I'll be right back," he said as he left the room.

Julie found some tennis magazines on Kevin's floor. She turned on the bedside lamp, turned off the overhead light, and lay on the bed. She flipped through the magazines as she waited for Kevin to come back.

She hadn't heard him enter the room, but suddenly he plunged beside her onto the bed causing her to bounce toward the wall away from him. She laughed.

"I love to hear you laugh," he told her.

She smiled at him and felt her face get warm.

"Whatcha doin'?" he asked as he looked at the magazines.

"I'm studying for my tennis lesson tomorrow," she answered.

"Did you learn anything?" he asked pulling a magazine out from under the pillows where it had shifted when he jumped on the bed.

"Um … no," she said smiling broadly, "but I know this great tennis instructor. He'll have me playing like a pro in no time just like he had be doing history like a history major. He has the most terrific legs too." She had rolled toward him as she spoke and returned to a position on her stomach next to him. She bumped his hip with her own.

Julie listened as Kevin explained the rules of tennis. He detailed how to win a game and how many games were needed to win a set. "The match is won by the player who wins the best of two or sometimes three sets," he explained.

"Wow. That all sounds very confusing."

"It's not that bad," he said as he laid the magazines on the floor. "Once you begin playing, you'll figure it out."

He turned over onto his back after pulling the sheet and blankets up over them. Then he turned out the light.

Julie snuggled next to him, placing her head on his shoulder. "Kevin," she said quietly, "do you *ever* go to church on Sunday?"

He didn't answer right away. "No," he finally said, "I don't."

"I miss going. I haven't been for three weeks," she said, yawning. "Usually, when I work on Sundays, I go to the evening service. Last Sunday I didn't because I was so tired."

"Tired, huh?"

"Mmhmm," she said, scrunching herself against him in her usual sleeping position. "Some great-looking guy kept me out all night for two nights."

Kevin kissed the top of her head. He chuckled. "That was very rude of him."

"Hmm," she said and yawned again. "Next Sunday, I'd like for you to go with me to the evening service. If you want to."

"I want to," he said and kissed her head again.

"Oh, good," she murmured.

"I love you," she heard him whisper right before she fell asleep.

Chapter 29

Julie was the type of person who would dwell constantly on an issue if she had a decision to make. If she had a major issue to consider, she rolled it over, under, and around in her mind until she came to a definite decision.

The current issue was Kevin Sanders. She tried not to think about it, about him saying he loved her, but she knew she had to decide one way or the other what she was going to do with their relationship. She didn't go with the flow or wait to see what happens very well. School work didn't even keep her from mulling over what she should do.

Since he had said those three little words, she had been letting what she knew about Kevin run through her mind again and again. She'd never once seen him lose his temper. Even all those days when stuff was messed up in the IV room, he just took care of business without losing his cool.

She thought about the history study sessions and the tennis lesson. He made everything fun, made her realize that there was more to living life than reaching your destination. He was teaching her how to play again.

The whole sex thing really had her astounded too. She *knew* he wanted her. He had flat out told her that he did. She was pretty sure he knew that she wanted him. She had never been so physically attracted to anyone. He didn't take advantage of that. The fact that he held himself back physically made her feel treasured, valued, and loved.

So what was she afraid of? They had similar career goals, and he was probably the most intelligent person she knew. How he remembered the stuff he did amazed her.

He had made his intentions clear. He loved her, and he wanted them to make a life together.

She was frightened because of her past. That was true, but her past doesn't have to predict her future. Kevin shouldn't have to pay because of her fiasco with Jeremy. Life was full of risks. She was beginning to think that a life with Kevin Sanders would be worth the risk, better than risking a life without him.

Over and over again Julie prayed for guidance about Kevin. Unfortunately, prayer had not been a part of her decisions concerning Jeremy. Not until the end, anyway, after the mess was already made. This time she wanted God in on it right from the start. The strange thing was, even though Kevin admitted to not going to church, she seemed to feel a sort of peace about her relationship with him. She didn't hear a big booming voice from heaven saying, "Have a relationship with Kevin Sanders!" or anything, but still there was a feeling that it was right.

They had talked about God, and he did say he believed. He also said he would go to church with her Sunday night. She didn't want to have another relationship where there was a difference in their feelings about God. It didn't work.

Maybe she was being entirely too clinical about this whole process. It wasn't very romantic to dissect feelings. Before she gave her heart to Kevin, though, she had to be sure it wasn't a mistake. She'd been caught up in passion before, Jeremy's passion and jealousy. It had been so wrong, so destructive.

It did not escape Julie's attention that Kevin didn't say those three little words at all during their phone conversations. It made her feel a bit sad, but she understood why he didn't. He'd already told her, and she had not responded in kind.

Kevin's priorities were changing. Thursday pharmacy parties no longer held any attraction for him. Besides wanting to avoid Cindy Smith, who never missed a party, he no longer had any desire to hang out with a bunch of drunken pharmacy students. Mitch had all but stopped going too, and Dave never had. Since the beginning of the semester, Kevin had been putting more time and energy into his studies. Julie's drive had inspired him to want to do the best he could instead of just getting by.

Friday he drove from Lexington to ECC. He parked in a visitor's space and headed for the science building. Organic lab was her last class for the day. He headed up the stairs and waited in the hall for Julie to finish.

He could see her through the glass in the door. Kevin watched her work. He saw Shannon next to her. He watched as Julie went around the counter to the station across from hers and Shannon's. There were two guys working at that station. It was clear she was trying to get them to understand something. She grabbed a piece of paper and started writing.

One of the guys waved his hands and shook his head. He walked over next to Shannon. The other guy remained focused on Julie. Kevin noticed the guy was nice looking, and he was attracted to Julie. It was obvious in the way he looked at her as she explained whatever it was she was explaining. Kevin couldn't blame him. He would've vied for a tutoring session or two if he had been in his shoes.

Julie was amazing to watch, so animated, talking with her hands and arms as she tried to make her point. Kevin could tell she had asked the guy a question. She was looking at him, her head to the side, nodding as he spoke. She smiled when he finished talking and gave him a reassuring pat on the arm. She began to make her way back to Shannon's side still smiling.

Kevin knew exactly when she saw him. Her eyes lit up, and her smile stretched all the way across her face. Kevin was breathless for a moment. He didn't care if she tutored a hundred guys as long as she saved that smile for him.

Julie must have said something to Mic, the chemistry professor, because she was speaking and looking toward where Kevin knew Mic's desk was. She came to the door, still beaming. She opened it and beckoned him inside.

"Hey, Kevin," she said happily, "come on in. Mic said it's okay." She took Kevin's hand and drew him through the doorway.

Mic had risen from his customary stool and was walking toward them. "Kevin!" he said in his distinctive accent as he shook Kevin's hand enthusiastically. He looked from Julie to Kevin and back. "This," he said pointing from one to the other, "this is good, very good."

Kevin noticed Julie blushing slightly.

To the class, Mic said, "Students, this is Kevin Sanders, one of the brightest students I have ever taught. He is a student at the University of Kentucky College of Pharmacy. Two years ago he was where you are now."

"You," Mic went on, pointing at Julie, "back to work."

Julie laughed as she headed back to her station.

"You," Mic said to Kevin, "come sit and tell me all about pharmacy school."

Kevin stepped up on the raised platform at the front of the lab and took a seat on the stool next to Mic. Kevin couldn't help cutting a glance at the guy Julie had been helping. He was not surprised to see the younger man looking back at him with apparent dislike. Kevin didn't blame the guy. He had already figured out what a gift he had in Julie. Lots of guys were going to envy him. He didn't care.

He and Mic talked while the students continued their work. They were still talking when Julie and Shannon finished the experiment and cleaned up everything. The two women stood nearby talking as they waited for Mic and Kevin to finish their discussion.

Both men stood. Mic exchanged good-byes with Kevin and his two current students. The three of them walked out into the hall together. Julie looped her arm through Kevin's as they made their way toward the stairs.

"Hey, Kevin," Shannon said. "How are you doing?"

"I'm good, Shannon. How'd your lab work turn out?"

"Well, we didn't blow up anything this time."

For a minute Kevin thought she was serious then realized they were teasing him when they both laughed. He held the door opened as they left the building. He took Julie's hand in his as they walked toward the lot where Julie and Shannon had parked that morning.

"Mitch told me he was visiting Bardstown tomorrow. You wouldn't know anything about that, would you?" Kevin asked.

"Would you believe," Shannon answered with blue eyes sparkling, "he is going with me to my grandparents' fiftieth anniversary party? My whole family, on both sides, will be there: uncles, aunts, cousins by the hundreds, old family friends. He will probably run back to Lexington so fast, the rubber will be worn off of his tires."

"I doubt that," Kevin answered. "I know Mitch pretty well. He wouldn't be going if he didn't think you were worth it."

Shannon gave him a shy little smile.

"You know," Kevin continued, "he talks about you all the time. I think he's really smitten. Next weekend you should come to Lexington with Julie when she comes to take her PCAT. I'm sure Nina and Mindy would be glad to have you stay with them if you don't feel comfortable staying with Mitch."

"I don't know. . . . " Shannon said uneasily.

"Oh, come with me," Julie urged. "You'd be great moral support. We can all do something fun after my test is over. Heck, you guys can do something fun while I take my test."

"Well, I'll talk to Mitch about it tomorrow," Shannon said as they came to the edge of the parking lot.

"I'll check with Nina and Mindy," Kevin said. "Would it be okay if I had one of them give you a call this week?"

"That'd be okay. I just hate to inconvenience them."

"They're from the South. Hospitality is in their blood. I'm sure they won't mind," Kevin said.

Julie and Kevin said good-bye to Shannon. She walked toward her car while Kevin and Julie made their way to Julie's. They both waved when Shannon drove by and honked. They were alone in the parking lot.

As they stood by Julie's car, she suddenly looked extremely excited, like she had some vast secret she was bursting to share.

"What is it?"

"Kevin, I have something to tell you." She was facing him. Both of her hands were clasped on his upper arms. Her elbows were resting in his hands. Her dark eyes were sparkling.

"Go ahead."

"Kevin Sanders, I'm in love with you. You are the most wonderful person I have ever known, and I want to spend the rest of my life with you."

She was gripping his arms. He could feel excitement coursing through her body. It felt like she was barely holding herself back from jumping up and down right there in the parking lot. He was speechless for a moment, trying to take this in.

"You are?" he finally asked.

She nodded her head up and down excitedly, smiling the entire time.

The realization hit him like lightening. He smiled and picked her up. He spun her around and kissed her. "I love you too," he told her and hugged her to his body. "I love you too."

Chapter 30

As Julie drove them off campus, she told him her grandmother was gone for the weekend to some kind of women's retreat with church. Kevin was not comfortable with the idea of her being by herself all the way out in the boonies, not with the psycho ex still bothering her. He weighed his options as they shopped at the grocery store for snack foods for dinner that night. He hadn't been to Hodgenville yet; he'd come straight to E-town from Lexington. All of his clothes and things were still in his car.

"I'm staying with you tonight," Kevin told her in a matter-of-fact tone as they carried the grocery bags to her car.

Julie gave him a surprised look. "Grams won't like it, Kevin. She is very conscious of what people say. The neighbors would see your car and say something to her."

"Does she know that Beavens guy has been calling you and stalking you? Do you honestly think she would want you to be alone down there at night when he might try to do something to you?"

Julie didn't answer right away. When she did respond, her voice was low. "She thinks he stopped calling. I haven't said anything about it in a while. I haven't told her that he's been down here. If I had, she wouldn't have left. I don't want her to give up what she wants to do."

"It's settled then," Kevin said as Julie started the car. "We'll go back to the college and get my car. I'll park it at the hospital. You'll pick me up there and take me home with you. My car won't be in your driveway, so no one will be the wiser. I'll ride with you to work tomorrow and go to my parents' house after you are safely inside the hospital. I'll give you directions, and you can drive to their house after you get off work; then I'll take you out to meet my family. It's a foolproof plan."

"Boy, you sure figured all that out fast! Are you really that concerned for me to be alone?"

"No, I just want to get you alone and have my evil way with you."

Julie laughed as she pulled into the spot next to Kevin's Mustang. "I love you, Kevin."

It amazed him to hear her say the words. "I love *you*," he answered and then leaned over and kissed her. He kissed her again, and again. He finally pulled himself away.

Julie followed him to the hospital where he left his car. Then she took him home with her. Kevin called the Sanders's house when they got inside. No one was home, but he left a message on the answering machine.

He and Julie spent a quiet evening together. While they watched television, they ate. They talked, they kissed, and they talked more.

Kevin told her that he wanted her to be his wife, but he wanted to wait until he could take care of her financially, which meant they'd have to wait until he was out of school and had a job. They were in Julie's bed. He was on his back. She was beside him with her chin supported by her left hand, which rested on his chest. She was wearing one of her big T-shirts over her panties.

Kevin felt the intimacy of the moment, the closeness. He could picture the two of them like this twenty years from now. They would be lying together, naked, after the kids had been put to bed. Perhaps they would have just finished making love. Or maybe they would talk and share about their day and then turn to each other and make love. Even without the lovemaking, this felt good, more than good. Being close to Julie made him feel that all was right with the world. His thoughts being what they were, he couldn't help but be surprised by Julie's question.

"Do you want to have children?"

He thought about what their children might be like, a little girl with Julie's eyes, a little boy who liked tennis. "Children, our children, would be wonderful. I do love kids. Truthfully, though, as long as I have you in my life, I cannot imagine wanting or needing anything else."

"I'd like to have children—someday. I want to have a career, though. That's very important to me."

"There's no reason why we can't have both," Kevin told her. "We have plenty of time."

She smiled.

Julie told him about being on birth control pills and why. He explained the mechanism of action of the hormones. She seemed fascinated as he explained the negative feedback, how it affected the pituitary gland, how the release of luteinizing hormone and follicle-stimulating hormone was stopped thus preventing ovulation.

"No ovulation, no baby," he said. "Of course, oral contraceptives are used for other reasons like your dysmenorrhea, even acne."

"You turn me on when you get all pharmaceutical."

"Do I?" he asked with raised eyebrows.

Julie's face took on a pink tint.

"I love you," Kevin said.

"I love you too."

They became quiet. Julie snuggled against him. He listened to the sound of her breathing as she fell asleep. It felt good to have her near him. He was glad he had stayed. He would do anything to protect her. He always wanted her to feel safe, secure, and happy.

Joann and John Sanders were having coffee at the kitchen table when Kevin went in the house Saturday morning. Kevin saw his parents look at each other as he poured himself a cup of coffee.

"Good morning," Kevin said, smiling as he sat at the table with them.

"Good morning, son," his dad said.

"Are you going out to the cabin this evening?" his mom asked.

The cabin was where his mom's side of the family had all their family functions. One summer when Kevin was still in high school his papaw had the bright idea of building a log cabin on his farm. The entire family took part in the building.

"I'll be there," Kevin answered, "and I'll be bringing someone with me."

His parents glanced at each other. His mom looked like she would burst. His dad was grinning at her.

"Who's coming with you?" his mother finally asked. "Is one of your friends from Lexington coming in?"

"No, she lives on the other side of Cecilia."

"She?" His mom choked on her coffee.

Kevin had never taken any girl to any family function. His parents had never once met a girl he dated. Of course, he'd never taken any girl, except Julie, on more than one date. Julie was his first real girlfriend.

"Her name is Julie McCourt. She works at the hospital, in the pharmacy. I worked with her all summer. She will be applying to pharmacy school at UK in January."

"Oh," his mom said.

His dad was still smiling. "We're looking forward to meeting Julie tonight," he said.

Julie had a pleasantly smooth day at work. She was a little nervous about meeting Kevin's family, but more than that, she was looking forward to spending more time with him. After work, she followed Kevin's directions to his parents' house. She automatically checked for any sign of Jeremy and was relieved when she saw none. When she pulled into the driveway, she saw Kevin's car but no other. She parked beside it and walked to the side door he had told her to use.

She didn't even get a chance to knock. She had just stepped up to the door when it flew open and Kevin dragged her inside. He started kissing her, a long, deep kiss.

"I missed you," he said as he held her close.

"I missed you," Julie said. "Please tell me your parents aren't here. I don't want them to walk in on us and have this be their first impression of me."

"They've already gone out to the cabin," Kevin told her. "We're going to meet everyone out there. If there's any chance you need to go to the bathroom, you should go now. There's no plumbing at the cabin, only an outhouse."

Julie made a face. "Okay. I'll go here. Where's the bathroom?"

Kevin held Julie's hand and led her through his parents' ranch-style home. They started in the kitchen. He took her around through the dining room, into the living room, and into the foyer.

"This is the front door we never use."

They went down the hall. He indicated a room on the right that had been his sister's. His parents' room and bathroom were through the last door on the left. His room was the last one on the right. He pulled her through the doorway. There was one UK print hanging on the wall. Besides that, the room didn't look at all lived in.

"Your parents' house is really nice. You better show me where the bathroom is so we can go. I don't want to be late the first time I meet your family."

He led her back into the hall and indicated the door right next to his as the bathroom. "Do you need any help?" he asked, following her into the room.

She laughed. "No!" she said, pushing him back out the door. "I've been doing this by myself for a long time now."

When she finished she was relieved when she opened the door to find the hall empty. She had pictured him standing right outside the door listening just to give her a hard time. When she found his room empty, she walked back toward the kitchen to find him waiting there.

"Ready?" he asked.

"Ready."

As he drove them to the farm, they talked about his family. He explained who everyone was that would be there and about the cabin his family had built together. They drove around the square in Hodgenville and took a road heading out of town the opposite direction they had just come. After a few miles, they turned right on a gravel lane next to an old, worn mailbox supported by a wooden post. The lane crossed a creek by a wooden bridge that made a *thump, thump, thump* sound as they crossed. The trees were dense on each side of the lane until the bridge. The leaves were beautiful fall shades, yellows, reds, oranges, and browns.

Julie looked around in silence, taking it all in. Past the bridge, the lane had fields on each side that looked to have been recently harvested.

"They grew corn here this year," Julie said without thinking.

"How do you know?" Kevin asked her curiously.

"I'm an Indiana farm girl, Kevin. I've seen more than my share of corn fields."

"Well, you're a Kentucky girl now," he said squeezing her hand, "even if you do talk funny."

"I don't talk funny! You're the one who talks funny." She laughed. "Kentucky's my home now, but I doubt that I'll ever sound like I belong here."

"I'll give ya some lessons, darlin,'" he said in a pronounced Southern drawl.

Julie laughed again.

"Be prepared," Kevin said. "My dad will tease you mercilessly about being a Hoosier. Don't let it bother you. He teases everybody. It means he likes you."

"He hasn't even met me yet. How do you know he'll like me?"

"He will. I'm sure of it."

Julie saw the cabin at that moment. It was beautiful, tucked in the woods, surrounded by all the fall colors.

"Oh, Kevin," she gasped. "It's beautiful out here."

He smiled and came around the car, took her hand, and led her up the steps to the porch that ran the entire length of the cabin. They opened the door to boisterous activity. Everyone inside seemed to be talking at once. Kevin pointed out his parents and grandparents before anyone noticed them. Julie couldn't help looking around. The place was wonderful! There was a large stone fireplace centered on the wall to the left. A fire was blazing in it. To the right was a long wooden table surrounded with various benches and mismatched chairs. Behind that, in the far corner on the right, sat a huge, old iron stove. It was actually being used to cook dinner. On the left side of the room, opposite the stove, was a wrought iron bed piled with handmade quilts. Scattered around the room were various other pieces of antique and rustic furniture. The place was lit with several candles and old-fashioned, glass kerosene lanterns.

Kevin's nephew, who she remembered from the park, was the first one to approach. Approach was putting it mildly. Actually, Kevin was tackled. Kevin picked up the little boy; both of them were laughing.

"Do you remember Miss Julie from the park?"

"Yes."

"Hello, Derrick. How are you?" Julie asked him.

"Fine. I'm seven now. I had my birthday. I'm in first grade," he said proudly. "Did you bring my friends with you?"

Julie assumed Derrick was talking about her cousins. She shook her head. "I'm sorry. They're at home with their mom and dad. Would you like me to bring them to play with you sometime?"

"Yes!" he cried as he dropped from Kevin's arms. Then he was off to play with another little boy who looked to be about the same age.

Kevin's mom and dad came up to them after that. "Julie," Kevin said, "this is my mom, Joann, and my dad, John."

"We're glad to have you," Joann said before she pulled her son down for a kiss.

"You didn't tell us she was a Yankee, son," Kevin's dad said, smiling and winking at her.

Kevin gave her a knowing nod. Julie smiled and said hello to both his parents. He guided Julie over to meet his grandparents who were already seated at the table with their backs to the stove. He leaned over and gave his grandmother a hug and a kiss and patted his grandfather's back.

"Mammaw, Papaw," he said, "this is my girlfriend, Julie McCourt. Julie, this is Mammaw Bootsie and Papaw Rodney."

"Welcome," Papaw Rodney said warmly. "We're glad you could come."

Julie was surprised when Kevin's grandmother took her hand and gave it a firm squeeze. Julie knelt down to be at the same level as the elderly couple.

"You have such a wonderful place here. I can't believe you guys built this."

Kevin's granddad gave her a proud smile and told her some stories about the building experience. Both his grandparents described stunts Kevin had pulled as a kid.

Throughout dinner, Kevin introduced Julie to the rest of his family. They politely interrogated her, but Julie didn't mind. They obviously cared a great deal for Kevin and each other. It warmed her heart. Her family gatherings were not like this.

After dinner, Julie held and fed the baby, Kevin's niece. Julie figured it was a test. She guessed she passed. The baby ate and fell asleep in her arms. After a while, someone took the baby from her. The little thing was popular, even while asleep.

After dinner, Derrick came over and sat in Kevin's lap. She started talking to him, and, before long, he moved over to her lap. He went into a rather involved account of the tribulations of first grade. Julie learned all about his teacher and his friends.

It was a very nice evening. Everyone told her to be sure to come back when she and Kevin stood to leave.

Joann walked out onto the porch with them. "I won't be home tonight either, Mom," Julie heard Kevin quietly tell his mother.

Julie was glad for the low amount of light on the porch because her face was blazing red. Kevin's mom didn't seem to be fazed by Kevin's news. She pulled her son down for a hug and a kiss and told Julie that she was glad she had come and that she was welcome back any time.

"Kevin, what is your mom going to think of me letting you spend the night with me?" Julie asked when they were in his car.

"I didn't tell her I was spending the night with you."

"I think she'll figure it out."

"We're big people. What we do is our business. Besides, we aren't doing anything but sleeping. Anyway, she really liked you. My whole family really liked you. I can tell."

"Your family is wonderful. You're fortunate to have them."

"I know," Kevin said honestly. "I'm fortunate to have you too."

Julie squeezed his hand.

Chapter 31

Julie didn't find the small, gift-wrapped box until Monday morning. It was on her dresser. She smiled as she unwrapped the box to find a new bottle of the same perfume her aunt and uncle had given her. She read the note Kevin had left.

> *Julie,*
> *I don't want you to ever run out. Please wear it whenever we're together.*
> *Love always,*
> *Kevin*

The next week, Kevin felt odd, different somehow. It had started over the weekend. He couldn't quite put his finger on it, whatever it was.

The time with Julie had been wonderful. Just like he suspected, his parents had adored her. They wanted to know when they would see her again. While neither of them came right out and asked him how serious he was about the relationship, Kevin got the feeling that somehow they knew Julie was to be a permanent part of the family.

So Kevin knew that whatever was off, wasn't Julie. Saturday night they had spent another wonderful night together. He left his car at the hospital as before. There'd been no contact from or sightings of Beavens, but Kevin was still more comfortable knowing Julie wasn't staying all the way out there alone. Sunday Kevin was waiting in the driveway for Julie when she got home from work. That evening he went with her to church. After church he stayed at her house later than he should have before driving back to Lexington in the early hours of the morning.

He came to the conclusion that it had something to do with that church service. After pondering the situation for a few days, he broke down and called Chad Daniels, Nina's youth pastor boyfriend.

The two men met for coffee Thursday afternoon. Somehow Kevin found that Chad understood how he felt when he hadn't even been able to figure it out himself. Chad asked Kevin if he had ever experienced a relationship with Jesus. Kevin knew about God and his Son but didn't know anything about a relationship with something or someone he couldn't even see. Kevin was only a little surprised when Chad pulled a small, well-worn New Testament from the back pocket of his Dockers. It must be a preacher thing to carry one around all the time. Chad read some scriptures with Kevin. He got the feeling Chad didn't even need the Bible he was holding to share the verses but used it for Kevin's benefit. Kevin knew this was what *it* had been; this is what he needed. He prayed with

Chad, or Chad prayed with him. Anyway, Kevin, for the first time in his life, actually talked to God. Right there in the middle of Denny's.

After praying, Chad talked to Kevin about becoming involved with other Christians and being part of a church. Kevin told him he was interested in attending church with Paul, Mindy, Nina, and him. Then he and Chad talked about football, about the upcoming basketball season, and about Nina and Julie.

"I'm going to ask Nina to marry me," Chad confided. "I've not told anyone else. Tomorrow I'm fixing her dinner at my apartment. I've already got her ring. I've been bursting to tell someone. I hope you can keep a secret."

Kevin smiled. "I can keep a secret. Do you think she'll say yes?"

For a moment Chad looked ill. When he realized Kevin was giving him a hard time, he said, "We have talked about it. I know she wants to marry me. The timing might throw her off, but I don't want to wait. I don't make a great deal of money, but I make enough to take care of us and pay her tuition until she's done with school. We haven't dated that long, but I know we are supposed to live our lives together. I'm ready to get married right now, but I'm sure she'll want to wait until summer at least. I pray we don't have to wait much longer than that, if you know what I mean."

Kevin knew exactly what he meant. It was funny to be friends with a pastor. Chad was a regular guy. He was a diehard UK fan, born and raised right here in Lexington, and he had wants and needs just like any other human.

He was a regular guy who loved God and wanted others to have that blessing too.

Kevin could barely contain himself waiting for Julie to call. Thursdays had become her nights to call, and Tuesdays were his. At eight thirty, when the phone rang, Kevin was sitting right next to the phone and picked it up on the first ring. He was dying to share his news and sort of rushed through the normal chit chat that always started their phone conversations.

"Kevin, is there something bothering you?"

"Well, nothing is bothering me, but I do have some news to share with you." He went on to tell of his encounter with Chad at Denny's.

Kevin waited for her to say something. She didn't, but he heard a snuffing sound like she was crying.

"Julie?" he said quietly. "Julie, are you okay?"

"Oh, Kevin, that is the most wonderful news! I'm so glad. I've been praying for you."

He smiled. It made him feel good to hear that, even though it wasn't a surprise that she had been.

"Know that now I will be praying for you too," he told her.

Friday, when Shannon and Julie arrived at Kevin's apartment, Mitch was there waiting for them. Well, not them. He was waiting for Shannon. Julie watched as Mitch wrapped his arms around her friend and gave her a sound kiss. When the kiss was over, Mitch continued to hold

Shannon as if he couldn't bear to let her go. Shannon looked happy, and Julie was glad.

Julie and Kevin spent the evening with Shannon, Mitch, Paul, and Mindy. They ordered pizza, played games, and watched movies. While they ate, Julie looked around at everyone in the room, realizing how intertwined her life was becoming with Kevin's. His friends were becoming her friends. Her friends were becoming his friends. His friend was dating her friend. It was all pretty cool. She realized that someone was missing.

"Mindy," Julie asked, "where's Nina?"

"Oh, Chad wanted her to himself tonight," she said, grinning. "I think something serious may be about to happen."

Kevin's lips tightened into a hard line, as if he was trying very hard not to smile, and he looked at the ceiling. Julie seemed to be the only one to notice. She gave him a what's-up look with her right eyebrow quirked upward.

He leaned over and whispered, "Chad is proposing tonight. He told me yesterday. No one else knows."

Julie mouthed a silent "Oh."

"What are you two whispering about?" Paul asked.

"I'm talking dirty to my woman," Kevin said quickly.

Everybody laughed, including Julie, as her face turned crimson.

Because Julie had to be at White Hall by nine o'clock for the PCAT Saturday morning, she and Kevin called it a night early. Julie felt self-conscious staying with Kevin when everybody knew she was staying with him. Nobody acted weird about it or said anything. When Paul and

Mitch walked Mindy and Shannon to the neighboring apartment, Kevin and Julie walked upstairs to get ready for bed. Kevin left the door unlocked for Paul.

It felt very natural to climb into bed with Kevin, to snuggle up, and to talk about anything and everything.

"Nervous?" Kevin asked as they lay facing each other, his hand sliding slowly up and down her arm.

"A little," Julie admitted, "but I feel like I'm as prepared as I can be. There's nothing to do now but get it over with."

"I know you'll do fine," Kevin told her and kissed her forehead.

For the three hours Julie was taking her test, Kevin was nervous. He was more nervous for her than he'd been when he took the blasted test himself. He tried to keep himself busy the whole time she was gone. He was relieved when he saw her walking down the sidewalk toward the parking lot where they had arranged to meet when she was done. She looked tired, and he exited the car to walk toward her. He hugged her right there on the sidewalk. Kevin could feel her lean into him.

After the PCAT was over, Kevin and Julie met the rest of their friends at Keeneland to watch the horse races. Keeneland was unbelievably beautiful. It was like being deep in the countryside instead a few miles from a city. The vast grassy areas were still a vibrant green while the trees were dressed in glorious colors of fall. The horses, of course, were also unbelievable.

It was a fun afternoon with lots of laughing, a little gambling, and good-natured teasing when someone's horse won the race. It started off with everyone admiring Nina's new ring. She glowed, and Chad looked extremely pleased with himself, smiling ear to ear. Kevin heard Julie thank Chad for praying with him.

Sunday Kevin surprised Julie by taking her to church. They went to the same church where Chad was youth pastor. Paul, Mindy, and Nina went. Even Shannon went. Of course, Mitch went because Shannon was there. The eight of them took up an entire pew.

Kevin liked sitting next to Julie in church. It was different this Sunday than it had been last Sunday too. Kevin was different. He was glad. It felt good holding Julie's hand during prayers and feeling her warmth beside him.

The sermon was on marriage. Kevin was paying attention. Kevin noticed even Mitch was paying attention. Kevin knew there had to be such things as miracles if Mitch was focused on what the pastor was saying during church.

One passage from Ruth in the sermon was unusual, unusual because the words spoken were from Ruth to her mother-in-law, Naomi. Kevin didn't know what that could possibly have to do with marriage. As the minister read, Kevin understood.

"Don't ask me to leave you and turn back," he read. "I will go wherever you go and live wherever you live. Your people will be my people, and your God will be my God. I will die where you die and will be buried there. May the Lord punish me severely if I allow anything but death to separate us!"

That was exactly how he felt about Julie. He wanted his home to be where hers was. He wanted their lives to be intimately interwoven. He prayed death wouldn't even separate them. He wanted to spend eternity with her in heaven.

He wished there was some way they could marry now, but he had no way to support them both. He'd always felt that a man could not truly be a husband until he could care for his wife—physically, emotionally, financially. When he heard, "This explains why a man leaves his father and mother and is joined to his wife, and the two are united into one," Kevin knew he was right. How can a man leave his parents if they still paid the bills? He really, really wanted to get to the two united into one part. He knew sex was supposed to be saved for marriage, but in his heart he had already committed himself to Julie. Did that count? He didn't know. He did know that being with Julie, but not *being with* Julie was getting more and more difficult. He didn't know how much longer he could hold out. He loved her. He would marry her when he could support them. Wasn't that enough?

Chapter 32

The following Friday, Julie was nervous about the dinner she had planned for Kevin. It was only hamburgers, French fries, and baked beans, but earlier that week when she had practiced, she had ruined the entire meal. The hamburgers had been black on the outside and raw on the inside. The fries were partially frozen, and the beans were scorched and stuck to the pan. Grams had given her some tips. Julie hoped Grams's pointers would keep her from botching the meal a second time.

It was all in the timing. As she worked in organic lab, she wondered why food couldn't be as easy as combining organic compounds in test tubes. Maybe if she cooked over a Bunsen burner she might have more luck.

She had an apple pie recipe to try too. Lisa had given it to her. Lisa, of course, was thrilled with Julie's relationship with Kevin. While Lisa never once said, "I told you so," Julie saw it on her friend's face whenever she talked about Kevin. Julie guessed she deserved that. Lisa had been right. Julie was so thankful it had worked out like it had.

Kevin was walking down the hall when Julie and Shannon walked out the door of the chemistry lab. Julie took the hand Kevin extended toward her. He pulled her the rest of the way to close the distance between them and gave her a quick kiss on the lips. Shannon gave Kevin a hasty hi and bye and took off like lightning ahead of Kevin and Julie.

"She's on her way to Lexington this afternoon," Julie told Kevin.

"I know. Mitch sprinted off after class today to get ready for her arrival. I've never seen him move so fast."

They both laughed as they walked down the stairs and toward the exit.

When Julie and Kevin got to the house, Grams was just leaving.

"I'm on my way to Derby Dinner Play House, dear," she told Julie. "Remember I told you I was going out tonight with my Bible study group."

"I remember, Grams. I hope you have a good time."

"Well, I'll be back late. You two behave yourselves," she said as she walked out the door.

"What if I don't want to behave?" Kevin asked Julie as he wrapped his arms around her.

Julie sighed and kissed him. "You don't have to be *that* good."

They kissed for a long time until Julie finally pulled away.

"I better start dinner. I'm making hamburgers, French fries, baked beans, and, for dessert, apple pie."

"I love apple pie," Kevin said. "Hey! I've got something for you. It's out in my car. I'll be right back." He was halfway out the door as he said the last part. He came back in carrying a denim apron with "Kiss the cook" embroidered on it. "Paul and I saw these in a cooking store this week. He got one for Mindy too." He passed the strap over her head, adjusted it, and reached around behind her to tie the apron in back. He stepped back and studied the effect. "Perfect," he said, "just perfect." Then he did what the apron said. He kissed her.

Because Julie wouldn't let him help, he sat on a bar stool and watched. He enjoyed Julie cooking for him. It was fun seeing her concentrate so hard on what she was doing. She was obviously out of her element, but she didn't let that stop her. Fleetingly, he wondered why she had never cooked for Beavens. Then he decided he didn't care. He was just glad she cooked for him.

Julie started on the pie first. When she had that in the oven, she started on the rest of the meal. She told Kevin how she had messed up everything earlier in the week. He could tell she was relieved when they sat down to eat and it was good. The apple pie was great, Kevin told her so, and he could tell Julie was very pleased with herself.

The two of them talked, teased, and laughed all through the meal preparation and into the cleanup. Julie washed, and he dried. Kevin was amazed how even the most everyday things were enjoyable when he was doing them with Julie.

When the phone rang, Kevin volunteered to answer it because Julie had her arms in soapy water up to her elbows. He was still chuckling as he picked up the receiver and said, "Hello, Young residence."

Kevin could hear someone breathing, but no one spoke. Kevin had a bad feeling, and his body tensed as he spoke again, "Hello. Is anyone there?"

Nothing. Then a gruff male voice said, "Who is this?"

"You called this number. You tell me who you're trying to reach."

There was a pause. Then the caller said, "Julie McCourt. I want to speak to Julie McCourt. Is she there?"

"That depends," Kevin said, "on who is calling."

Julie turned to look at Kevin, soap and water dripping from her hands. Her eyes questioned him.

"This is Jeremy Beavens, and I want to speak to Julie."

Kevin gave Julie a short nod in answer to her unspoken question. He watched as every bit of color drained from her face. She shook her head back and forth slowly mouthing, "No, no," over and over.

"Julie doesn't want to speak to you, Beavens. I suggest you get over it, move on, and leave her alone."

"I suppose you're the new guy," Beavens said in a snide tone. "I guess you like another man's leftovers." He let loose an evil laugh. "She's used goods, dude, used goods."

If Kevin could put his hands around the guy's neck, he would kill him. He would gladly kill him. He just took a deep breath and brought his emotions under control, conscious of Julie's eyes still on him. He wasn't about to let her be any more upset than she was already.

When Kevin spoke, his voice was tight and controlled. "I'm going to tell you this one time and one time only. She doesn't want to have anything to do with you. I want you to leave her alone. Stay away from her, or you will answer to me. I will not let you hurt her. Don't call her again. Don't come down here anymore."

For a long while the line was still. Kevin could tell Beavens was still there. He could hear him breathing.

Beavens finally spoke. "I'll kill you. I'll kill both of you. If I can't have her, no one will have her. I'll see her dead before I'll let her be with someone else."

Before Kevin could answer, the line went dead. Kevin hung up the phone.

"What did he say?" Julie asked her voice barely above a whisper.

"Has he ever threatened you? Said that he wanted to kill you?"

"Well," Julie said turning away from him to lay the towel she had used to dry her hands on the counter, "he's told me more than once that if he can't have me, no one could."

Kevin walked toward her, placed his hands on her upper arms, and squeezed gently. "Julie," he said quietly as he turned her to face him, "he said he's going to kill us." After a moment, Kevin continued. "I think it's time to call the police."

Julie nodded and stepped away from Kevin to pull the phonebook out of a drawer. She laid it on the counter near the phone and sat down.

"I'll call," Kevin said as he sat next to her. He found the number for the Hardin County Sheriff's Office. Before he dialed the number, he placed his hand over Julie's on the counter. He kept squeezing gently until she looked at him.

Her eyes were glistening with tears. It broke Kevin's heart, and he wished again that he could kill Jeremy Beavens.

"I'm so sorry, Kevin. I'm so, so sorry."

"Julie," he murmured, "this is not your fault. None of this is your fault. He's crazy. Normal people don't threaten to kill ex-girlfriends."

Julie knew Kevin was right about Jeremy being crazy, but she did not agree with it not being her fault. She should have never become involved with Jeremy. She should have been able to see the signs of the drug use. And for Kevin's sake, she should have never started dating him. How could she ever make this right?

Busy with her own thoughts, Julie only halfway listened as Kevin called the sheriff's office. "They're sending out a deputy to take our statements," he said.

Kevin stood up and drew Julie off her stool and folded her in a warm, protective embrace. "It's going to be okay," he told her. "I promise. I'm not going to let anything happen to you."

She pulled away far enough to look at his face. "I'm not worried about me, but I couldn't bear it if anything happened to you. This is part of the reason I didn't want to date again, Kevin. You should stay away from me." Tears were streaming down her face.

"Julie, don't shut me out. Don't let him come between us. I know from things you've told me about him that he wants to manipulate and control you. Don't let him. Don't let him win this."

He studied her face for a moment, searching for … something. "Do you love me, Julie?"

"I'll always love you, no matter what."

"Then don't shut me out. Let me help you fight him. Let's face this together."

"I don't know what you see in me, Kevin Sanders. Why would someone as wonderful as you want to fool with someone like me?"

"Well, I could tell you all the reasons I love you, but it would take hours. Besides, you would be so full of yourself that no one would be able to live with you. Since I very much want to live with you, I better keep the reasons I love you to myself."

Julie smiled. She couldn't help it.

As they finished washing and putting away the dishes from dinner, there was a knock on the front door. Kevin followed her into the living room, and, after looking through the window, she opened the door to a uniformed officer.

The deputy introduced himself as Steve Phillips. He was tall and muscular and maybe a few years older than her. He told Julie he knew her grandmother. Everyone knew Grams.

"She fed me many a meal when I was in elementary school. She makes the best cinnamon rolls and dinner rolls that I've ever tasted, but don't tell my wife I said that.

After the introductions were over, Deputy Phillips was all business. He took their statements and asked Kevin questions about the phone conversation with Jeremy. He took down Jeremy's first, middle, and last name in his small notebook. He also wrote down a physical description that Julie gave him of Jeremy along with a description of Jeremy's truck. He seemed only slightly disappointed when neither Julie nor Kevin could give him a license number.

"Well, I'll check this out, folks. I'll get back with you later tonight and let you know what I find. I'll put out an alert for Hardin County and Elizabethtown for officers to be on the lookout for Mr. Beavens's vehicle. You should probably stay in tonight, Miss McCourt, just to be on the safe side. It'd probably be best if you weren't here alone." This last sentenced was directed to Kevin.

"I'll be here with her," Kevin answered.

The deputy said his good-byes, telling Julie to wish her grandmother well for him. Kevin shut and locked the door behind Steve Phillips. It was dark now, and Kevin turned on the porch light.

He turned to Julie and said, "Let's go watch the movies I brought. What do ya say?"

"Okay."

Julie followed Kevin into the kitchen where he turned on the porch light by the back door. He made sure the door was locked.

Julie popped some microwave popcorn and took two Cokes out of the refrigerator. They walked down the steps and snuggled together on the couch after Kevin started the movie. Hearing Kevin's laughter mix with her own and feeling him close beside her almost made it possible for Julie to push thoughts of Jeremy from her mind.

The first movie had just ended when the phone rang. They both stiffened. Kevin went across the room and answered the phone.

Kevin murmured yes or no or "I see" occasionally, but Julie could not discern anything from that.

After Kevin hung up the phone, he stood frozen for a minute. "When did you last hear from Beavens?"

She had to think about it. "It was September sixteenth, or maybe the seventeenth, because he called after midnight. I remember that he called after our second date."

"Apparently," Kevin said taking a seat next to her again, "he's been in jail on drug charges since about that time, until a couple of days ago, anyway. He was out on parole, but missed his first meeting with his parole officer. That meeting was today. Phillips is concerned that Beavens is either already down here or on his way. They—the county, city, and state police—are watching for his truck. Since he broke his parole agreement, Phillips said they would arrest him if he turns up down here. That's why the state police are involved. They would be the ones to return him to the state line and to the Indiana State Police. Phillips said the county would have patrols go by here through the night. I don't want to leave you, even after Ann gets home. Do you think your grandmother will let me stay?"

"I think under the circumstances she will want you to stay. She'll want you to sleep in the other bedroom. In fact, I'll go ahead and get the bed ready." Julie stood and walked toward the room next to hers.

"I'm going to call and let my parents know I won't be there tonight. After that I'm going out to my car to get my stuff."

When Kevin went outside, the first thing he did was look across the road to see if there was a gray truck parked in the field. No such luck. That would've been too easy. Kevin took his bag out of his car, being aware the whole time of his surroundings. He locked his car, checked Julie's to be sure it was locked, and went back in the house. He shut and locked the kitchen door, taking one more look at the yard from the window.

Downstairs, Kevin found Julie in the spare room finishing up the bed by putting a clean pillowcase on a pillow. Kevin took the pillow from her hands, dropped it on the bed, and placed his hands on her hips as she faced him. "You know, I feel a fit of sleepwalking coming upon me."

"I didn't know you sleepwalked."

Kevin looked at her with raised eyebrows. He smiled as the familiar blush colored her cheeks. "I don't," he said, "but I can't be this close to you and not sleep with you. After the weekends sharing a bed with you, I have trouble sleeping by myself Monday through Thursday, especially on Monday."

"I have that same problem," Julie admitted. "Don't worry. Once Grams is asleep, she's out. I'll sneak you into my room."

Chapter 33

Grams had not cared that Kevin stayed. In fact, after she heard about their evening, she seemed very glad he was there. She did make a point of making sure Julie prepared the guest bed for him.

"Already done, Grams." Julie felt a tiny amount of guilt, but she wasn't exactly telling a lie. She had fixed the bed; Kevin just wasn't going to use it.

Julie didn't think she'd be able to sleep. Once she was curled up next to Kevin, though, she felt so safe and secure that she slept like a baby until her alarm went off.

It was still dark outside as Kevin drove her to work. Julie watched for Jeremy. She was thankful when they reached the hospital without a sign of him. Kevin insisted on walking her all the way to the pharmacy. Before Julie opened the pharmacy door, Kevin stopped her. He looked up and down the hallway before he gave her a quick kiss.

"Please be careful today," she told him.

"I'll be careful. *You* be careful." Kevin kissed her again. As the heavy door closed, Julie looked back to see Kevin waving from the hallway. She smiled and waved good-bye.

She was able to get into the familiar routine of her work and push Jeremy from her mind. She even had the pleasant surprise of finding Lisa working this weekend. Julie looked forward to talking with her at lunch. She wanted to tell her how right she had been about Kevin.

Lisa was too swamped to take lunch with the unit dose techs. It wasn't until the afternoon when the carts had been exchanged that Lisa had a chance to talk to Julie. The two of them had just sat down with a couple of Diet Cokes when Julie looked up to see someone she hadn't seen in nearly eight months. He was still tall, dark, and handsome, she had to admit, but now he also looked scary as hell. His black hair, coated with some sort of hair gel, reflected the light from the florescent fixtures in the cafeteria. It was even longer than she remembered. Julie could feel the blood drain from her face.

Lisa turned in her seat. "Jeremy," Lisa mumbled. "What is he doing here?" Lisa stood and took Julie's arm and pulled her to her feet. "Come on. Let's get out of here."

Leaving their drinks on the table, the two of them walked toward the door, which was blocked by Jeremy. When he reached inside his long, black denim coat, Julie knew he was going to pull out a gun and shoot her right there in the middle of the hospital cafeteria. Her heart skipped a beat, and the first thought to cross her mind was that she would never see Kevin again.

When he pulled out a single yellow rose instead of a gun, Julie closed her eyes and let out a breath she hadn't known she was holding. When she opened her eyes, she looked straight up into his. "Why are you here, Jeremy? You have to know I don't want you here."

"Oh, Julie," he said in a voice that was sickeningly soft, "you know you don't mean that. I've come to take you home, back to Indiana with me where you belong."

He stepped toward her, extending the rose. Julie automatically took a step away from him. At the same time, Lisa tightened her grip on her arm and pulled her to the side. Lisa's movement brought them closer to the door and farther from Jeremy, but he also shifted, closing the distance. He held the rose directly under Julie's nose. She could smell it. She wanted to ram it down his throat. From the corner of her eye, Julie could see Lisa trying to wave down a security guard on the other side of the large room.

Jeremy didn't seem to notice. Julie looked back into his eyes and realized why. The blue of his irises had all but engulfed his pupils. Julie knew enough to realize that the appearance of Jeremy's eyes was not natural. It had to be drug induced. He was strung out on something, and his behavior was going to be completely unpredictable. She had to get away from him. She had to get Lisa away from him. She needed to somehow call the police. *Why in the world didn't that security guard pay attention?*

Julie forced herself to stand a little straighter and stare at Jeremy. "I'm not going anywhere with you, Jeremy. Not now. Not ever," she said with calm she did not feel. "I am, however, going back to work." With that she walked around and away from him pulling Lisa with her.

Behind her, Julie heard Jeremy roar, "I will hunt you down, Julie. I will hunt you down and kill you. You will *never* belong to anyone but me!"

That got the security guard's attention. He was a big guy, thankfully, and he made his way over to Jeremy. Julie looked back to see the man place a beefy hand on Jeremy's arm, keeping him from following them. Lisa walked behind her. Julie could feel Lisa's hand on her back as they hurried to the pharmacy. Julie was so embarrassed. Few people had been in the cafeteria, but every one of them had been focused on Julie, Jeremy, Lisa, and eventually the security guard.

"I'm so sorry, Lisa," Julie said when they were safely inside the pharmacy.

"Oh, honey, don't you apologize to me. This is not your fault."

Julie quickly told Lisa about last night.

"You go back to the unit dose area and call the police," Lisa told her. "I'm going out there to see if he's gone. Is Kevin picking you up?"

When Julie nodded in reply, Lisa said, "I'll look for him while I'm out there."

Julie felt a tear run down her cheek. Lisa reached out to pat her arm.

"Why would Kevin want to fool with all this, Lisa? He should walk away from me."

"Don't be silly," Lisa said softly. "Kevin loves you. I think he's loved you for a long time now."

"But why? I don't deserve it."

"Sure you do. You're a wonderful person. Just because you were involved in the past with a man who has chosen to destroy himself with drugs doesn't mean you're a bad person. You deserve good things, Julie. You are going to get through this and be a better person because of it. Now, go call the police. I'm going out to the hall to check things out and find Kevin." Lisa gave Julie an encouraging smile, patted her arm again, and headed toward the pharmacy door.

Julie called the sheriff's office. She was told that Deputy Phillips would call her back shortly. She gave the direct line to unit dose as the callback number. After she hung up, she paced back and forth in front of the phone. She hit the palm of her left hand with the fist of her right hand, making a rhythmic slapping sound as she walked. She looked at her watch. She looked at the clock on the wall. She blew out her breath. She looked around for something to do. Noticing that some of the unit dose bins were not completely full, she filled them from the overstock area on the back shelves. Once every bin was completely full, she went to her locker and removed the bag with a change of clothes she had packed that morning. She changed quickly in the pharmacy restroom. She wished there was a shower. She couldn't help feeling dirty from being that close to Jeremy.

Kevin and Lisa were walking into the unit dose area as Julie stepped out of the restroom. Kevin's face looked tense and worried, but it seemed to loosen as his eyes met hers. He came to her and held her for a moment before asking if she was all right. Julie managed to nod but was afraid to speak for fear of crying.

Kevin rubbed his hands up and down her upper arms. "Hey," he said gently, "I'm not going to let him hurt you."

She wanted to tell him that she was not frightened for herself. She felt so much shame for being in this mess and for involving Kevin. She had no idea how to express how she felt, so she nodded again.

"The security guard who was in the cafeteria followed Jeremy out to the parking lot," Lisa explained. "He said it appeared that Jeremy was trying to hide behind the dumpster but took off when he saw the guard. The guard watched him drive out of the parking lot and was able to get his license plate number." Lisa handed Julie a slip of paper.

Julie took the paper and finally found her voice. "Thanks, Lisa. You're such a good friend."

The phone rang. It was Steve Phillips. Julie related the events that occurred in the cafeteria. She read the license number to him and listened as he read it back.

"Did anyone else hear him threaten you?"

"Yes," Julie answered. "There were other people in the cafeteria at the time. One of my co-workers was there with me, and the security guard who followed him out heard what he said."

Deputy Phillips came to the hospital and took statements from the security guard and Lisa. He told Julie and Kevin that every officer in the county and surrounding areas would be watching for Jeremy. Then he walked the three of them out to the parking lot and saw them safely to their vehicles.

From the driver's seat of his car, Kevin watched Lisa and the deputy drive out of the parking lot. He put the keys in the ignition but didn't start the car. Julie was facing the passenger side window. He couldn't see her face. Her hands were in her lap, and Kevin watched as she twisted and untwisted her fingers over and over again.

He reached over and covered both her hands with one of his. The twisting stopped, and she looked at him. Her face was pale and tight. With his other hand, he reached over and rubbed that spot above her nose.

"You know, I'm really not looking forward to you having a wrinkle the size of the Grand Canyon there when you're sixty." He grinned at her.

Her face softened. Kevin could almost make out a smile.

"I need to run by KFC for some coleslaw before we head to Hodgenville. Do you mind?"

"No, I don't mind. As long as I'm with you, I don't care where we go."

Kevin was relieved to see the color come back to her face. He smiled, and this time, she smiled back. He started the car and headed down the road.

"Doesn't your mom cook?"

"Sure she does. She's a great cook. She just cheats on her coleslaw."

Julie laughed, and Kevin felt like a weight had been lifted off him. He hoped the police found Beavens quickly, locked him up, and threw away the key.

Still sitting at the drive-thru window, Julie took the KFC bag from Kevin and set it on the floor behind his seat. He dropped the change into Julie's hand when she turned around. As Kevin pulled into traffic on Dixie Highway, she slipped the bills into his wallet and put the coins in the console between their seats.

Julie was laughing at something Derrick had done at school when she saw the truck. It was barreling straight at her. Evidently Kevin had seen it before she had; she could feel the car changing direction before her brain registered what was happening.

Everything was in slow motion. There was no noise at all. Suddenly, real time kicked in and Julie was surrounded by the sounds of crumpling metal and breaking glass. Her body flung violently forward. The windshield rushed at her face. She felt the seatbelt tighten and jerk but not before her body thudded loudly against the dash. Everything stopped. Something pushed against the back of her seat, pinning her between the seat and her seatbelt. Her chest was only inches from the dash.

She turned toward Kevin. The side of his face was covered with blood. "Kevin!" she screamed. She tried to reach the buckle release but could not.

"I'm okay," he said gently. "Stay calm."

"Kevin, you're bleeding. We need to stop the bleeding. Can you unbuckle my seat belt? I think I can reach my bag if you unbuckle me. I can use my blouse in there to stop the bleeding."

"Are you hurt, Julie?"

Kevin released his seatbelt and struggled with hers. Her entire upper body hurt, but the pain radiating from her right arm was the greatest. She tried to move it and had to bite her lip to keep from crying out. "My arm hurts," she answered. "I think it hit the dash or the dash hit it."

Once Kevin got her unbuckled, she wrestled her bag loose enough from under the seat to dig out her blouse. Working awkwardly with her left hand she wiped the blood from Kevin's face. There was a small but deep cut near his right eyebrow. "Does it feel like there's any glass or anything in it?" Julie asked as she pressed on the gash. When Kevin shook his head, she pushed with more force trying to stop the flow of blood.

"Julie, I smell gasoline. We need to get out of the car. I don't think I'm hurt anywhere else. I'll get out and help you over the console. We're not going to be able to open your door."

When Kevin got out, Julie shifted over to the driver's seat, holding her right arm up and against her chest. Her arm felt as if it was going to explode, and she had to work hard to keep from crying. Kevin reached into the car and gently pulled her out. She tried to reach up with her left hand to wipe the blood from around his eye, but he brushed her hand away. He looked her over, and the expression on his face was grim. She looked down to where Kevin had focused his attention. Her arm was already swollen. Her shirt sleeve was stretched tightly over her Popeye-sized bicep. Her fingers tingled, and she thought the pressure of the shirt was cutting off the circulation in her arm. Kevin reached back into his car and took a pocketknife from his console. He very carefully cut the sleeve off of her shirt at the seam. Her arm looked awful. He continued to study it with a troubled expression on his face.

"Kevin, I'm fine, but you're bleeding. Here, wrap this around your head and use the sleeves to tie it." She used her good arm and the front of her thigh to roll the body of her shirt up toward the sleeves to make a bandage of sorts. She pressed it against the cut on his head while he did as she had instructed.

People and cars were all around them. She heard someone say they had called an ambulance.

"I'm going to check on Beavens. You stand over there away from the car," Kevin told her sternly.

"I'm coming with you. He might try to hurt you."

Kevin started to argue but she insisted. Julie followed Kevin as he made his way around his Mustang to the truck Jeremy had plowed into them. Jeremy's bumper had crushed into Kevin's backseat on the passenger side.

Kevin opened the truck door. Jeremy didn't move. His eyes were opened but looked empty. Julie watched as Kevin checked for a pulse, first on his neck and then on his wrist. "There's no pulse," she heard him say even though he seemed to be talking to himself. "I've got to get him out of the truck."

"Can we move him? I mean should we?" she asked.

"Well," Kevin answered as he quickly looked over the man slumped in the truck, "if we don't, he'll die for sure. We need to start CPR."

Jeremy wasn't brawny, but he was tall. Julie was sure he would be heavy. She knew she wouldn't be able to help lift him with her arm in the shape it was. Thankfully, a man from the crowd stepped forward to help. Carefully, Kevin pulled Jeremy from the truck, supporting his neck and upper back as he did. The other man took his feet, and together they carried Jeremy away from the crash site.

As Kevin struggled to lower Jeremy to the ground, Julie heard him talking under his breath. She couldn't make out what he was saying, but it sounded like he was praying. She started praying, too. Kevin knelt on the ground and gave two rescue breaths, he checked again for a pulse before beginning chest compressions.

Facing Kevin, Julie dropped down on the ground beside Jeremy's lifeless body. "I know CPR. I'll do the breathing." Kevin gave her a short nod. She used her left forearm to push down on Jeremy's forehead and her left fingers to pinch his nose closed. She gave the breaths when Kevin completed his first round of compressions. She used her right hand to check for a pulse as she breathed, trying not to wince in pain from moving it.

"Still no pulse," she called, and Kevin continued compressions.

They continued for what seemed like hours. Kevin was becoming short of breath and his face was flushed. Blood had soaked through the shirt tied around his head. Her own feet had grown numb from being in a kneeling position, and her arm was throbbing. Eventually, she heard sirens approaching.

There was a flurry of activity as EMTs and police arrived on the scene. The medical personnel listened as the man who had helped remove Jeremy from his truck explained why Kevin had wanted to move him. The medical technicians took over from Kevin and Julie and quickly had Jeremy secured in an ambulance. Other technicians evaluated the two of them. Julie saw police officers talking to the people who had gathered. Others were directing traffic around the area.

Kevin watched Julie's face as they rode toward the hospital. He wanted to reach over and rub away the tightness he saw on her forehead but couldn't from where he lay in the ambulance. Neither of them spoke. Julie didn't look at him. She stared at the floor.

The ER personnel let Kevin and Julie stay in the same trauma room. One of the nurses was a friend of his mom. She offered to call his and Julie's families to let them know what was going on. After a nod from Julie, he accepted her offer.

He had to have twelve stitches to sew up the gash in his head. Julie's arm was not broken, just badly bruised. She stood next to him, holding a cold pack against her bulging arm as he sat on the examination table. They were alone together for the first time since the accident.

"You're going to have a scar," she said as her eyes focused on the area above his right eye.

He reached up to touch the wound. The area was still numb, but with his fingers he could feel the bumps where the skin had been brought back together and feel the crustiness of his own blood. It felt like the stitches ran along his eyebrow. He doubted it would be noticeable once it healed. It really didn't matter to him.

"I don't think it will mess up my good looks. Do you? Mitch is always saying how chicks dig scars. What do think? Are scars sexy?"

She didn't even crack a smile. If anything, she looked like she might cry.

"Come on, Julie," he said quietly. Gently, he pushed on her good arm so that she stood directly in front of him. He kissed her between the eyebrows and let his lips rest against the area. He felt her body shudder.

"Are you angry with me, Kevin?" Her voice was barely a whisper.

Kevin eased her away and lifted her chin so that she looked in his eyes. "I am not angry. Would you please let that go? I don't blame you for what happened. None of this is your fault. I want you to stop thinking that it is. Don't say another word about any of this being your fault. I just thank God that we're not hurt any worse than we are. We could've been dead. That was apparently what Beavens was shooting for."

Julie put down the cold pack, took his hand in her left, brought it to her lips, and kissed his fingers.

Over Julie's head, Kevin saw Deputy Phillips in the doorway. The officer cleared his throat and paused before coming into the room. Julie blushed and let go of Kevin's hand. She picked up her ice and sat down in a plastic chair next to the exam table.

The deputy took a seat in another chair after dragging it over next to them. His face was grim.

"Mr. Beavens is dead," Phillips said flatly. He looked from Kevin to Julie. Neither of them spoke.

"There will be an autopsy, but if the drugs we found in his truck are any indication of what he had in his body…well, there's not much chance he would've had long to live, car accident or not." He pulled his notebook out of his pocket before he spoke again. "According to several of the witnesses who were questioned, Beavens accelerated into your car, Mr. Sanders. I need to get a statement from each of you about the accident for my report. Just to put your mind at ease, Mr. Sanders, no fault for the situation will be placed on you. In fact, I'd like to commend you for performing CPR on a man who, more than likely, was trying to do you and Miss McCourt extreme bodily harm."

Chapter 34

Julie could not believe Jeremy was dead. She was ashamed to admit, even to herself, that she was relieved at his passing. Her emotions were so confused. She felt guilty and angry. She had no idea how to bring closure to this part of her life. She wanted to move past it, but she didn't know how. She prayed and read her Bible. Nothing seemed to help. She couldn't sleep well, and when she did sleep, she had nightmares, horrible nightmares. In some she had died. Sometimes Jeremy was there, like a ghost taunting her. In the worst one, she could see Kevin covered in blood and screaming in pain.

After that one, she knew she had to talk to someone. She didn't think Grams would understand, and Kevin had already told her to stop talking about her guilt. She needed an impartial counselor—someone trained to listen and talk to people in turmoil. In a moment of inspiration, she thought of Chad.

She dialed Nina's number; Nina answered after three or four rings.

"Kevin told us about the accident. How's your arm?"

"It's still sore, but I can use it now." Julie paused a moment. She wasn't sure how much Nina knew about the circumstances involved in the accident. "Um, I called to ask a favor. I really need to talk to someone about … about what's happened. I was wondering if maybe Chad would mind doing some counseling."

"I don't think he'd mind at all. He's right here. I'll get him for you."

When Chad came to the phone, he put her at ease and prayed with her. Julie went right into the details of her problem. She explained to him what had happened. From the questions and comments Chad made, Kevin hadn't told them the sordid details about Jeremy. She explained, as best she could, about her guilt and anger. She told Chad that she didn't think she was worthy of Kevin.

Calmly, Chad said, "Julie, I honestly think that had it not been for you, Kevin would not have a relationship with Christ. It's a blessing to have an influence on someone for God's sake."

He was right. She felt an overwhelming sense of thankfulness. While Chad had been the one to read scriptures and pray with Kevin, she had played a part as well. She had invited him to church. She had prayed for him. She realized she had not been counting her blessings, only looking at the negatives.

"You need to forgive, Julie. You need to forgive Jeremy, even though his time on earth is done, and you need to forgive yourself. God will help you. Forgive, and then you can heal."

He prayed with her again. Julie felt such relief. She had probably been carrying this weight around since she had known Jeremy. It felt unbelievably good to let it go.

"Thank you so much, Chad. I'm sorry for taking up so much of your time and keeping you from Nina. It's okay with me if you tell her what we talked about. I don't want you to have any secrets from her."

She spoke with Nina for a couple more minutes, apologizing for keeping her from Chad. Nina told her not to worry. As soon as Julie hung up the phone, it rang again.

She knew it was Kevin.

"Hello, Kevin."

"How did you know it was me?"

"It's Tuesday," she said laughing.

"It's good to hear you laugh. Everything is okay, right? I've been trying to call, but the line was busy."

"Everything is great. I've been talking to Nina and Chad. He helped me work out some things. I feel so much better."

"I'm glad. I've been really worried about you."

"I love you, Kevin, and I always will."

"I love you too."

That night Julie had only pleasant dreams.